The Complete Strategy & War Collection (Vol. 6)

Sevastopol Sketches & Hadji Murat
— Tolstoy's Lessons in Courage and Command

A Modern Translation

Adapted for the Contemporary Reader

Leo Tolstoy

Translated by Tim Zengerink

Table Of Contents

Preface - Message to the Reader

What If You Could Help Rebuild the Greatest Library in Human History?

Thousands of years ago, the Library of Alexandria stood as the crown jewel of human achievement — a sanctuary where the collected wisdom of every known civilization was gathered, preserved, and shared freely.

And then, it was lost.

Through fire, conquest, and the slow erosion of time, humanity lost not just books — but ideas, dreams, discoveries, and stories that could have changed the world forever.

Today, the Library of Alexandria lives again — and you are invited to be a part of its restoration.

Our mission is simple yet profound:

To rebuild the greatest library the world has ever known, and to translate all timeless works into every language and dialect, so that no seeker of knowledge is ever left behind again.

By joining our movement to rebuild the modern Library of Alexandria, you become part of an unprecedented mission:

- **Unlimited Access to the Greatest Audiobooks & eBooks Ever Written:**

  Instantly explore thousands of legendary works—Plato, Shakespeare, Jane Austen, Leo Tolstoy, and countless more. All instantly available to read or listen, placing a complete literary universe at your fingertips.

- **Beautiful Paperback & Deluxe Editions at Printing Cost**

  Own any title as an elegant paperback, deluxe hardcover, or stunning collectible boxset—offered to you at true printing cost, delivered straight to your door. Build your personal Library of Alexandria, crafted for beauty, built for durability, and worthy of proud display.

- **Fresh Translations for Modern Readers—in Every Language & Dialect**

  Enjoy timeless masterpieces reimagined in clear, contemporary language—no more outdated phrases or obscure references. Alongside the original versions, we're tirelessly translating these classics into every language and dialect imaginable, ensuring accessibility and understanding across cultures and generations.

- **Join a Global Renaissance of Literature & Knowledge**

  You directly support expanding our library, publishing deluxe editions at true cost, translating works into all global languages, and bringing humanity's greatest stories to people everywhere. By joining today, you're not just preserving a legacy of masterpieces; you set in motion a powerful wave of literary accessibility.

Become a Torchbearer of Knowledge.

Join us for free now at **LibraryofAlexandria.com**

Together, we will ensure that the light of human wisdom never fades again.

With gratitude and a shared love of knowledge,
The Modern Library of Alexandria Team

Visit:

www.libraryofalexandria.com

Or scan the code below:

Introduction

The Human Face of War:
Tolstoy's Tactical Truths and Moral Clarity

War is not merely a matter of strategy, terrain, or firepower. It is a human event, full of contradiction and suffering, shaped not only by generals and empires but by ordinary men confronting fear, honor, futility, and death. Few writers have captured this truth with the clarity, depth, and force of Leo Tolstoy. In The Complete Strategy & War Collection (Vol. 6), we turn from the abstractions of doctrine to the intimacy of the battlefield through Tolstoy's Sevastopol Sketches and Hadji Murat.

These two works offer something rare: not only philosophical insight and psychological depth, but a writer's unflinching witness to war's reality. They are neither patriotic epics nor polemics—they are meditations on courage, leadership, loyalty, betrayal, and the moral cost of empire. They show war from the trenches and from the command tent, from the perspectives of soldiers and insurgents, officers and civilians. Through these narratives, Tolstoy expands our understanding of strategy—not just as a means of victory, but as a mirror of values, motives, and consequences.

Tolstoy served in the Russian army during the Crimean War, where he experienced firsthand the confusion and brutality of combat. His observations became the foundation for the Sevastopol Sketches—a series of literary reports that combine journalism, fiction, and ethical inquiry. Decades later, after embracing pacifism, he returned to the theme of war in Hadji Murat, a novella that presents the life and death of a legendary Caucasian rebel caught between imperial Russia and his own fractured homeland.

Together, these texts confront the reader with questions no strategy manual can ignore: What is victory worth? What is courage without conscience? How do systems of command preserve or destroy human dignity? And what role does the storyteller play in making sense of it all?

This introduction explores the literary, strategic, and ethical dimensions of these works, drawing lessons from Tolstoy's unique vantage point—both as a soldier and as one of history's greatest moral novelists. His contribution to the theory of war lies not in maxims, but in empathy. His battlefield is not only physical, but spiritual.

Sevastopol:
Glory, Horror, and the Confusion of Command

Tolstoy wrote the Sevastopol Sketches in 1855, during the siege of Sevastopol in the Crimean War, where Russia defended its naval stronghold against a coalition of British, French, and Ottoman forces. The siege became a symbol of Russian resilience and sacrifice—but Tolstoy's account undermines simplistic heroism.

The three sketches—Sevastopol in December, Sevastopol in May, and Sevastopol in August—offer evolving perspectives. The first presents the atmosphere of the city under siege: the wounded in the hospitals, the bravado of officers, and the quiet dread beneath the surface. The second begins to unravel patriotic illusion, showing the disorganization of the military command, the incompetence of bureaucrats, and the pointless waste of life. The third, written after Tolstoy had witnessed more suffering, is his most profound indictment: a literary act of disillusionment that strips war of its glory.

Tolstoy explores the psychology of command—how leaders justify inaction, how decisions are made under pressure, how soldiers cope with terror by clinging to routine and camaraderie. He also challenges the reader directly, breaking the fourth wall to ask, "Who is to blame?" His answer is radical for the time: no one and everyone.

War is a system too large for any single man to control, and yet every individual bears moral responsibility for its perpetuation.

In these sketches, the city of Sevastopol becomes a character: wounded, proud, and ultimately sacrificed for strategic illusions. Tolstoy uses shifting viewpoints to show how perspective shapes perception. To the general staff, a battle is a position gained or lost. To the infantryman, it is a burst of mud, blood, and death.

The strategic lesson is profound: commanders must see more than maps and orders—they must understand the human costs their decisions impose. Tolstoy's realism teaches that leadership in war is not only logistical—it is moral. Victory gained through blindness is no victory at all.

Hadji Murat:
Resistance, Loyalty, and the Tragedy of the Individual

Hadji Murat, written in the late 1890s but published posthumously in 1912, is a mature work of fiction that blends history, biography, and philosophy. Set during Russia's conquest of the Caucasus, it tells the story of a real historical figure: Hadji Murat, an Avar warrior and former lieutenant of the Islamic leader Imam Shamil. Murat defects to the Russians after a power struggle with Shamil, hoping to rescue his family. The novella follows his fate as he becomes a pawn in the imperial game.

Unlike the panoramic sweep of War and Peace, Hadji Murat is tightly focused, cinematic in its imagery, and psychologically intense. It is a study of divided loyalties and personal honor in a world dominated by political calculation. Murat is caught between two empires—Shamil's theocratic tyranny and Russia's bureaucratic despotism. He navigates them both with skill, but neither side offers him true refuge.

Tolstoy portrays Murat as courageous, intelligent, and proud—a man shaped by war, but not broken by it. His downfall is not a result of weakness, but of being trapped within a system that does not value his individuality. In his isolation, we see the tragedy of the honorable man in a dishonorable war.

The Russian officers who interact with Murat range from respectful to condescending. Tolstoy uses these interactions to critique imperial arrogance. The Russian command views Murat as a tool, an asset to be managed. But Murat never forgets his mission: to reunite with and save his family. His death—lonely, brave, and defiant—is one of the most poignant in Tolstoy's canon.

Strategically, Hadji Murat offers a counterpoint to doctrinal thinking. It shows that war is not only waged between nations or ideologies, but within the hearts of men. It emphasizes the limits of command: even the most skilled generals cannot control the will of those they presume to manipulate. It also questions the ethics of empire—what is gained when loyalty is purchased, when local customs are trampled, and when resistance is interpreted only as rebellion?

Tolstoy's Murat is not a hero in the traditional sense. He is not flawless, nor purely noble. But he is real—and in his defiance, we see a different kind of power: the dignity of conscience amid the machinery of conquest.

The Ethics of Strategy:
What Tolstoy Teaches Us About Power and Leadership

Tolstoy's contribution to the study of war does not lie in tactical innovation or structural theory. It lies in his insistence that we look at war not from the top down, but from the inside out. He humanizes every aspect of conflict—from the grand movements of empires to the flicker of thought in a soldier's mind.

In the Sevastopol Sketches, he reveals how courage and confusion coexist. He shows how bureaucracy suffocates initiative, how miscommunication breeds catastrophe, and how war, far from being an instrument of progress, is often a symptom of societal decay.

In Hadji Murat, he examines loyalty, identity, and the futility of trying to preserve honor within systems built on betrayal. He warns that the use of war for political ends often destroys the very human values those ends claim to defend.

Taken together, these works offer a framework for ethical strategy. Not ethics as a constraint on power, but as its refinement. Tolstoy demands that leaders ask not only "What works?" but "What is right?" and "What endures?" He reminds us that leadership is not only about control—it is about responsibility.

His narratives also emphasize the importance of perception. War is experienced differently by each participant. Strategy that ignores these subjective realities risks collapse. Morale, misunderstanding, and morale again—these are as decisive as numbers and arms.

Most importantly, Tolstoy invites us to see every soldier, every rebel, every peasant not as a statistic or obstacle, but as a person. This shift—from abstraction to attention—is the foundation of any ethical or effective approach to power.

Welcome to The Complete Strategy & War Collection (Vol. 6). May Tolstoy's portraits of command, courage, and conflict guide you toward a deeper understanding of leadership—not as domination, but as a form of listening, reckoning, and enduring moral vision.

Sevastopol

Leo Tolstoy

Sevastopol in December, 1854

The first light of morning is starting to appear over Sapun Mountain. The dark blue sea has already lost the night's shadows, waiting for the sun to make its surface shine. A cold mist drifts in from the bay. There is no snow—everything looks dark and bare—but the morning frost bites at the skin and crunches underfoot. The steady sound of the sea fills the air, broken only now and then by the distant boom of cannons firing in Sevastopol. The ships remain in darkness, and the clock has just struck eight bells.

To the north, the quiet of night slowly fades as the city wakes up. A guard patrol marches past, their weapons clanking. A doctor rushes toward the hospital. A soldier steps out of his underground shelter, splashes icy water on his sunburned face, then quickly crosses himself as he prays toward the brightening east. A heavy wagon, loaded to the top with bodies, creaks its way to the cemetery.

Down by the wharf, the air is filled with the mixed smells of coal, damp wood, manure, and raw meat. Piles of supplies—firewood, sacks of flour, iron bars, and tools—are stacked all around. Soldiers from different regiments, some carrying muskets, others without, crowd the area. They smoke, argue, and haul heavy loads onto a steaming ship docked nearby. Small two-oared boats, packed with all kinds of people—soldiers, sailors, traders, and women—come and go from the shore.

"To the Grafsky dock, Your Excellency? Right this way," a few retired sailors call out, standing in their boats, ready to offer a ride.

You pick the nearest boat and step carefully over the muddy remains of a dead brown horse lying beside it. You climb aboard and take a seat at the back. As the boat pulls away from shore, the sea around you begins to shine under the morning sun. In front of you, an old sailor in a thick coat and a young boy with white-blond hair row in silence, their movements steady and strong.

You look around at the busy bay, where ships of all sizes are scattered across the water. Small boats appear as tiny black dots, drifting on the vast blue waves. In one direction, the bright buildings of the city glow with the warm pink light of sunrise. The white line of the dock stands out against the water, while sunken ships rest nearby, their dark masts sticking out like lonely reminders of battles lost. In the far distance, enemy warships rock gently on the clear horizon. Foam swirls in the water, bubbling up where the oars slice through the waves. Voices echo across the bay, blending with the deep booms of cannon fire, which seem to be growing louder in Sevastopol.

It is impossible not to feel something stir inside you—a sense of pride, of strength. The thought that you are here, in Sevastopol, makes your heart beat faster.

"Your Excellency, you're steering right toward the Kistentin," the old sailor warns, glancing back to check your direction and shifting the rudder slightly.

"All the cannons are still on it," the young boy adds, eyeing the ship as the boat glides past.

"Of course. It's a new one. Korniloff used to live on board," the sailor says, looking at the ship as well.

A long silence follows. Then, suddenly, a thick cloud of white smoke rises high over the South Bay, followed by the sharp blast of an exploding bomb.

"Look! It just hit!" the boy exclaims, watching as the smoke spreads across the sky.

"He's using his new cannons today," the old man says calmly, spitting into his hands before gripping the oars. "Come on, Mishka! Row harder—we'll catch that barge."

Your boat moves swiftly across the bay's rolling waves, gaining speed. Before long, you pass a slow-moving barge piled high with sacks, its oars handled awkwardly by exhausted soldiers. As you approach the Grafsky Wharf, you see boats of all sizes docking and unloading their passengers and cargo.

The shore is crowded with gray-uniformed soldiers, black-coated sailors, and women dressed in different colors. Some women sell bread rolls, while Russian peasants with steaming samovars call out, offering hot sbiten. Nearby, rusty cannonballs, broken bombs, and heavy iron cannons of different sizes are scattered across the steps. A little further ahead, in an open square, large wooden beams, gun carriages, and sleeping soldiers lie in the dirt. Horses stand tied to carts, while green-painted cannons and ammunition chests sit stacked in piles. The area is packed with people—soldiers, sailors, officers, women, children, and merchants. Wagons filled with hay, sacks, and barrels arrive constantly. Cossacks weave through the crowd, officers on horseback move past, and a general rides by in a small carriage.

To the right, a street is blocked off by a barricade, with small cannons poking through its openings. A sailor sits beside them, casually smoking his pipe. On the left, a grand-looking building with Roman numerals carved above the entrance stands, its steps crowded with soldiers and stretchers stained with blood. Everywhere you look, signs of war surround you.

Your first reaction is a strange discomfort. The city feels like a mix of order and chaos—a grand, beautiful place that has become a battlefield. The scene is not inspiring but unsettling, as if everyone is lost in confusion, running around without knowing what they're doing.

But then, as you look more closely at the people, your impression changes. See that young soldier from a distant village leading three brown horses to the water? He hums a tune to himself, calm and focused, moving through the crowd as if it doesn't exist. He knows his job—whether it's feeding the horses or carrying weapons—and he does it with quiet confidence, just as he would back home in Tula or Saransk.

You see the same attitude on the face of a neatly dressed officer in spotless white gloves, in the relaxed expression of the sailor smoking by the barricade, in the patience of the stretcher-bearers waiting outside the former Assembly Hall, and even in the young woman lifting her pink dress as she carefully steps across the muddy street.

Yes, if this is your first time in Sevastopol, you might be surprised. You won't see fear, panic, or even excitement on anyone's face. No one here seems overwhelmed, terrified, or even filled with heroic determination. Everything appears normal—business as usual. The merchants go about their trade, and life carries on. For a moment, you might wonder if you had the wrong idea about Sevastopol's defenders. Maybe the stories of their courage and sacrifice were exaggerated. Maybe this city isn't as heroic as you expected.

But before you start doubting, go to the front lines. Stand on the bastions and see the men defending Sevastopol with your own eyes. Or, if you want to understand the true cost of war, step into that building over there—the former Assembly Hall. Look at the soldiers on the roof holding stretchers. Inside, you will see something that will stay with you forever.

The moment you open the door, a strong smell fills the air, and your eyes take in a painful sight. Forty or fifty wounded men, many missing limbs, lie in hammocks or directly on the floor. Some groan in pain, while others lie still, too weak to move.

Your first instinct is to stop, to turn away. The sight is overwhelming, and you hesitate on the threshold. But don't let that feeling hold you back. There's no shame in coming to see these men. There's no shame in showing them kindness. In fact, they welcome it. They long to see a caring face, to share their stories, and to hear words of comfort.

You walk between the rows of wounded soldiers, looking for someone who seems less burdened by pain—someone you can talk to. Finally, you stop beside an older soldier sitting up in his hammock. He is thin and weathered, but his eyes are kind, and he looks at you with quiet patience, as if inviting you to speak.

"Where were you hurt?" you ask cautiously.

You feel uncertain, not only because you feel sorry for them but because these men have been through things you can't even imagine. Their pain makes you feel both respect and a quiet sense of unease—you don't want to say the wrong thing, but you also wonder if you even deserve to stand among them.

"In the leg," the soldier replies. But as you look at the blanket covering him, you realize his leg is gone above the knee.

"Thank God," he adds. "Now I can go home."

"How long ago were you wounded?"

"Six weeks ago, sir."

"Does it still hurt?"

"No, not really. Sometimes I feel a dull ache in my calf when the weather is bad, but it's not too bad."

"How did it happen?"

"At the fifth bastion, during the first attack. I had just aimed a cannon and was about to move to a different spot when something hit my leg. It felt like I had stepped into a hole—like my leg was suddenly gone."

"Did it hurt right away?"

"Not at all. It just felt like something burning hot had struck me."

"And then?"

"Then… nothing. Just a strange pulling feeling, like my skin was tightening. The most important thing, sir, is not to think about it. If you don't dwell on it, it's not so bad. People suffer more from their thoughts than from the pain itself."

At that moment, a woman in a gray-striped dress and a black headscarf approaches. She joins the conversation, eagerly telling you about the soldier—how much he suffered, how he was in terrible condition for four weeks, and how, even when he was injured, he made the stretcher-bearers stop so he could watch a volley of fire from their battery. She talks quickly, her eyes shining with excitement. She tells you how a grand duke visited him, gave him twenty-five rubles, and how the soldier said he wanted to return to the bastion to help guide the younger men, even if he couldn't fight himself.

As she speaks, she glances between you and the soldier, who has turned his face away and is quietly picking at the lint on his pillow as if he isn't listening.

"This is my wife, sir," the soldier says with a slight smile, as if to apologize. His expression seems to say, You know how women are— she's making too much of it.

At that moment, you begin to truly understand the defenders of Sevastopol. Standing before this man, you feel an unexpected sense of shame. You want to say something meaningful, to express how much you respect him, how much you admire his courage. But no words seem right. Nothing you say would be enough. So you simply stand there, silently honoring his quiet strength and resilience.

"Well, I hope you recover soon," you finally tell him before moving on.

Nearby, another wounded soldier lies on the floor, his body twisted in unbearable pain. He has pale, swollen cheeks and light-colored hair. His left arm is stretched out, as if frozen in agony. His mouth, dry and cracked, barely manages to release heavy, labored breaths. His lifeless blue eyes stare upward. From under the thick blanket, his bandaged right arm—what's left of it—sticks out. The strong smell of death lingers in the air, and the burning fever inside him seems to radiate outward, making you shiver.

"Is he unconscious?" you ask a woman standing nearby. She looks at you kindly, as if you were a close relative.

"No, he can still hear," she whispers. "But he's not doing well." She sighs and lowers her voice. "I gave him some tea today. Even though he's a stranger, I couldn't just let him suffer. But he barely drank any of it."

You lean in closer. "How are you feeling?" you ask gently.

At the sound of your voice, the wounded man slowly moves his eyes, but they are distant, unfocused. He doesn't seem to see you or understand the question.

"It feels like something is eating away at my heart," he murmurs weakly.

A bit further down, you see an older soldier sitting up, changing his shirt. His skin is rough and dark, almost like dried wood. He is painfully thin, his body just skin and bone. His right arm is missing, cut off at the shoulder. Even so, he moves quickly, trying to tidy himself up. But his sunken eyes, deep wrinkles, and weak posture show the hardship he has been through for many years.

On the other side of the room, you see a young woman lying in a cot. Her delicate face is pale, except for the feverish redness on her cheeks.

"That's our little sailor girl," your guide tells you. "She was hit in the leg by a bomb on the fifth bastion."

"Was it amputated?"

"They had to cut it off above the knee," he replies.

If you have the courage, step through the door on the left. In that room, doctors are treating wounds and performing surgeries. You will see them, their sleeves stained with blood up to the elbows, their faces pale and serious, working over a patient. The wounded man, his eyes wide open, mumbles nonsense under the effects of chloroform, sometimes saying simple, heartbreaking words. The doctors are performing an amputation.

You watch as a sharp, curved knife cuts into healthy, pale skin. Suddenly, the patient regains consciousness, screaming in pain and shouting curses. The surgeon throws the severed limb into a corner. Another injured man, lying nearby on a stretcher, flinches and groans—not just from his own pain, but from the terror of knowing he might be next.

Here, you see war—not the heroic image with marching drums, flags waving, and generals on horseback. This is war as it truly is— filled with blood, suffering, and death.

When you leave this place of pain, you will feel relief. The fresh air will seem cleaner, your own health will feel like a gift. But at the same time, you will feel small, humbled by the suffering you just witnessed. Without hesitation, you will walk toward the bastion.

"What does my life matter compared to all this death and pain?" you may think.

But soon, the sight of the clear blue sky, the shining sun, and the busy streets of the city will push those thoughts away. You will pass an open church, see soldiers going about their tasks, and life will seem normal again.

Maybe you will cross paths with a funeral procession—a fallen officer being carried from the church in a pink-lined coffin, with music playing and flags waving. Perhaps you will hear distant gunfire from the bastion. But these things won't bring back the same feelings you had before. The funeral will seem like a grand military event, not a reminder of real death. The sounds of war won't feel as personal as they did inside the hospital.

As you walk past the barricades and the church, you enter one of the busiest parts of the city. Shops and inns line the streets, their signs swaying in the breeze. Merchants call out their goods, women in bonnets and scarves stroll by, and officers walk past, dressed neatly, carrying themselves with confidence. Everything around you speaks of normal life, as if the war isn't happening just beyond the city's edge.

If you step into the inn on the right, you will hear sailors and officers chatting about the latest battles. They swap stories about the previous night's fight, a woman named Fenka, and the events of the 24th. They complain about the rising cost of food and argue over which cutlets are the worst. They talk about comrades who have been lost, mentioning their names like it's just another part of the day.

"Damn it, things are rough today!" a young naval officer exclaims in a deep voice. He has no beard, pale eyebrows and lashes, and wears a green knitted sash.

"Where?" another asks.

"The fourth bastion," the young officer replies. At that moment, you find yourself paying closer attention to him, feeling a sense of respect. When he mentions the fourth bastion, you assume he is about to describe the heavy shelling, the constant gunfire, or the destruction.

But he doesn't.

Instead, he complains about the mud.

"It's impossible to get across the battery," he grumbles, pointing at his boots, which are covered in thick mud up to his calves.

Another officer chimes in. "My best gunner was killed today. Took a shot right to the forehead."

"Who? Mitiukhin?"

"No," the officer replies, before suddenly turning to the innkeeper. "Are you bringing my veal or not? Thieves!"

"It wasn't Mitiukhin. It was Abrosimoff," he continues, his voice more casual. "Such a fine guy... He was in the sixth attack."

At another corner of the table, two infantry officers sit over a plate of cutlets and peas, sharing a bottle of sour Crimean wine called "Bordeaux." One of them, a young officer with a red collar and two stars on his uniform, is telling the other, who has a black collar and no stars, about the battle at Alma. The young officer has clearly had too much to drink. You can tell by the way he hesitates while speaking, the unsure look in his eyes as if wondering whether he is being believed, and the way he makes himself the center of the story, exaggerating the danger and his own role in it. But these kinds of stories, which will be told for years to come all over Russia, don't interest you. You would rather see the bastions for yourself, especially the fourth, which people describe in so many different ways.

Whenever someone says they have been at the fourth bastion, they say it with a mix of pride and satisfaction. When someone mentions they are going there, you can sense either nervousness or a forced indifference. If someone wants to tease another, they joke, "You must be stationed at the fourth bastion!" And when stretchers pass by and you ask where the wounded came from, the answer is often, "The fourth bastion."

There are two completely different opinions about this feared place. Those who have never been there believe it is a death trap, a place where no one survives. But those who live there—like the young midshipman with white eyebrows—speak about it casually. They will tell you whether it's muddy or dry, whether their dugout is warm or cold, as if it's just another assignment.

While you've been sitting in the inn, the weather has changed. The fog that hovered over the sea has thickened into damp, heavy gray clouds, hiding the sun. A cold mist falls from the sky, wetting the rooftops, streets, and the soldiers' coats.

You pass through another barricade and step onto the main street. Behind this barricade, the houses on both sides are abandoned. The shop signs are gone, the doors are boarded up, and the windows are shattered. Some buildings have missing corners, others have holes in their roofs. They look like tired old warriors, battered and broken, standing with silent pride. The street is littered with cannonballs, and deep craters filled with rainwater mark the spots where bombs have hit.

As you walk, you pass groups of soldiers, sharpshooters, and officers. Occasionally, you see a woman or a child, but they are no longer dressed in fine bonnets and coats. Instead, you see a sailor's daughter wrapped in an old fur cloak, wearing a soldier's boots.

Soon, the houses disappear, replaced by piles of rubble—broken stones, wooden planks, collapsed clay walls, and scattered beams. Ahead, on a steep hill, you see a vast stretch of black, muddy ground cut through by trenches. This is the fourth bastion.

Fewer people are around now. No women. The soldiers you see walk briskly with a sense of purpose. Here and there, you notice drops of blood on the road. You will almost certainly come across four soldiers carrying a stretcher, on which lies a pale, motionless face and a uniform soaked in blood. If you ask, "Where was he hit?" the men carrying him will answer gruffly, "In the leg" or "In the arm"—if the wound isn't too bad. If the soldier on the stretcher is already dead or gravely wounded, they won't answer at all.

As you climb the hill, the sudden shriek of a cannonball or bomb nearby jolts you. The sound is different from how it seemed back in the city. There, the gunfire was just background noise. Here, it feels immediate—real. For a moment, a bright memory from home flashes in your mind. Suddenly, you become aware of yourself in a way you weren't before. You stop focusing on everything around you and instead feel a rising discomfort, an unsettling sense of uncertainty.

Despite this instinct to hesitate, you push it down. Especially when you see a soldier jogging past you, laughing, waving his arms as he slides down the muddy slope. Without thinking, you straighten your posture, lift your chin, and keep climbing.

At the top of the hill, rifle shots begin to whistle past you—some to the right, others to the left. You consider stepping into the trench running alongside the path for cover. But when you glance inside, you see that it is filled with thick, yellowish, knee-deep mud that stinks of filth. You quickly realize why everyone is choosing to stay on the path, and you follow their lead.

After walking a few hundred steps, you reach a chaotic, muddy space surrounded by defensive walls, wooden barriers, and dugouts. Heavy iron cannons are scattered around, cannonballs stacked in neat piles. At first glance, everything looks thrown together without order.

To your right, a group of sailors sits together, talking. In the middle of the open area, half-buried in the mud, lies a broken cannon. A soldier struggles to walk across the sticky ground, dragging his boots with effort. Everywhere you look, there are traces of battle—shattered dishes, unexploded bombs, loose cannonballs, and signs that men have been living in these trenches for weeks. All of it is sinking into the thick, wet mud.

Nearby, you hear the dull thud of a cannonball striking the ground. The air is filled with the terrifying sounds of gunfire—some bullets hum past like buzzing insects, others whistle sharply, while some make a low, eerie whining sound. The booming of rifles and cannons echoes through the air, shaking you from the inside out.

"So this is the fourth bastion, the place everyone fears," you think. A little pride stirs in you, but it's quickly drowned out by a much stronger feeling of quiet fear. But you're wrong—this isn't the fourth bastion. It's the Yazonovsky redoubt, a much safer area, nowhere near as dangerous as what lies ahead.

To reach the fourth bastion, you need to turn right and follow the narrow trench where the foot soldier just went. Along the way, you might pass stretchers carrying the wounded, sailors and soldiers digging with shovels, and the mine supervisor inspecting the area. You'll see tiny dugouts where only two men can squeeze in by crouching. Inside, sharpshooters from the Black Sea battalions rest, eat, smoke their pipes, and go about their daily lives. The same thick, foul-smelling mud is everywhere, along with scattered camp supplies and discarded metal scraps.

After walking about three hundred more steps, you'll reach another battery—an open area filled with deep craters, surrounded by defensive walls, cannons, and mounds of earth. Here, you might spot five sailors playing cards behind a protective barrier, while a naval officer, noticing you are new and curious, will be happy to show you around.

This officer, sitting calmly on a cannon, rolls a cigarette with yellow paper as if he has all the time in the world. He walks around with ease, moving from one gun position to another, speaking in a relaxed manner without a hint of nervousness. Despite the bullets flying overhead more frequently now, his composure makes you feel calmer too. You start to listen more closely and ask questions with genuine interest.

If you ask, he will tell you about the bombardment on the 5th. He'll explain how only one cannon in his battery was still usable and how, out of all the gunners, only eight men remained. Still, by the next morning, on the 6th, they managed to fire every cannon again. He'll tell you about a bomb that struck a sailor's dugout, instantly killing eleven men. Then, he'll point through an opening in the barrier, showing you the enemy's batteries and trenches, just thirty or forty fathoms away.

But be careful—when you hear the bullets whizzing around you, you might feel tempted to peek through the opening to see the enemy for yourself. If you do, you won't see much. And if you manage to spot something, you'll be shocked to realize that the plain white stone wall so close to you—the one with thin puffs of smoke rising from it—is the enemy. That's him, as the soldiers and sailors say.

The officer might even fire a few shots while you're there, either to impress you or just for his own satisfaction. "Call the captain and his crew to the cannon!" he orders. At once, fourteen sailors step up, moving with energy and ease. One shoves his pipe into his pocket, another munches on a biscuit, while another clatters his boots loudly on the wooden platform.

Watch their faces, their posture, their movements. The lines on their sunburned skin, their strong cheekbones, their broad shoulders, and the way they carry themselves all show the qualities that make Russia powerful—simplicity and strength. But here, on these faces, you also see something else. The hardships of war have left a mark— not just in exhaustion and suffering, but in a quiet sense of dignity, deep emotion, and unwavering determination.

Suddenly, a deafening explosion shakes not just your ears but your entire body, making you flinch. A moment later, you hear the high-pitched whistling of the shot as it flies through the air. Thick smoke from the gunpowder covers the platform, hiding the sailors moving around it. You hear excited voices among them, talking about the shot. There's an energy in their tone, a feeling you didn't expect to see—a mix of anger and revenge against the enemy, buried deep inside each man.

"It hit the opening! Looks like it took out two of them—see, they're carrying them off!" someone shouts with excitement.

"Now they're mad. They'll fire back soon," another sailor says. And sure enough, moments later, you see a flash and a puff of smoke in the distance. The sentry standing on the barrier shouts, "Cannon!" Then, a ball whistles past you, slams into the ground, and sends dirt and rocks flying everywhere.

This shot fuels the battery commander's rage. He orders another cannon to be loaded, then a third. The enemy fires back, and suddenly, you are fully caught up in the action, watching and listening with intense focus.

Once again, the sentry shouts, "Cannon!" and you hear the same loud blast, followed by another explosion of dirt and debris. Then, the word "Mortar!" rings out. This time, the slow, eerie whistling of a bomb fills the air. It sounds almost steady, even oddly pleasant, making it hard to connect it with danger. But then, as it gets closer, the sound grows faster and sharper. You spot a black sphere tumbling through the sky before it crashes into the ground, followed by a massive explosion you can feel in your chest. Fragments fly in every direction, stones whip through the air, and mud rains down around you.

As strange as it seems, you feel a mix of fear and excitement. When you hear the incoming shot, your mind instantly tells you, This one will hit me. But your pride keeps you standing tall—no one around you can see the fear cutting through your heart. Then, when the shot lands without touching you, a wave of energy rushes through you. For a brief moment, there's a strange thrill in facing life and death so closely. You almost want the next cannonball or bomb to land even nearer.

But then, another shout of "Mortar!" breaks through the air. A whistle, a shriek—and then a terrible sound as a bomb explodes. This time, you hear something different—the painful groan of a wounded man.

You rush toward him along with the stretcher-bearers. He looks almost unrecognizable, covered in blood and dirt, his body twisted unnaturally. A large piece of his chest has been torn away. At first, his face is frozen in fear, as if his mind hasn't caught up with what happened. There is also a strange, almost forced expression of pain, the kind people make when they know they are supposed to be suffering but haven't fully felt it yet. But as they lift him onto the stretcher, something changes. His expression shifts into something deeper—his eyes shine, his jaw tightens, and his head lifts slightly, though with difficulty.

As the stretcher-bearers prepare to carry him away, he suddenly stops them. With a weak but steady voice, he calls out to his fellow sailors, "Farewell, brothers!"

He struggles to say more, trying to leave them with something meaningful, something powerful. But all he can manage is a second, trembling "Farewell, brothers!" before they carry him off.

One of the other sailors steps forward, places the wounded man's cap back on his head, and then, without hesitation, waves a hand as if to say goodbye and calmly returns to his post at the gun.

"That happens to about seven or eight men every day," the naval officer says when he sees the look of horror on your face. He stretches, yawns, and casually rolls himself a cigarette, as if what just happened was nothing out of the ordinary.

You have now seen the defenders of Sevastopol where they fight, and as you walk back, you barely notice the cannonballs and bullets still whistling through the air. You continue calmly, your heart filled with a deep, powerful feeling.

The strongest and most reassuring thing you take away from this is the unshakable strength of the Russian people. And it's not because of the trenches, barricades, cannons, or clever military strategies— those things may be important, but you don't really understand them. Instead, you've seen this strength in the faces, words, and spirit of the men defending Sevastopol. They do their duty so naturally, without hesitation, as if it costs them nothing. It makes you certain they could do a hundred times more if needed—maybe even anything.

You realize that their motivation isn't for medals, promotions, or recognition—things you might have imagined before. Instead, it comes from something much deeper, something rarely spoken of but always present. It is a love for their country, hidden in the heart of every Russian, though few admit it openly. These men endure constant danger, endless work, hunger, and filth—not because they are forced to, but because they believe in something greater than themselves.

Now, for the first time, the stories you've heard about the early days of the siege feel real. Back then, there were no strong defenses, no large army, no reason to believe the city could hold. And yet, not a single person doubted that Sevastopol would not fall. Now, you truly understand why. You can picture those soldiers—just like the ones you have seen today—standing firm in the face of impossible odds. You can almost hear the voice of Kornilov, the great leader, as he looked at his men and declared, "We will die, my children, but we will not surrender Sevastopol." And the soldiers, men not given to fancy words, simply shouted back, "We will die! Hurrah!"

What once sounded like an old legend now feels completely real. You finally believe it, because you have seen the spirit of those very same men, still standing, still fighting, not for a city, but for their homeland.

This chapter of Sevastopol's history, with the Russian people as its heroes, will leave a lasting mark on the country for generations.

Night is falling. The sun, breaking through the gray clouds at the last moment before setting, bathes everything in a warm, crimson glow. The sky turns soft purple, the greenish sea stretches wide, dotted with ships and boats rising and falling with the waves. The white buildings of the city shine in the fading light, and the people walking through its streets seem almost golden in the sunset. Across the water, the faint sound of an old waltz drifts from the regimental band playing on the boulevard. Mixed with it, from the bastions, come the sharp echoes of gunfire—two sounds that, in this strange moment, blend together as one.

Sevastopol in May, 1855

I

Six months have gone by since the first cannonball shot from Sevastopol's walls and crashed into the enemy's defenses. Since then, thousands of bombs, cannonballs, and bullets have flown between both sides, bringing constant destruction. Death has never left this place, lingering over the battlefield without pause.

Thousands of men have sought glory and failed. Thousands more have found it, filled with pride. And thousands now rest in graves, their bodies wrapped in canvas or laid in red coffins. Yet the battle goes on. Gunfire still rings out from the bastions, and on clear nights, French soldiers in their camp watch Sevastopol's battered walls with unease. They see the dark shapes of Russian sailors moving along the defenses, counting the gun openings and the cannons, knowing they are ready to fire.

At the same time, a Russian officer stands at the telegraph station, peering through his telescope at the enemy's side. He studies the dark shapes of the French soldiers at their batteries, the lines of tents, the troops marching over the green hills, and the white smoke rising from their trenches.

And still, soldiers from different countries, speaking different languages, continue to pour into this battlefield, each with their own reasons for being here. They come with the same eagerness, though their hopes and dreams are as different as the nations they come from.

The question that diplomats failed to settle remains unanswered, and neither blood nor gunpowder has brought a solution.

II.

In the boulevard of the besieged city of Sevastopol, near the pavilion, a regimental band played lively music. Soldiers and women strolled through the streets, enjoying the moment. That morning, the bright spring sun had risen over the English fortifications, passed over the bastions, then over the city and the Nikolaevsky barracks. Now, as it set, it cast a golden glow over the calm sea, making the waves shimmer like silver.

A tall infantry officer with a slightly hunched posture stepped out of a small naval hut on the left side of Morskaya Street. He pulled on a glove that wasn't exactly clean but was still in decent condition. With his eyes fixed on the ground, he walked up toward the boulevard, lost in thought.

His face was plain, not particularly clever-looking, but it showed honesty, good judgment, and a simple, steady nature. He moved a little awkwardly, lacking grace, and his worn cap, faded lilac-colored cloak, polished boots, and the gold chain peeking from under his coat suggested he was either a German officer—though his features were unmistakably Russian—or an adjutant, or maybe a regimental quartermaster. If he were, he would likely be wearing spurs. Perhaps he had transferred from the cavalry for the war, or even from the Guards. In fact, he was an officer who had switched from cavalry service, and as he climbed the boulevard, he was thinking about a letter he had just received from an old comrade—now retired and living in the countryside.

The letter brought back memories of the man's wife, Natasha—a pale, blue-eyed woman whom the officer had always considered a dear friend. One passage in particular stood out in his mind:

"When the newspaper arrives, Pupka (the name my wife still goes by) runs straight to the front hall, grabs it, and rushes to the arbor or the drawing room—remember how you and I used to spend our winter evenings there when the regiment was in our town? She reads about your heroic deeds with such excitement you wouldn't believe it. She talks about you all the time. 'There's Mikhaïloff,' she says. 'He's such a wonderful man! I could kiss him if I saw him. He's fighting on the bastions, and I just know he'll be awarded the Cross of St. George. He'll be in the papers...' and so on and so on. I swear, I'm starting to get jealous of you."

Another part of the letter amused him:

"We get the news terribly late, and even though there's plenty of gossip, not all of it is true. For example, some young women who play music—you remember them—said yesterday that Napoleon had already been captured by our Cossacks and sent to Petersburg. You can imagine how much I believe that. Also, a visitor from Petersburg—a government official, a very charming man, and, since there's no one else around, one of our only sources of entertainment—told us that our army has taken Eupatoria. He claims the French have been completely cut off from Balaklava, that we only lost 200 men, while the French lost 15,000! My wife was so thrilled that she celebrated all night. She insists she has a feeling you were part of the battle and that you must have distinguished yourself."

Despite the exaggerated words, the jokes, and the gossip, Captain Mikhaïloff felt a deep, bittersweet warmth as he thought of Natasha. He could picture her sitting in the arbor in the evenings, speaking with him about life and feelings. He remembered the many card games with his friend, how his comrade would get frustrated when he lost, and how Natasha would laugh at them both. Their friendship had always meant a great deal to him—though perhaps he felt it was Natasha who had truly understood him. As these memories filled his mind, he smiled and pressed his hand against the pocket where he had tucked the letter.

From these memories, his thoughts drifted into daydreams.

"Just imagine how excited Natasha will be," he thought as he walked along the narrow path. "She'll be reading the newspaper one day and suddenly see my name—'Captain Mikhaïloff was the first to climb onto the cannon and was awarded the Cross of St. George!'

He pictured himself being promoted to full captain, then to major—after all, many officers had already been killed in battle, and many more would be lost before the war was over. From there, new battles would come, and with his experience, he could be given command of a regiment. Then, he imagined himself as a lieutenant colonel, then a colonel with the Order of St. Anna around his neck.

Soon, he was a general, standing in his grand office, granting an audience to Natasha, now a widow after his friend's passing.

At that moment, the music from the boulevard grew louder, and the busy crowd came into focus. His daydream vanished in an instant, and he found himself back in reality—a regular infantry staff captain, walking through the boulevard as before.

III.

He first walked toward the pavilion, where the regimental band was playing. Since there were no music stands, other soldiers from the same regiment held the sheet music for the musicians. A small crowd had gathered around them—cadets, nurses, and children, more interested in watching than actually listening.

Around the pavilion, sailors, adjutants, and officers in white gloves stood, sat, or walked about. Along the wide boulevard, officers of all ranks strolled, along with women—most wearing headscarves, some without, and very few in bonnets. Strangely, there were no old women among them—only young, cheerful ones. Further down, in the shady paths lined with fragrant white acacia trees, small groups of people sat or wandered quietly.

Captain Mikhaïloff wasn't expecting a warm welcome on the boulevard, and he didn't get one. No one seemed particularly happy to see him—except, perhaps, for two fellow captains from his regiment, Obzhogoff and Suslikoff, who greeted him enthusiastically. However, Obzhogoff was dressed in camel-hair trousers, without gloves, and his coat was so worn out that it was embarrassing to walk with him. His flushed face was covered in sweat. Suslikoff, on the other hand, spoke so loudly and excitedly that it was uncomfortable to be seen with him—especially in front of the officers in white gloves. Mikhaïloff had just exchanged nods with one of those officers, an adjutant, and he might have done the same with another staff officer since they had met twice before at a mutual friend's house.

Besides, what was the point of walking with Obzhogoff and Suslikoff when he had already run into them six times that day? That wasn't why he had come to the boulevard.

He wanted to join the group of officers he had nodded to, not to show off in front of Obzhogoff, Suslikoff, or Lieutenant Pashtetzky, but because these men were interesting. They always had the latest news, and he was curious to hear what was happening.

But something held him back.

What if they ignore me? he thought. What if they just nod and keep talking among themselves as if I'm not there? Or worse—what if they just walk away, leaving me standing there alone like a fool?

He hesitated, watching them from a distance.

The word aristocrats came to mind—not in the sense of nobility, but as a way to describe a higher, more exclusive social group. In Russia, this idea had spread everywhere—to merchants, officials, writers, and officers. No matter where you went, people used the word.

To Captain Obzhogoff, Mikhaïloff himself was an aristocrat. But to Mikhaïloff, Adjutant Kalugin was one—simply because he was an adjutant and had the privilege of addressing other adjutants informally. To Kalugin, Count Nordoff was an aristocrat, because he served as an adjutant on the Emperor's staff.

Vanity! Mikhaïloff thought. Vanity everywhere!

Even here, among men ready to die for a noble cause, standing on the edge of life and death, vanity still existed. It was a disease of the modern age. Why had past generations never talked about this obsession? Why had Homer and Shakespeare written about love, honor, and suffering, while today's literature seemed filled with stories of arrogance and self-importance?

Mikhaïloff walked past the group twice, unsure of himself. The third time, he finally gathered the courage to approach them.

The group consisted of four officers: Adjutant Kalugin, whom Mikhaïloff knew; Adjutant Prince Galtsin, who was an aristocrat even to Kalugin; Colonel Neferdoff, one of the well-connected society men who had rejoined the army just for this campaign; and Captain Praskukhin, another officer from the same background.

Luckily for Mikhaïloff, Kalugin was in a great mood. The general had just spoken to him in a friendly manner, and Prince Galtsin—who had recently arrived from Petersburg—was staying with him. Feeling confident, Kalugin didn't mind shaking Mikhaïloff's hand.

Praskukhin, however, hesitated. He had met Mikhaïloff many times at the bastion, drank his wine and vodka, and even owed him twenty rubles and fifty kopecks from a card game. But he had only recently been introduced to Prince Galtsin, and he didn't want to damage his image by acknowledging a simple infantry staff captain. So instead of shaking hands, he simply gave Mikhaïloff a brief, polite nod.

"Well, Captain," Kalugin said, "when are we going back to the bastion? Remember when we met at the Schwartz redoubt? Things got pretty intense there, didn't they?"

"Yes, it was tough," Mikhaïloff answered, recalling how he had carefully made his way through the trenches that night while Kalugin walked boldly past, his sword clanking like a hero's. "I was supposed to go tomorrow, but one of our officers is sick…"

He was about to explain that it wasn't his turn to go, but since the commander of the eighth company was ill and only a junior officer remained, he had volunteered to take his place and was heading to the bastion today. However, Kalugin didn't let him finish.

"I have a feeling something big is going to happen in the next few days," Kalugin said, turning to Prince Galtsin.

"You don't think anything will happen today?" Mikhaïloff asked, glancing between them.

No one answered. Prince Galtsin simply frowned slightly, looked past Mikhaïloff's cap, and after a brief pause, said, "That girl in the red kerchief is gorgeous. You don't happen to know her, do you, Captain?"

"She lives near my quarters. She's a sailor's daughter," Mikhaïloff replied.

"Let's go take a better look at her," Galtsin said, linking arms with both Kalugin and Mikhaïloff. He was certain that this simple gesture would feel like an honor to Mikhaïloff, and he was right.

Mikhaïloff was actually superstitious and believed it was bad luck to be distracted by women before battle. But wanting to fit in, he pretended to be just as interested, though neither Kalugin nor Galtsin really believed him. The girl, however, was surprised—she had seen the staff captain pass by her window many times before, always blushing.

Praskukhin trailed behind them, trying to stay involved in the conversation. He kept touching Prince Galtsin's shoulder and making comments in French. But since the narrow path could only fit three people, he had to walk alone. On their second lap around the boulevard, he managed to link arms with Servyagin, a well-known and respected naval officer who had just joined them, eager to be part of the aristocrats' circle.

Praskukhin happily grabbed onto Servyagin's strong, battle-worn arm, feeling proud to be seen with him. But when he whispered to Galtsin that Servyagin was famous for his bravery, the prince wasn't impressed. After all, he had been on the fourth bastion the night before, had seen a bomb explode just twenty steps away, and considered himself just as much of a hero. He knew that reputations were often exaggerated, so he paid little attention to Servyagin.

Mikhaïloff was so pleased to be part of this group that he completely forgot about the letter from T—— and the heavy thoughts of his upcoming assignment at the bastion. He stayed with them until they started talking only among themselves, avoiding eye contact with him—a silent hint that he was no longer welcome. Eventually, they moved on without him.

Even so, Mikhaïloff didn't feel upset. He was still pleased with the evening's events. As he walked past Yunker Baron Pesth—who had spent his first night in a bomb shelter at the fifth bastion and now carried himself like a war hero—he wasn't even bothered by the arrogant way the young man straightened up and tipped his hat, full of self-importance.

IV.

As soon as Staff-Captain Mikhaïloff stepped into his quarters, his thoughts completely changed. He looked around the small, simple room with its uneven dirt floor. The windows were crooked, covered with scraps of paper to keep out the wind. His old bed stood in the corner, with a rug nailed above it that showed an image of a woman on horseback. Two Tula pistols hung on the wall. Nearby was the cadet's messy cot, covered with a faded chintz blanket. His servant, Nikita, stood up from the floor, scratching his head with his greasy, unkempt hair sticking out.

Mikhaïloff's eyes landed on his worn-out coat, his extra pair of boots, and a small bundle on the table. A piece of cheese stuck out from it, next to the neck of a vodka bottle he had set aside for his trip to the bastion. That's when it hit him—tonight, he was heading back to the front lines with his company.

"I just know I'm going to die tonight," he thought. "I can feel it. And the worst part is, I didn't even have to go—I volunteered. It's always the ones who volunteer who get killed. And what if Nepshisetsky isn't even really sick? Maybe he just made it up, and now someone else is going to die in his place. Probably me."

Then, another thought crossed his mind. "But if I survive, I might get promoted. The regimental commander seemed pleased when I stepped up to go instead of Nepshisetsky. Maybe I'll become a major. If not that, then at least I might get the Order of Vladimir. This will be my thirteenth time going to the bastion... Thirteen—that's bad luck. They're definitely going to kill me. I feel it."

He tried to reassure himself. "But someone had to go. The junior officer couldn't. And no matter what happens, the honor of the regiment—of the whole army—is at stake. It's my duty... my sacred duty."

Mikhaïloff didn't realize that he had felt this same sense of doom every time he went to the bastion before. He also didn't know that every soldier on their way to battle felt the same fear, though some more than others. Telling himself that duty came first helped calm him. He sat at his table and wrote a farewell letter to his father. Ten minutes later, after finishing the letter, he stood up, his eyes wet with tears. Whispering every prayer he knew, he started getting dressed.

His lazy, often-drunk servant, Nikita, slowly handed him his new coat. His usual coat, the one he always wore to the bastion, still hadn't been mended.

"Why isn't my coat fixed? You never do anything but sleep, you useless fool!" Mikhaïloff snapped.

"Sleep?" Nikita grumbled. "I work like a dog all day. Even when I stop, I still don't get to rest."

"You're drunk again, aren't you?"

"Not on your money, so what's the problem?"

"Shut up, idiot!" Mikhaïloff yelled, his patience snapping. At first, he had been lost in thought, but now Nikita's rude attitude had pushed him over the edge. He had known this servant for twelve years, even spoiled him at times, but tonight, he was fed up.

"I'm an idiot, huh?" Nikita muttered. "Why are you calling me that, sir? At a time like this? That's not right."

Mikhaïloff suddenly remembered where he was about to go. His anger faded, and shame took its place.

"You drive me crazy, Nikita," he said more gently. "Just leave the letter for my father on the table, and don't touch it." His face turned red as he spoke.

"Yes, sir," Nikita replied, his mood changing. The alcohol in his system made him soft, and he blinked like he was about to cry.

As Mikhaïloff stepped onto the porch, he turned and said, "Goodbye, Nikita."

At those words, Nikita suddenly lost control of his emotions. He sobbed and rushed forward, grabbing his master's hand and kissing it.

"Goodbye, sir!" he cried.

An old sailor's wife, standing nearby, couldn't help but be moved by the moment. Wiping her eyes on her sleeve, she began talking about how hard life was, about how even officers had their struggles. Then she launched into the same story she had told Nikita a hundred times—how her husband had been killed in the first bombardment, how her house had been destroyed (the one she was living in now wasn't hers), and how she had been left a poor widow.

But as soon as his master was out of sight, Nikita lit his pipe and sent the landlord's daughter to fetch some more vodka. It didn't take long for his tears to dry. Before the night was over, he was already arguing with the old woman about some bucket she had supposedly broken.

Meanwhile, as Mikhaïloff marched through the fading daylight with his company, his mind raced with new thoughts.

"Maybe I won't die... maybe I'll just get wounded," he told himself. "But where? How bad? Here? Or here?" He touched his chest and stomach, trying to imagine what kind of injury he might survive.

"If it's my leg, maybe I'll make it through. But if it's my side—or if a shell hits me—then it's over."

The captain made it safely through the trenches and reached the fortifications. In the darkness, he worked with a sapper officer to get his men started on their tasks. Then, he sat down in a small pit behind the protective barrier.

The gunfire was light—only occasionally did flashes of light burst from their batteries, followed by answering shots from the enemy. Every so often, the glowing trail of a bomb arched across the starry sky. But none of the bombs landed near him; they all fell farther back and to the right of the rifle pits where he was sitting.

Feeling a bit more relaxed, he took a sip of vodka, ate some cheese, and lit a cigarette. After a short prayer, he got comfortable and tried to fall asleep.

V.

Prince Galtsin, Lieutenant-Colonel Neferdoff, and Praskukhin—who hadn't been invited but still tagged along without anyone speaking to him—followed Adjutant Kalugin to his quarters for tea.

"You never finished telling me about Vaska Mendel," Kalugin said, taking off his cloak and settling into a soft chair by the window.

He unbuttoned the stiff collar of his freshly starched shirt and made himself comfortable. "How did he end up getting married?"

"Oh, that's a wild story! Back then, it was all anyone in Petersburg could talk about," Prince Galtsin said, laughing as he moved away from the piano and sat on the windowsill beside Kalugin. "I know every detail—it's absolutely ridiculous."

He launched into a lively and entertaining story about a scandalous romance, but since it has no relevance to us, we'll skip it. What's worth noting, though, is how different these men seemed now compared to when they were on the boulevard. Gone was the arrogance they usually displayed toward the infantry officers. Here, among their own, they were relaxed, friendly, and even playful— especially Kalugin and Galtsin, who now acted like cheerful, carefree young men.

The conversation drifted to people they knew from Petersburg and their fellow officers.

"What about Maslovsky?"

"Which one? The uhlan from the bodyguard or the horse guard?"

"I know both. The one in the horse guards was just a kid when I first met him, fresh out of school. What rank is the older one now? Captain?"

"Oh, yes, he was promoted a while ago."

"Is he still running around with that gypsy woman?"

"No, he left her..."

And so the conversation went, hopping from one name to another, full of gossip and stories.

Then, Prince Galtsin sat at the piano and sang a gypsy song with impressive skill. Praskukhin, though no one had asked him, joined in as a backup singer. He did such a good job that they asked him to do it again, which he happily did.

A servant entered, carrying tea, cream, and biscuits on a silver tray.

"Serve the prince," Kalugin ordered.

"It's funny when you think about it," Galtsin said, taking his tea and looking out the window. "We're in a city under siege, yet here we are, drinking tea with cream and living in rooms as nice as anything in Petersburg."

"If not for that," said the old lieutenant-colonel, who always found something to complain about, "this endless waiting would be unbearable. Every day, men are dying—constantly—and it never seems to end. And if we had to live in the mud like the others, that would be truly miserable."

"And what about our infantry officers?" Kalugin asked. "They're out there on the bastions, living with the soldiers, eating the same food as them. What about them?"

"What about them? They don't change their clothes for ten days straight," the colonel said. "But they're true heroes—remarkable men."

Just then, an infantry officer entered the room.

"I... I was sent... May I report to His Excellency from General N.?" he asked hesitantly, bowing awkwardly.

Kalugin stood up but didn't return the salute. Instead, he looked at the officer with a forced, polite smile that was more insulting than welcoming. In a formal tone, he told the officer to wait, then immediately turned back to Galtsin and started speaking to him in French.

The poor infantry officer, left standing in the middle of the room, had no idea what to do with himself.

"It's urgent, sir," the officer said after a brief pause.

"Ah, well then," Kalugin replied, putting on his cloak and walking him to the door.

When he returned, he said in French, "Well, gentlemen, I think tonight is going to be intense."

"A battle?" they all asked eagerly.

"I'm not sure yet—you'll find out soon enough," Kalugin answered with a mysterious smile.

"My commander is at the bastion," Praskukhin said as he fastened his sword. "I'll probably have to go."

No one responded. It was his own responsibility to know whether he was needed or not.

Praskukhin and Neferdoff left to report to their posts. "Goodbye, gentlemen!" Kalugin called from the window as they rode off, hunched over their Cossack saddles. The sound of their horses' hooves soon faded into the dimly lit streets.

"Tell me honestly," Galtsin asked in French as he and Kalugin leaned on the windowsill, watching bombs arc through the air, "is something really happening tonight?"

"Well... you've been to the bastions before, haven't you?" Kalugin asked.

Galtsin nodded, though he had only been once.

"Then you know there's a trench right in front of our fortifications," Kalugin continued, explaining the battle plans as best he could, even though he wasn't a strategist. He mixed up military terms, but that didn't stop him from confidently describing how things would unfold.

Meanwhile, the enemy gunfire grew louder. "They're really hammering our defenses now. Look at that—was that ours or theirs?" he asked as they watched a bomb explode in the air. The flashes of gunfire lit up the dark blue sky, sending smoke curling into the night.

"It's actually a beautiful sight, isn't it?" Kalugin remarked. "Sometimes you can't even tell the difference between the stars and the bombs."

"Yeah, I was just thinking that," Galtsin said. "I thought that one was a star, but then it fell and—there! It just exploded. That big star over there—what's it called? It looks exactly like a bomb."

"You know, I've gotten so used to seeing them that I think starlit nights back home will always remind me of bombs," Kalugin said.

After a short silence, Galtsin asked, "Should I be going out there too?"

"Come on, don't even think about it," Kalugin said. "Your time will come, just wait."

"Really? You don't think I should go?"

Before Kalugin could answer, a sudden burst of rifle fire drowned out the cannons. The shots flickered like fireflies along the line of battle, flashing without pause.

"This is it—the real fight has started," Kalugin said. "That's the sound of rifle fire. I can't hear it without feeling something deep in my gut."

Then came a long, roaring cheer—hundreds of voices shouting together from the bastion.

"Was that them or us?" Galtsin asked.

"I don't know," Kalugin replied. "But it's turned into close combat—the gunfire has stopped."

At that moment, an officer rode up to the house, his Cossack galloping hard. He jumped off his horse and ran inside.

"Where are you coming from?"

"The bastion. The general is needed immediately," the officer said, out of breath but still calm as he hurried to the door.

"What's happening?"

"They attacked our trenches... at first, they took them. The French sent in reinforcements, and we only had two battalions to fight back," the officer explained, still catching his breath.

"Did we retreat?" Galtsin asked.

"No," the officer said sharply. "Our battalion pushed them back, but our regiment commander was killed. We lost a lot of officers. I was sent to request reinforcements."

Kalugin and the officer left to deliver the report to the general.

Five minutes later, Kalugin was riding off on a Cossack's horse, sitting in that exaggerated style that adjutants always seemed to find impressive. He trotted toward the bastion to give orders and wait for the final outcome of the battle.

Meanwhile, Galtsin, feeling the unease of watching a battle unfold without taking part in it, wandered into the street and started pacing back and forth with no real purpose.

VI.

The soldiers carried the wounded on stretchers or helped them walk by supporting their arms. The streets were completely dark, except for the occasional light shining from a hospital window or a small fire where officers gathered. The deep booms of cannons and sharp cracks of rifle fire still echoed from the fort, with bright flashes lighting up the night sky. Every now and then, the sound of a horse's hooves, the painful groans of an injured man, or the quiet voices of stretcher-bearers broke the silence. A few frightened women stood outside their homes, watching the explosions with worry.

Among them were Nikita, the old sailor's widow—who had forgiven him for their earlier fight—and her ten-year-old daughter.

"Lord, Holy Mother of God," the old woman whispered with a sigh as she watched the fiery bombs streak across the sky. "What a terrible thing! It wasn't like this during the first attack. Oh, look! That one just exploded—cursed thing—right over our house in the suburbs."

"No, mama, it's farther away. They're falling in Aunt Arinka's garden," the little girl corrected.

"And where is my master now?" Nikita mumbled, still a little drunk. "Oh, how I love that master of mine! I don't even know why— I just do! If—God forbid—they kill him in this awful fight, I swear I don't know what I'll do! He's such a good man—words can't describe it. Would I trade him for one of those officers who just sit around playing cards? Never! Not in a million years!" Nikita pointed toward the window of his master's house, where, in his absence, Yunker Zhvadchevsky had invited some friends over to celebrate his new medal. Inside, Sub-Lieutenant Ugrovitch and Sub-Lieutenant Nepshisetsky, who was suffering from a cold, were drinking together.

"They look like little stars!" the girl suddenly said, breaking the silence that followed Nikita's speech. "See? They shoot across the sky just like real stars. Look, there's another one! Mama, why do they do that?"

"They're going to destroy our house," the old woman sighed, not answering her daughter's question.

"And when Uncle and I went there today," the girl continued excitedly, "we found a huge cannonball right inside the house, near the cupboard! It smashed through the wall! It's so big, I couldn't even lift it."

"People who had money or family left the city," the old woman said bitterly. "But I had no one, and now they're destroying the only home I had left. Look at them, still firing, those heartless men. Lord, have mercy!"

"And when Uncle and I stepped outside, a bomb flew right at us! It hit the ground and exploded—dirt went everywhere! A piece of the shell almost hit us," the girl added, her voice high with excitement.

VII.

Prince Galtsin saw more and more wounded soldiers—some being carried on stretchers, others walking while helping each other, talking loudly as they moved.

"When they charged at us, brothers," said a tall soldier with two rifles slung over his shoulder, speaking in a deep voice, "they shouted 'Allah, Allah!' and just kept coming. You take one down, and another takes his place—there was no stopping them. I've never seen so many of them before…"

Before he could finish, Galtsin interrupted.

"You were at the bastion?"

"Yes, sir."

"What happened there? Tell me."

"Well, sir, they attacked in full force. They climbed over the walls, and that was it. They took over completely."

"What do you mean, took over? Didn't you push them back?" Galtsin asked, frowning.

"How could we push them back when they came at us with everything they had? They killed most of our men, and no reinforcements came."

The soldier was mistaken—our troops were behind him, not lost—but it's common for wounded soldiers to think their side has suffered a terrible defeat, no matter the outcome.

"But I was told the enemy was pushed back," Galtsin said, frustrated. "Maybe they were driven out after you left? When did you leave?"

"I just came from there, sir," the soldier replied. "It doesn't seem likely. The trenches are in their hands now… they won."

"You're not ashamed to give up the trenches so easily? This is disgraceful!" Galtsin snapped, frustrated by what seemed like a lack of care.

"What could we do against so many?" the soldier muttered.

"And sir," added a soldier lying on a stretcher, who had just caught up with them, "how could we hold out when almost all of us were dead? If we had the numbers, we would've fought to the last man. But what else could we do? I took down one of them, then I got hit…" His face twisted in pain. "Oh—easy, brothers! Go slower! Ahh!" he groaned.

"There seem to be too many men leaving the bastion," Galtsin said, his eyes narrowing as he spotted another soldier with two rifles. "Why are you walking away? Stop right there!"

The soldier paused and removed his cap with his left hand.

"Where are you going, and why?" Galtsin demanded.

But as he stepped closer, he saw the soldier's right arm wrapped in a blood-soaked bandage, and the realization made him freeze.

"I'm wounded, sir," the soldier answered.

"Wounded? Where?"

"Must've been a bullet, right here," the soldier said, pointing to his arm. "Not sure yet. And something hit me in the head." He bent forward, showing the back of his hair, matted with dried blood.

"And whose gun is that other one?" Galtsin asked, glancing at the second rifle.

"It's a fine French one, sir! I took it in battle. And I wouldn't have left if I weren't helping this man—he might collapse," he added, nodding toward another soldier ahead, limping heavily and leaning on his rifle.

Suddenly, Galtsin felt deeply ashamed of himself for doubting them. His face flushed, and he turned away without saying another word. Without looking back, he hurried toward the place where the wounded were being treated.

When he reached the entrance, he had to push through a crowd of injured men and stretcher-bearers carrying the wounded inside and taking the dead out. But as soon as he stepped into the first room, he took one look around and immediately turned back.

The sight was too horrifying.

VIII.

The large, dark hall was lit by only a few candles held by doctors as they moved through the crowded room, tending to the wounded. Stretcher-bearers kept carrying in more injured men, laying them wherever they could find space on the packed floor. Some soldiers lay pressed against each other, their blood mixing as more kept arriving. The few empty spots were already stained with dark puddles.

The air was thick and heavy, filled with heat from so many bodies, the strained breathing of the wounded, and the damp steam rising from the stretcher-bearers' hard work. The candlelight flickered weakly in the suffocating room. A low chorus of moans, sighs, and ragged breathing echoed throughout the hall, sometimes interrupted by sudden, sharp cries of pain.

Nurses moved quickly through the room, stepping carefully over bodies as they brought medicine, water, and bandages. Their expressions were not of empty pity, but of calm and determined care.

Doctors with rolled-up sleeves knelt beside the wounded, their assistants holding candles to help them see. They examined wounds, felt for broken bones, and performed painful procedures, ignoring the desperate groans and pleas of the soldiers. One doctor sat by the door, writing down names and injuries.

"Iván Bogaeff, private, third company of the S— regiment. Complicated leg fracture," called a doctor from across the hall as he pressed on a crushed leg.

"Turn him over."

"Ooh, my fathers, please, no!" the soldier begged, crying out in pain.

"Head injury," another doctor reported as he examined an unconscious officer.

"Lieutenant Colonel Semyon Neferdoff, N— infantry regiment. Hold on, Colonel, this is the only way to treat you," he said as he carefully removed pieces of bone from the man's head with a tool.

"Ah! Stop! Please, for God's sake, hurry—!" the colonel screamed before his voice turned into a painful wail.

"Chest wound," another doctor announced. "Sevastyan Sereda, private. What regiment? Never mind, it doesn't matter... he's dying. Take him away."

The soldier's eyes rolled back as his breath became shallow. The doctor moved on.

Outside the door, around forty stretcher-bearers stood quietly, waiting to take the wounded to the hospital and the dead to the chapel. They watched without speaking, letting out deep sighs every now and then.

IX.

On his way to the bastion, Kalugin passed many wounded soldiers, but he knew from experience that seeing them could shake his confidence before a battle. So, instead of stopping to ask questions, he tried not to look at them at all. At the bottom of the hill, he spotted an orderly racing past on horseback.

"Zobkin! Stop a moment!" Kalugin called out.

"What is it?" the orderly replied, barely slowing down.

"Where are you coming from?"

"The trenches."

"How bad is it there?"

"Terrible!" the orderly shouted before galloping away.

Even though there wasn't much gunfire, the cannons were roaring louder and more often than before. Kalugin felt a wave of uneasiness. A sudden thought of death crossed his mind, something that often happens before a battle. But Kalugin saw himself as a fearless man. He pushed the feeling away and reminded himself of a story about one of Napoleon's officers. The officer had been wounded while leading an attack, but when Napoleon asked if he was hurt, he simply said, "I beg your pardon, Sire, I am dead," before falling from his horse.

Kalugin liked that story—it made him feel like he could be just as brave. He gave his horse a sharp kick, sat a little straighter in the saddle, and glanced back at his orderly to make sure he was keeping up. He wanted to look as bold and confident as possible as he rode to the spot where he had to dismount.

Four soldiers sat on nearby rocks, smoking.

"What are you doing here?" he snapped.

"We just carried a wounded man back, sir, and stopped to rest," one of them answered, quickly hiding his pipe and taking off his cap.

"Resting, are you? Get back to your posts!" Kalugin ordered, then walked up the hill through the trenches, passing more injured soldiers along the way.

When he reached the top, he turned left and suddenly found himself alone. Splinters from exploding shells zipped past him, and another bomb soared overhead, heading straight toward him. Panic hit him. He ran a few steps and threw himself onto the ground. But when the bomb exploded far away, he felt embarrassed. He quickly stood up, glancing around to see if anyone had noticed. Luckily, no one had.

Once fear sets in, it doesn't leave easily. Kalugin, who had always bragged about his courage, found himself moving quickly, almost crawling through the trench. "This is bad," he thought, stumbling as he went. "I'm definitely going to be killed." His heart pounded, sweat dripped down his back, and he was breathing heavily. He didn't even try to fight his fear anymore.

Then, he heard footsteps ahead. Instantly, he straightened up, raised his head, and slowed his pace, making sure his sword clanked loudly as he walked. He didn't want to look afraid. He met an officer and a sailor coming toward him. When the officer suddenly shouted, "Get down!" and pointed at a glowing bomb hurtling toward them, Kalugin only lowered his head slightly, too proud to duck.

"Wow, he's fearless!" the sailor whispered to the officer, impressed that Kalugin hadn't even flinched. He had watched the bomb explode and could tell that its fragments wouldn't reach them.

Just ahead, Kalugin saw the casemate where the bastion commander was stationed. But as he crossed the last open stretch, his vision blurred, and his body filled with dread. His heart pounded harder, his face flushed, and he had to force himself forward to reach the shelter.

"Why are you so out of breath?" the general asked after Kalugin delivered his orders.

"I walked here quickly, sir," Kalugin replied.

"Would you like some wine?"

Kalugin nodded, took the glass, and lit a cigarette. By then, the fight had ended. Only the steady roar of cannon fire remained, rumbling from both sides.

Inside the bunker, General N., the commander of the bastion, sat with six other officers, including Praskukhin, discussing different details of the battle. The room was surprisingly comfortable, with blue curtains, a sofa, a bed, a table covered with papers, a clock on the wall, and religious icons with a small lamp burning in front of them. The thick wooden beams of the ceiling and the muffled sound of gunfire outside made Kalugin wonder how he had let himself feel so afraid earlier. He was frustrated with himself and wanted another chance to prove his courage.

"I'm glad you're here, Captain," Kalugin said to a naval officer who had just entered. The man wore a staff officer's cloak, had a thick mustache, and bore the St. George Cross. He had come to ask the general for men to help repair two gun openings that had been destroyed.

"The general wanted me to check if your cannons can fire grapeshot into the trenches," Kalugin added when the captain finished speaking with the general.

"Only one of my guns can do that," the captain replied gruffly.

"Let's go check anyway," Kalugin suggested.

The captain frowned and muttered, clearly annoyed. "I've been out there all night, and I came here just to get a little rest. Can't you go on your own? My assistant, Lieutenant Kartz, is there—he'll show you everything."

The captain had been commanding one of the most dangerous batteries for six months. Even before they had bunkers, he had lived in the bastion among the sailors since the start of the siege. He was known for his bravery, so his refusal surprised Kalugin. "So that's what reputation is worth," he thought.

"Well, I'll go alone then, if that's all right," Kalugin said, trying to make a joke. But the captain ignored him.

What Kalugin didn't consider was that he had spent maybe fifty hours total on the bastion, while the captain had been there nonstop for six months. Kalugin was driven by a need to impress others, to build his reputation, and to feel the thrill of danger. But the captain had already been through all that. At first, he had wanted to prove himself too. He had shown courage, taken risks, and even earned recognition. But after so much time in battle, those feelings had faded. Now, he simply did his duty. He understood that after six months in the bastion, his chances of survival were slim, and he wouldn't risk his life unless absolutely necessary. In contrast, the young lieutenant who had only been in the battery for a week and was now showing Kalugin around seemed ten times braver than the captain.

After inspecting the battery, Kalugin returned to the bunker and nearly bumped into the general in the dark as the general and his staff climbed up to the watchtower.

"Captain Praskukhin," the general said, "go to the first lodgement and tell the second battery of the M— regiment to stop their work. They are to leave quietly and join their regiment at the base of the hill, where they are being held in reserve. Do you understand? Lead them there yourself."

"Yes, sir," Praskukhin answered before running off toward the lodgement.

The gunfire outside was starting to slow down.

X.

"Is this the second battalion of the M— regiment?" Praskukhin asked as he rushed forward, accidentally bumping into soldiers carrying heavy sacks of earth.

"Yes, sir," one of them replied.

"Where is your commander?"

Mikhaïloff, thinking the question was for the company commander, crawled out of his trench. Seeing Praskukhin, he assumed he was speaking to a superior officer and quickly saluted.

"The general has ordered… that you… move back as quickly and quietly as possible… not all the way back, just to the reserve line," Praskukhin said nervously, glancing toward the enemy's position.

When Mikhaïloff recognized Praskukhin and understood the situation, he lowered his hand, gave the necessary orders, and the battalion began to move. The soldiers picked up their weapons, pulled on their coats, and set off.

Anyone who has never been in a battle cannot understand the overwhelming relief of leaving a dangerous position after hours under enemy fire. For three long hours, Mikhaïloff had been sure he would not make it out alive. He had convinced himself that his fate was sealed and that he no longer belonged to this world. Yet, as he finally led his men away from the lodgement alongside Praskukhin, he had to resist the urge to break into a run.

"See you later," said the major of another battalion, who was staying behind and had shared some cheese with Mikhaïloff while they had been hiding behind the earthworks. "Safe journey."

"Thanks. Hope things stay quiet for you now," Mikhaïloff replied.

But just as he spoke, the enemy, having noticed movement in the trenches, increased their fire. The Russian cannons answered, and another heavy exchange began. The stars shone faintly in the night sky, but the darkness was thick. Only the flashes of gunfire and the glow of exploding bombs lit the scene for brief moments. The soldiers marched in silence, staying close together. Their boots thudded in rhythm on the dry ground, bayonets clinked as they knocked against each other, and every now and then, a young soldier whispered a nervous prayer.

"Lord, Lord! What is happening?" one muttered.

Now and then, a wounded man groaned, followed by a desperate cry for a stretcher. In Mikhaïloff's company alone, twenty-six men had been killed that night by artillery fire.

Lightning flashed far off on the horizon. A sentry called out from the bastion, "Cannon!" A shell whistled overhead, crashing into the ground ahead and sending dirt and rocks flying.

"Why are they moving so slowly?" Praskukhin thought, glancing behind him again and again as he walked beside Mikhaïloff. "Maybe I should run ahead—I already delivered the message. But no, if I do, they'll think I'm a coward. Whatever happens, I'll stay with them."

"Why is he walking right behind me?" Mikhaïloff wondered. "Every time he's around, something bad happens. That one is coming right at us…"

After walking several hundred more yards, they ran into Kalugin, who was on his way to the bunker, swinging his sword confidently. The general had sent him to check on the work being done at the fortifications. But when Kalugin saw Mikhaïloff, he realized that instead of heading straight into the dangerous area, he could just ask Mikhaïloff for an update.

Mikhaïloff gave a full report. Satisfied, Kalugin walked with them for a short distance before turning into a trench that led to the bunker.

"What's happening?" asked an officer who was sitting alone at a table, eating his supper.

"Seems like nothing major. I don't think there will be any more fighting tonight."

"How so? The general just went up to check the defenses. A new regiment has already arrived. Listen… the firing has started again. You should stay here," the officer said, noticing that Kalugin was about to leave.

Kalugin hesitated. "I really should go," he thought. "But I've already put myself in enough danger today. The fighting is intense."

"Maybe I'll just wait here," he said instead.

About twenty minutes later, the general returned with his officers. Among them was Baron Pesth, but Praskukhin was missing. The Russian forces had successfully taken and secured the lodgement.

After getting a full report, Kalugin and Pesth left the bunker.

XI.

"There's blood on your cloak. Did you fight up close?" Kalugin asked.

"Oh, it was awful! Just imagine…" Pesth began excitedly, jumping into his story. He talked about leading his company, how his commander had been killed, how he had stabbed a French soldier, and how, without him, they might have lost the battle.

The basics of his story were true—the commander had died, and he had killed an enemy soldier—but the details were exaggerated. Pesth wasn't trying to lie on purpose. During the battle, everything had been a blur, and now he could hardly remember what had happened. It all felt distant, like something he had seen in a dream, so he filled in the gaps in a way that made himself look braver.

What had really happened was this:

The battalion Pesth was assigned to had stood near a wall for two hours, waiting under enemy fire. Then the commander gave an order, the officers passed it down, and the battalion moved forward, marching past their protective cover. They walked about a hundred steps before stopping and forming into groups. Pesth, assigned to the right flank of the second company, stood there without knowing what was happening or why. His heart pounded, a chill ran down his spine, and he stared straight ahead into the darkness, dreading what might come next.

Since the firing had stopped, his fear lessened, but he still felt strange standing out in the open, away from the safety of the fortress. The commander gave another order, the officers whispered to their men, and suddenly, the soldiers in front of him disappeared. They had been ordered to lie down. Pesth quickly dropped to the ground too, pricking his hand on something sharp as he did.

Only one man remained standing—his company commander. The short officer paced in front of the group, waving his sword and shouting nonstop.

"Stay close together! Don't shoot—use your bayonets! We'll show them what we're made of! For our Tsar!"

"What's our commander's name?" Pesth whispered to a fellow soldier lying beside him. "He's fearless!"

"That's Lisinkovsky," the soldier replied. "He's always like this in battle."

At that moment, a sudden flash of light lit up the night sky, followed by a deafening explosion. Rocks and debris flew into the air. A second later, a heavy stone crashed down and crushed a soldier's foot. The French had spotted them.

"So they're using bombs now!" Lisinkovsky shouted. "Just wait until we get close—you'll feel the sharp end of a Russian bayonet!" He yelled so loudly that the battalion commander had to tell him to be quiet.

Then the first company stood up, followed by the second. They fixed bayonets, and the battalion began moving forward.

Pesth was so terrified that he barely remembered what happened next. He staggered forward like a man in a daze. Suddenly, blinding lights flashed all around him. Gunfire roared. Something whizzed past his ear. Everyone screamed and charged. He screamed too and ran, simply because everyone else was running. Then he tripped and crashed into something on the ground—it was the wounded company commander.

Lisinkovsky, mistaking Pesth for an enemy, grabbed his leg and held on tightly. Panicked, Pesth kicked free and scrambled to his feet. Then someone ran into his back, almost knocking him down again.

"Run him through! What are you waiting for?!" a voice shouted.

Pesth instinctively grabbed a gun and stabbed his bayonet into something soft.

"Ah, Dieu!" came a terrible cry.

Only then did Pesth realize he had stabbed a French soldier. A wave of cold sweat covered him. He shuddered as if he had a fever and immediately dropped the gun. For a brief moment, he felt sick.

But then another thought struck him—he was a hero! He had fought bravely! He grabbed the gun again and ran forward with the others, yelling "Hurrah!"

After about twenty steps, they reached the trench. There, he found his fellow soldiers and the wounded company commander.

"I stabbed one!" he blurted out.

"You're a brave man, Baron," the commander said.

XII.

"Did you hear? Praskukhin was killed," Pesth said as he walked with Kalugin.

"That can't be!"

"It's true. I saw it happen."

"Well, I have to go," Kalugin said quickly.

As Kalugin walked back, he felt satisfied. "That went well," he thought. "For the first time, I had real success on duty. The battle was intense, and I made it out in one piece. There will be awards, and I'll probably get a golden sword. I deserve it."

After reporting everything to the general, he returned to his room, where Prince Galtsin was waiting. Galtsin had arrived much earlier and was reading a book he found on Kalugin's table.

Kalugin felt an overwhelming sense of relief to be back in safety. He changed into his nightshirt, lay down on the couch, and started telling Galtsin about the battle. Of course, he told the story in a way that made him look like a brave and skilled officer—though he believed that should already be obvious to everyone. The only person who might have disagreed was Praskukhin, who, ironically, had admired Kalugin but had secretly told a friend the night before that Kalugin seemed afraid of going to the bastions.

Meanwhile, just before Praskukhin's death, he had been walking with Mikhaïloff when they parted ways with Kalugin. As they moved to a safer area, Praskukhin started to calm down. Then, suddenly, a bright flash lit up the sky behind them.

"Mortar!" a soldier shouted.

Another voice in the battalion called out, "It's coming straight at the bastion!"

Mikhaïloff turned around. A fiery point of light hovered in the sky, too high to tell exactly where it would land. But within a second, the bomb dropped lower, moving faster, its fuse burning brightly as it whistled through the air.

"Get down!" someone shouted.

Praskukhin and Mikhaïloff threw themselves to the ground. Praskukhin shut his eyes tight. He heard the bomb smash into the ground nearby.

A second passed—an eternity in his mind—but nothing happened. Had he panicked for nothing? Maybe the bomb had landed farther away than he thought. He opened his eyes and saw Mikhaïloff lying completely still beside him. Relief swept over him—until he spotted the burning fuse, twisting just a few feet away.

Terror filled his entire body. His thoughts raced.

"Who will it hit—Mikhaïloff or me? Maybe both? If it's me, where will it land? If in my head, I'm done for. But if it's my leg, they'll amputate. I'll make sure they give me chloroform... I could survive. But maybe only Mikhaïloff will die, and I'll tell the story of how we were walking together when he was killed, and his blood splattered on me. No—it's closer to me! I'm going to die!"

Suddenly, he remembered the 20 rubles he owed Mikhaïloff. Then, another unpaid debt in Petersburg. A song from the night before played in his mind. He pictured a woman he loved in a lilac-ribboned hat. He thought of a man who had insulted him five years ago, someone he had never gotten revenge on. All these memories swirled in his mind, tangled with the overwhelming fear of death.

"But maybe it won't explode," he thought. With desperate courage, he forced his eyes open.

At that moment, a blinding red flash filled his vision. A deafening blast struck his chest like a hammer. His body reacted on its own— he tried to run but tripped over his sword and collapsed to the ground.

"Thank God! It's just a bruise," was his first thought. He tried to move his hands to touch his chest, but his arms felt trapped, and his head throbbed as if something was squeezing it. Shapes of soldiers moved in and out of his blurry vision, and he found himself counting them.

"One, two, three soldiers… and an officer wrapped in his cloak," he thought. A bright flash filled his eyes. Was it gunfire? Mortars? Cannons? It had to be cannons. Another flash. More soldiers passed. Four, five, six, seven.

Suddenly, fear gripped him. What if they stepped on him? He wanted to yell, to tell them he was hurt, but his throat was so dry his tongue stuck to the roof of his mouth. A deep thirst burned inside him.

Then he noticed a wet, warm feeling spreading across his chest. It reminded him of water, and for a second, he wanted to drink it—whatever it was. "I must have scraped myself when I fell," he thought.

Panic rose in him. The soldiers were getting closer. Were they going to trample him? He gathered all his strength to call out, "Take me with you!" But instead of words, a horrible groan escaped his lips. The sound of it scared him.

More red flashes flickered in his vision. It felt like stones were being stacked on his chest, pressing down harder and harder. The flashes dimmed, the weight grew heavier.

He struggled to push the weight off. He stretched his body—and then everything went dark. No sights, no sounds, no thoughts.

He had been killed instantly, a piece of shrapnel tearing through the center of his chest.

XIII.

Mikhaïloff saw the bomb and immediately dropped to the ground. Like Praskukhin, in just a few seconds, his mind raced through countless thoughts. He silently prayed, repeating, "Let Your will be done!"

"Why did I even join the army?" he wondered. "Why did I transfer to the infantry for this campaign? I could have stayed with the Uhlans in T., spent time with Natasha... and now, here I am."

He started counting to himself—"One, two, three, four"—thinking that if the bomb exploded on an even number, he would survive, but if on an odd number, he would die. "It's over. I'm dead," he thought when the explosion came. He felt a sharp pain in his head.

"Lord, forgive me," he whispered, clasping his hands together. Then everything went dark.

When he came to, the first thing he felt was warm blood trickling from his nose and a throbbing pain in his head, though it wasn't as bad as before. "Is this my soul leaving my body?" he thought. "What happens next? Lord, take me in peace." But then something strange occurred to him—if he was dying, why could he still hear soldiers' footsteps and gunfire so clearly?

"Get the stretchers! The captain is down!" shouted a voice above him. It was his drummer, Ignatieff.

Someone grabbed his shoulders. Mikhaïloff forced his eyes open and saw the deep blue night sky, the scattered stars, and two bombs whistling through the air. He saw Ignatieff, soldiers carrying stretchers, the dirt walls of the trench. In that instant, he realized—he was still alive.

A piece of debris had hit his head, only slightly injuring him. His first feeling was almost regret—he had prepared himself for death so completely that waking up to the sounds of battle, surrounded by blood and chaos, felt disappointing. Then came relief—he was alive. And finally, the overwhelming urge to get away from the bastion as soon as possible.

The drummer wrapped a handkerchief around his head and helped him up. "Come, sir, let's get you to the medics."

Mikhaïloff took a few steps but then stopped. "Wait… where am I going? Why?" His mind cleared. "My men are still out there. They'll be out of range soon, so I should stay with them," a voice inside told him.

"No, brother," he said, pulling away. "I won't go to the hospital. I'll stay with my men."

"You should get it checked, sir," Ignatieff urged. "It might not seem bad now, but if you don't treat it, it'll get worse. It's already swelling—really, sir."

Mikhaïloff hesitated but then thought about the many soldiers with serious wounds waiting for help. "The doctor will probably just laugh at this scratch," he thought. He made up his mind and rejoined his men, ignoring the drummer's protests.

"Where's Officer Praskukhin? He was with us," Mikhaïloff asked another officer leading the group.

"I don't know. Probably dead," the lieutenant muttered.

"How do you not know? He was right next to us. Why didn't you bring him?"

"How could we?" the lieutenant shot back. "We barely got out ourselves!"

"How could you leave him, Mikhaïl Ivánowitch?" Mikhaïloff said angrily. "If he was alive, you should've carried him. And if he was dead, you still should've brought him."

"I'm telling you, I saw him. He didn't make it," the lieutenant insisted. "But if you want, send some men to check."

Mikhaïloff sat down, his head throbbing. "I should go back," he thought. "Maybe he's still alive." He glanced at the soldiers. "It's our duty, Mikhaïl Ivánowitch," he said.

The lieutenant stayed silent.

"If he didn't bring him before, sending men back now would be useless. They'd just risk their lives for nothing," Mikhaïloff thought. "It's my fault for not checking earlier. I should go myself."

He turned to his men. "We have to go back for the officer in the ditch," he ordered, though his voice was not as firm as usual. He could tell they didn't want to go. Since he hadn't called on anyone directly, no one moved.

"Maybe Praskukhin is already dead," he reasoned. "I can't force them into danger for nothing. But I have to be sure. It's my responsibility."

"Mikhaïl Ivánowitch, take the men forward. I'll catch up," he said. He pulled up his cloak, pressed his hand to the image of Saint Mitrofaniy he always carried, and ran back through the trench.

After finding Praskukhin's body, he made his way back, exhausted, supporting his aching head with one hand. By the time he caught up, the battalion had reached a safer area at the base of the hill. But the gunfire hadn't completely stopped—random shells still crashed into the ground nearby.

"I'll have to go to the hospital tomorrow," Mikhaïloff thought as a medic wrapped his bandage tighter. "I'll at least put my name down."

XIV.

Hundreds of bodies, still covered in fresh blood, lay motionless in the damp, flower-filled valley between the bastion and the trench. Just two hours earlier, these men had dreams, hopes, and fears—big and small. Now, their limbs were stiff and lifeless, scattered across the battlefield and the chapel floor in Sevastopol.

Hundreds more clung to life, writhing in pain, whispering prayers or cursing through dry, cracked lips. Some lay among the dead in the valley, while others groaned on stretchers, cots, or the blood-stained hospital floor.

And yet, just like every morning before, the dawn appeared over Sapun Mountain. The stars faded, a white mist spread from the dark, restless sea, and the sky in the east glowed red. Streaks of pink stretched across the horizon, and the bright, beautiful sun rose again, as if nothing had changed—promising warmth, love, and happiness to the world.

XV.

The next day, the military band played on the boulevard once again. Officers, cadets, soldiers, and young women strolled near the pavilion and under the drooping branches of blooming white acacias, just like before.

Kalugin, Prince Galtsin, and a colonel walked arm-in-arm, discussing the battle from the day before. But instead of focusing on the fight itself, most of their talk was about the parts they had played in it. Their expressions were serious, almost somber, as if they were deeply affected by the losses. But since none of them had lost anyone truly close to them, their sadness was more of a formal act— something expected of them.

In reality, Kalugin and the colonel wouldn't have minded another battle like that, as long as it meant a medal or a promotion. They were both good men, but ambition drove them. And really, if you asked any young officer, you'd find plenty who would risk hundreds of lives just for the chance to earn a medal or a higher rank.

"No, I'm sure it started on the left flank. I was there myself," said the colonel.

"Maybe," Kalugin replied. "I was farther to the right. I went there twice—once looking for the general and another time to check the trenches. It was rough."

"Kalugin would know," Galtsin said to the colonel. "You know, V. told me today that you're a brave man."

"But the losses were terrible," the colonel added. "I lost four hundred men in my regiment. I'm lucky I made it out alive."

Just then, Mikhaïloff appeared at the far end of the boulevard, walking toward them with his head wrapped in a bandage.

"What happened, Captain? Are you hurt?" Kalugin asked.

"Just a small wound. A stone hit me," Mikhaïloff replied.

"Has the flag been lowered yet?" Prince Galtsin asked, not looking at anyone in particular.

"No, not yet," Mikhaïloff answered quickly in French, wanting to show he could speak the language.

"Is the truce still in place?" Galtsin asked him again, but this time in Russian, as if to say, Why struggle with French when you could just speak your own language? Then, without another word, the officers walked away, leaving Mikhaïloff alone once more.

Feeling isolated, just like the night before, he gave polite nods to passing officers, some of whom he didn't care to approach, and others he didn't feel comfortable speaking to. Finally, he sat down near the Kazarsky monument and lit a cigarette.

Meanwhile, Baron Pesth arrived, bragging about how he had helped arrange the truce and spoken with French officers. He claimed one had told him, "If daylight had lasted just thirty more minutes, we would have taken back those trenches." He proudly repeated his reply: "Sir, I won't argue, just so I don't have to call you a liar."

But in reality, he had barely spoken during the truce, even though he had desperately wanted to chat with the French soldiers. Instead, he spent most of the time pacing up and down, asking the same question over and over: "What regiment are you from?" They answered, and that was it.

At one point, when he wandered too far, a French sentry, not realizing he understood French, muttered, "Look at this guy, spying on our defenses." That was enough for Pesth. Losing interest in the truce, he went home, where he made up the conversation he later bragged about.

Elsewhere on the boulevard, Captain Zoboff talked loudly, while Captain Obzhogoff, looking rather unkempt, wandered nearby. An artillery captain, who didn't try to impress anyone and was happy being liked by the cadets, also stood among the usual crowd.

Everything seemed the same as the day before. But some faces were missing—Praskukhin, Neferdoff, and a few others. No one really talked about them now. Their bodies hadn't even been properly washed, laid out, or buried yet.

XVI.

White flags were raised over both the Russian fort and the French trenches. In the valley between them, fallen soldiers lay across the field, their gray or blue uniforms torn and their boots missing. Workers moved through the area, lifting bodies onto carts. The air was heavy with the smell of death.

People from Sevastopol and the French camp gathered to watch. They stood close together, their faces full of curiosity. Some even smiled as they talked.

A young Russian officer, struggling with his French but managing to communicate, examined a soldier's cartridge box.

"What is this bird for?" he asked, pointing to the emblem.

"That's the Imperial eagle, Monsieur. It belongs to a regiment of the guard," the Frenchman explained.

"And you? Are you from the guard?"

"No, Monsieur, I serve in the Sixth Regiment of the Line."

The officer then pointed to the man's wooden cigar holder. "Where did you buy this?"

"At Balaklava, Monsieur. It's simple, made of palm wood."

"Nice," the officer said, more focused on using the words he knew than on the conversation itself.

"If you would like to keep it as a souvenir, I would be honored," the Frenchman offered, politely blowing out his cigarette and handing over the holder with a small bow. The officer accepted and exchanged his own in return. The soldiers standing around them, both Russian and French, smiled in approval.

Nearby, a bold Russian soldier in a pink shirt, his cloak draped over his shoulders, approached a Frenchman, followed by two grinning comrades. He gestured for a light for his pipe. The Frenchman stirred his own short pipe, shaking out a glowing ember for him.

"Tobacco good!" the Russian soldier said. The group chuckled.

"Yes, good tobacco. Turkish tobacco," the Frenchman responded. "And your tobacco—is Russian tobacco good?"

"Russian, good," the soldier replied confidently, making everyone laugh. Then, eager to use the little French he knew, he patted the Frenchman's stomach and blurted out, "Bon jour, Monsieur."

The French soldiers laughed along with him.

"They are not very handsome, these Russian brutes," one French zouave muttered to his comrades.

"What are they laughing about?" another asked, his dark features and accent showing he was Italian.

The Russian soldier in pink looked at the zouave's decorated uniform and grinned. "Caftan good," he said, admiring the embroidery. Another round of laughter erupted.

"Back to your posts! Move it, now!" a French corporal shouted. The soldiers, still grinning, reluctantly returned to their lines.

Meanwhile, a young Russian cavalry officer wandered among the French officers, chatting with them. The conversation turned to a Count Sazonoff.

"I knew him well, Monsieur," said a French officer with one epaulet. "A true Russian count! We admire men like him."

"There's a Sazonoff I know," the Russian officer replied, "but I don't think he's a count. A short, dark-haired man, about your age."

"Yes, yes, that's him exactly!" the French officer said eagerly. "Ah, how I would love to see that dear count again! If you happen to meet him, please give him my regards—Captain Latour," he added, with a polite bow.

The Russian officer glanced at the bodies lying in the valley and changed the subject. "This is terrible, isn't it? Last night's battle was brutal."

"Awful, Monsieur! But your soldiers—they are brave men. It is an honor to fight such warriors."

"It's true that your men don't hold back either," says the cavalry officer with a polite nod, convinced that he is being charming.

But enough of that.

Instead, look at this young boy, about ten years old, wearing an old cap—probably his father's—shoes without socks, and loose pants held up by a single suspender. As soon as the truce began, he climbed over a wall and wandered through the valley, curiously staring at the French soldiers and the bodies scattered on the ground. He picked blue wildflowers that covered the field. On his way home, holding a large bundle of them, he pinched his nose to block out the awful smell in the air. When he reached a pile of bodies that had been collected, he stopped and stared at one, a headless corpse, lying closest to him. He stood frozen for a long time, then stepped forward and nudged the stiff arm sticking out. The arm swayed slightly. He kicked it again, harder this time. The arm swung, then dropped back in place. The boy let out a terrified scream, buried his face in the flowers, and ran toward the fort as fast as he could.

Yes, the white flags wave from both sides, the valley is covered with the dead, the golden sun sets over the deep blue sea, and the water shimmers under its light. Thousands of people gather, talk, and even smile at each other. And yet, why don't the people—who claim to follow the great law of love and self-sacrifice—fall to their knees in regret when they see the destruction they have caused? Why don't they embrace each other with tears of joy, like true brothers? No. Instead, they find comfort in the idea that they did not start this war, that they are only defending their homeland.

The white flags are lowered. Once again, the weapons of death and suffering scream through the air. Once again, innocent blood is spilled, and the sounds of pain and curses fill the battlefield.

That is all I have to say for now. But a heavy thought lingers in my mind. Maybe I should not have spoken. Maybe these are uncomfortable truths that live inside every person, truths that should remain hidden, like a barrel of wine that must not be shaken or it will spoil.

Who is good? Who is bad? There is no clear answer.

Kalugin, with his flashy courage and need for praise, is not the hero or the villain. Neither is Praskukhin, an empty-headed man who died in battle for his country. Nor is Mikhaïloff, shy and uncertain, or Pesth, still just a child without strong beliefs.

The real hero of this story—the one I admire, the one I have tried to show in all its honesty, the one that has always mattered and always will—is the truth.

Sevastopol in August, 1855

I

Near the end of August, a small cart moved slowly along the rough, dusty road to Sevastopol, stirring up thick clouds of dust. The cart was an old-fashioned type, somewhere between a Russian carriage and a simple wooden wagon. A soldier sat in the front, gripping the reins. His coat was wrinkled, and his officer's cap had lost its shape from wear. Behind him, perched on top of some bundles covered by a military coat, sat an infantry officer wearing a light cloak.

The officer was a broad and stocky man, more thick than tall. His body was solid and compact, with no clear waistline but also no extra weight—his face was lean and sunburned, giving him a tired, worn-out look. His features were strong but heavy, with deep lines that made him seem older. His small, sharp brown eyes were both bold and watchful. A thick mustache covered his upper lip, though the ends were kept short from his habit of chewing on them. His chin and cheekbones were covered in dark stubble from two days without shaving.

He had been wounded in the head by a piece of shrapnel back in May and had just been released from the Simferopol hospital. Now, feeling strong again, he was on his way back to rejoin his regiment. He could hear gunfire in the distance, but he wasn't exactly sure where his unit was—whether they were in Sevastopol, up in the northern defenses, or near Inkerman.

The sound of battle echoed through the hills, sometimes distant, sometimes so close that it made the air tremble. A deep explosion would shake the ground, followed by a series of quick, sharp cracks like drumbeats. Then everything would blend into a thunderous roar, growing louder, like a storm rolling in with heavy rain. It was clear that the bombardment was fierce.

The officer urged his driver to go faster, eager to reach his regiment. Along the road, they passed a long line of carts carrying wounded soldiers away from Sevastopol. The wagons were full of men in torn gray coats, navy uniforms, and red-fezzed volunteers, along with bearded militia fighters. Thick dust swirled around them as the carts moved slowly past. The officer squinted through the dust, studying the faces of the injured.

"There's one of our men," the driver said, pointing to a wagon carrying wounded soldiers.

At the front of the cart, a bearded Russian man in a wool cap sat sideways, fixing the lash on his whip. Behind him, five soldiers were packed in. One, pale and thin, with his arm in a sling and his cloak draped over his shirt, sat upright and tried to salute the officer. But remembering his injury, he quickly scratched his head instead. Another soldier lay flat on the cart's wooden floor, only his hands gripping the side and his knees wobbling as the cart bumped along. A third, with a swollen face and a bandaged head, dangled his legs over the side, resting his elbows on his knees and staring off into the distance. The officer called out to him.

"Dolzhnikoff!"

The soldier blinked, recognized his officer, and pulled off his cap. His voice was so deep and hoarse it sounded like twenty men speaking at once.

"Here, sir!"

"When were you wounded, brother?"

The soldier's tired, glassy eyes lit up with recognition.

"I wish you good health, sir!" he said in the same deep, slow voice.

"Where is our regiment now?"

"They were in Sevastopol, sir, but they were supposed to move on Wednesday."

"Move where?"

"I don't know for sure, but I think to the northern side. Today, sir," the soldier added in a weary tone, putting his cap back on, "they've been firing clear across, mostly using bombs. Even near the bay, they're fighting hard. It's terrible today—"

His words were lost in the noise of the passing carts, but his face and tone made it clear—he was speaking with the bitterness of someone who had suffered.

The officer, Lieutenant Kozeltzoff, was not like most officers. He didn't simply follow what others did. He lived his life as he pleased, and others followed his lead, believing he was always right. He had many small talents—he could sing well, play the guitar, tell stories, and write official reports with ease. But his strongest trait was his self-confidence. It gave him an air of authority, whether he was dealing with his fellow officers or lower-ranked soldiers.

"Bah! Why am I even listening to this guy?" Kozeltzoff muttered, shaking off the uneasy feeling that had crept into his chest. Seeing so many wounded men, combined with the distant roar of the battle, left a heavy weight on his mind. "That soldier is just talking nonsense. Keep moving, Nikolaeff! Are you asleep?" he snapped at his driver, adjusting his coat as if shaking off his thoughts.

Nikolaeff pulled the reins, clucked his tongue, and the cart picked up speed.

"We'll stop to eat for a moment, then keep going. We need to get there today," the officer said, urging the driver forward.

II.

As Lieutenant Kozeltzoff entered the street lined with the crumbling stone walls of Tatar houses in Duvanka, he was stopped by a line of carts carrying bombs and ammunition to Sevastopol. The road was crowded. Two infantry soldiers sat on a pile of rubble near a broken garden wall, eating watermelon and bread.

"Have you come from far, comrade?" one of them asked, chewing as he spoke, while looking at a soldier with a small knapsack who had paused nearby.

"I've come from my home province to join my regiment," the soldier replied, adjusting the sack on his back and glancing away from the watermelon. "Just two weeks ago, we were all working in the fields, gathering hay. Then they rounded us up and sent us here, but now we don't even know where our regiment is. They say our men moved to Korabelnaya last week. Have you heard anything, comrades?"

"They're in the city now," the other soldier answered, an older man from the reserves, as he dug into a pale, unripe watermelon with his knife. "We just came from there this afternoon. It's awful, brother."

"How so?" the traveler asked.

"Can't you hear the gunfire today? It's everywhere—nowhere is safe. So many of our men have been killed," the old soldier said, waving his hand and adjusting his cap.

The traveler shook his head, clicked his tongue, and pulled a pipe from his boot. Without adding fresh tobacco, he stirred the burnt bits left inside, lit a piece of tinder from another soldier's pipe, and nodded.

"Only God knows what will happen, comrades. Goodbye," he said, shifting his sack and continuing down the road.

"Hey, wait a bit," the soldier with the watermelon called out, as if sure the traveler should stay.

"No point," the traveler muttered as he weaved through the carts and moved on.

III.

The station was crowded when Kozeltzoff arrived. The first person he saw on the porch was a thin, young man—the station supervisor—arguing with two officers who had followed him outside.

"You won't just wait three days—you'll have to wait ten! Even generals have to wait, gentlemen," the supervisor said, clearly trying to annoy them. "And I'm not giving you any horses."

"Then don't give horses to anyone if you don't have any!" the older officer snapped, gripping his glass of tea. He made sure not to use words that would sound too polite. "So why did you give them to some servant with luggage?"

"Now, think about it, sir," the younger officer said hesitantly. "We're not traveling for fun. We wouldn't have been called if we weren't needed. I'll have to report this to the general. You're not treating military officers properly."

"You always make things worse," the older officer interrupted in frustration. "You're only getting in my way. You need to know how to talk to these people. Look at him, he has no respect! I said we need horses now!"

"I'd be happy to help, sir, but where am I supposed to get them?" the supervisor replied.

There was a brief silence before he grew more agitated, waving his arms as he spoke.

"I get it, sir, I really do. But what can I do? Just let me make it to the end of the month, and you'll never see me here again. I'd rather be on Malakhov Hill, I swear, than stuck here! They can do whatever they want with me! There's not a single team of fresh horses, and they haven't had a bite of hay in three days." With that, he disappeared behind the gate.

Kozeltzoff entered the room with the officers.

"Well," the older officer said calmly to his companion, though he had been furious just moments before, "we've been traveling for three weeks, we can wait a little longer. We'll get there eventually."

The small, smoky room was so packed with officers and luggage that Kozeltzoff struggled to find a place to sit. Finally, he found a spot by the window, rolled himself a cigarette, and started listening to the conversations around him.

Near the door, at a small, greasy table, sat a group of young officers. The table was cluttered with two samovars covered in greenish spots, scattered papers, and sugar wrapped in pieces of newspaper. A young officer without a mustache, wearing a brand-new, quilted summer coat, was pouring tea.

Four young officers like him sat around the room. One had rolled up his coat to use as a pillow and was fast asleep on a couch. Another stood at the table, cutting up roasted mutton for an officer missing an arm.

Two other officers sat by the stove—one in an adjutant's cloak, the other in an infantry uniform with a satchel slung over his shoulder. From the way they stared at the others and the relaxed way the one with the satchel smoked his cigar, it was clear they were not frontline officers. They seemed pleased about it. They didn't show open disdain, but there was a smug confidence about them, a quiet sense of superiority, likely due to their connections with generals or their personal wealth.

A young doctor with thick lips and an artillery officer with sharp German features sat near the couch, counting their money.

Near the door, four officers' servants sat among trunks and bags, some dozing, others busy organizing belongings.

Kozeltzoff didn't recognize a single face, but he listened with interest. The young officers, who looked like they had just come from military school, caught his attention. They reminded him of his younger brother, who had recently graduated and should have arrived in Sevastopol to join an artillery unit.

However, the officer with the satchel, whose face seemed familiar, gave him a bad feeling. He looked bold and arrogant. Kozeltzoff disliked him immediately. He left his spot by the window and sat near the stove, thinking to himself that if this man said anything rude, he'd be ready to put him in his place. As a seasoned frontline soldier, he had always resented officers who worked in the staff, and he could tell right away that these two belonged to that group.

IV.

"But this is so frustrating," said one of the young officers. "We're so close, yet we can't get there. There might even be a battle today, and we won't be there to fight."

His sharp voice and the way his face flushed slightly showed his nervousness, as if he was always worried about saying the wrong thing.

The one-armed officer gave him a slight smile. "Don't worry, you'll get there soon enough," he said.

The young officer looked at the older man's tired face with respect. The empty sleeve of his coat made him seem calm and indifferent, as if saying, "I've been through it all. I know exactly how this goes."

"So what should we do?" the young officer asked his companion in the short coat. "Stay here overnight or try to move on with our own horses?"

His companion shook his head. "No, we should wait."

"Imagine this, captain," said the young officer pouring tea. He turned to the one-armed man while picking up a knife the officer had dropped. "We heard that horses were extremely expensive in Sevastopol, so we bought one together in Simferopol."

"They probably overcharged you," said the older officer.

"I'm not sure," the young officer replied. "We paid ninety rubles for the horse and harness. Was that too much?" He looked around, hoping for opinions, including from Kozeltzoff, who was watching him closely.

"It depends. If the horse is young, then no," Kozeltzoff said.

"Really? Because we were told we paid too much. She limps a little, but they said it would go away. They also said she's strong."

"What academy did you come from?" asked Kozeltzoff, hoping to find out about his brother.

"We just finished at the academy of the nobility. There are six of us, and we volunteered to go to Sevastopol," the talkative young officer explained. "But we don't even know where our battery is. Some say it's in Sevastopol, others say Odessa."

"Couldn't you find out in Simferopol?" Kozeltzoff asked.

"They didn't know there either. One of us even went to headquarters, and they were rude to him. It was really frustrating!"

As he spoke, he noticed the one-armed officer taking out a cigarette machine. "Would you like me to roll one for you?" he asked eagerly, almost as if trying to impress him.

"Are you coming from Sevastopol too?" he continued, turning toward Kozeltzoff. "Oh wow, that's incredible! You have no idea how much we admired you and all the heroes of Sevastopol back in Petersburg!" His voice carried admiration and a bit of flattery.

"And now you might have to turn back?" asked another officer.

"That's what we're afraid of," the young officer admitted. "You see, after buying the horse and everything we needed—like a coffee pot and some other essentials—we don't have much money left," he added in a lower voice, glancing at his companions. "If we do have to go back, we don't know what we'll do."

"Didn't they give you money for travel expenses?" asked Kozeltzoff.

"No," the young officer whispered. "They promised to give it to us here."

"Do you have the certificate?"

"I know that's the important thing," he said. "But my uncle in Moscow—he's a senator—told me they would give it to us here. Otherwise, he would've given me money himself. So they will give it to us, right?"

"Of course they will," said Kozeltzoff.

"I think so too," the young officer said, though his tone suggested he had already asked the same question at every station and had received different answers each time. It seemed he wasn't sure what to believe anymore.

V.

The housekeeper, a plump woman around forty, walked into the room carrying a bowl of beet soup.

"Who ordered beet soup?" she called out.

The room fell silent, and all eyes turned to her.

"Oh, it was for Kozeltzoff," said a young officer. "We should wake him up. Get up, it's time to eat," he said, nudging the person asleep on the sofa.

A young man, about seventeen, with bright black eyes and rosy cheeks, jumped up quickly and stood in the middle of the room, rubbing his eyes.

"Oh, excuse me," he said to the doctor, who he had accidentally bumped into while getting up.

Lieutenant Kozeltzoff immediately recognized him and walked over.

"Don't you recognize me?" he asked with a smile.

"A-a-a-! This is unbelievable!" the younger brother exclaimed, then threw his arms around him.

They hugged twice, but when they went for a third, they both hesitated as if wondering, "Why exactly three times?"

"I'm so happy to see you!" said the older brother, looking at him. "Let's step outside and talk."

"Forget the soup. You eat it, Federsohn," the younger one said to his friend.

"But you were hungry," his friend pointed out.

"I'm not anymore."

Once outside on the porch, the younger brother eagerly asked, "How are you? Tell me everything!" He kept repeating how happy he was to see him but didn't say much about himself.

After a few minutes of conversation, the older brother finally asked why he hadn't joined the guards as everyone had expected.

He explained that he wanted to get to Sevastopol as soon as possible. If things went well there, he could get promoted faster than in the guards. In the guards, it could take ten years to become a colonel, but here, Todleben had been promoted from lieutenant colonel to general in just two years. And if he got killed, well, that was just how it was.

"You're something else," his brother said, smiling.

"But the real reason," the younger brother admitted, smiling and blushing as if confessing something embarrassing, "is that I felt ashamed to stay in Petersburg while people are dying for our country here. And... I wanted to be with you," he added, looking even more embarrassed.

"How silly you are!" the older brother said, pulling out his cigarette case and avoiding his gaze. "It's a shame we can't be stationed together."

"Tell me honestly, is it really that bad in the bastions?" the younger one asked suddenly.

"It's scary at first, but you get used to it. It's not so bad. You'll see for yourself."

"And do you think Sevastopol will fall? I don't believe it will."

"Who knows?"

"But one thing really bothers me. Can you believe it? A whole bundle of my things was stolen on the way here, and my shako was in it! Now I don't know what I'm going to do. How can I even show up like this?"

The younger Kozeltzoff, Vladimir, looked a lot like his older brother, Mikhail, but in the way a budding flower resembles one that is already in full bloom. His chestnut hair was thick and curled slightly at his temples. At the back of his neck was a light-colored patch of hair—something nurses called a sign of good luck. His face had the same fair complexion, but instead of staying one shade, it constantly flushed with color, reflecting his emotions. His eyes were like his brother's but wider and brighter, often glistening as if holding back moisture. A soft golden fuzz was beginning to grow on his cheeks and above his lips, which often curled into a shy smile, revealing dazzling white teeth.

He was broad-shouldered and strong, dressed in an open jacket that revealed a red shirt with the collar folded back. As he leaned on the porch railing, cigarette in hand, his face full of excitement, he looked so cheerful and full of life that anyone would have enjoyed watching him.

He admired his older brother deeply, looking up to him like a hero. But in some ways—like speaking French, behaving in high society, or dancing—he thought his brother was lacking. He even hoped that, with time, he might help him improve in those areas.

His experiences so far had mostly come from life in Petersburg, where a kind older woman had taken a liking to him and invited him for holidays, and from Moscow, where he had once attended a grand ball at a senator's house.

VI.

After talking for a while, the brothers fell into silence, realizing that, despite their love for each other, they didn't have much in common.

"Gather your things, and let's go," the older brother said.

The younger one suddenly blushed, hesitated, and looked uneasy.

"Are we heading straight to Sevastopol?" he asked after a brief pause.

"Of course. You don't have much, and we can carry everything ourselves."

"Alright, let's go right away," the younger one replied with a sigh and went inside.

But instead of packing, he stopped in the hallway, his head lowered in thought.

"Straight to Sevastopol, right into the danger zone, with bombs flying—terrifying! But it had to happen sooner or later. At least I'll be with my brother."

It was only at that moment, when he knew there was no turning back, that the reality of the danger he had been chasing fully hit him. He tried to shake off his fear and stepped into the room, but time passed, and he still hadn't come out. Eventually, his brother opened the door to check on him. The younger Kozeltzoff was talking to an officer, looking as guilty as a child caught misbehaving. When he saw his brother, he became even more flustered.

"I'll be right there!" he called, waving his hand. "Just wait for me outside."

A few minutes later, he finally came out and walked up to his brother, taking a deep breath.

"Listen, I can't go with you," he said.

"What? What are you talking about?"

"I'll tell you the truth, Misha. None of us have any money, and we owe that staff captain you saw in there. It's so embarrassing!"

The older brother frowned and remained silent for a while.

"How much do you owe?" he asked, avoiding eye contact.

"Not a huge amount, but still... I feel awful about it. He paid for three of my travel stages, and we finished all his sugar. And... we played cards. I lost some money there too."

"This is bad, Volodya. What would you have done if you hadn't run into me?" the older brother asked, his voice serious.

"I was thinking I'd get my travel pay in Sevastopol and pay him back then. That should work, right? It's probably better if I go with him tomorrow."

The older brother took out his purse, his fingers slightly trembling as he pulled out two ten-ruble bills and a three-ruble note.

"This is all I have," he said. "How much do you owe?"

He wasn't entirely truthful—he still had four gold coins sewn into his sleeve for emergencies, but he had promised himself not to touch them.

It turned out that the younger brother owed eight rubles in total, including his card game loss and the borrowed sugar. The older brother handed him the money but couldn't help making a comment.

"You shouldn't play cards if you don't have the money for it."

"What were you playing for?" his brother asked.

The younger brother stayed quiet. The question felt like an insult. He was already embarrassed about what he had done, and now his brother's words made him feel even worse. A mix of shame, frustration, and disappointment filled him, especially since it was coming from someone he looked up to. His throat tightened, and he couldn't bring himself to speak. Without looking at the money, he took it and walked away to rejoin his comrades.

VII.

After buying two jugs of vodka from a soldier at the bridge in Duvanka, Nikolaeff pulled on the reins, and the cart jolted over the rough, rocky road lined with trees, following the Belbek River toward Sevastopol. The two brothers sat close together, their legs brushing against each other, but neither said a word. Both were thinking about the other, yet neither wanted to break the silence.

"Why did he insult me?" the younger brother wondered. "Couldn't he have just kept quiet? He acted like I was some kind of thief. And now he's angry, so we're probably not even on good terms anymore. But it would have been great to be in Sevastopol together—two brothers, fighting side by side. He's the tough, silent type, and I would have shown that I'm not just a kid anymore. In a week, I'd prove myself. I'd stop blushing over every little thing, I'd stand tall, and even though my mustache is barely growing now, it would be full by then." He ran his fingers over the soft fuzz above his lip. "Maybe we'll get there today and head straight into battle. My brother must be fearless, one of those men who don't talk much but are braver than everyone else. I wonder if he's pressing me against the side of the cart on purpose. Maybe he knows I feel awkward and is pretending not to notice."

His mind kept racing. "When we get there, we'll head straight to the bastion. My brother will join his company, and I'll take my position. Then, suddenly, the French will attack. I'll start firing, taking down enemy after enemy, but they just keep coming. I run out of bullets—there's no escape! Then, my brother charges forward with his sword. I grab my gun and rush after him with the soldiers. The French surround him—I won't let them! I take down one, then another, saving him. But then I get hit in the arm. I switch my gun to the other hand and keep fighting. And then—my brother is shot right beside me.

I stop for a moment, staring at him in shock, then stand tall and shout, 'Follow me! We have to avenge him! My brother was the bravest man I knew, and I lost him—let's make the enemy pay!' The soldiers cheer and charge forward. The entire French army, even their commander, Pelissier, comes at us. We fight with everything we have, but I get hit again, then again, until I finally collapse, barely alive. Gortchakoff arrives and asks what I want. 'Nothing,' I whisper. 'Just lay me next to my brother—I want to die beside him.'

They carry me to his lifeless body, and with my last breath, I say, 'You never understood what true loyalty to our homeland means. Now you have lost two men who truly loved their country. May God forgive you!' And then—I die."

Who knew how much of that would come true?

Lost in his thoughts, he suddenly turned to his brother and blurted out, "Have you ever been in hand-to-hand combat?" forgetting that he had decided not to speak to him.

"No, never," the older brother replied. "Our regiment has lost two thousand men, all from gunfire at the front. I was wounded there too. War isn't anything like you imagine, Volodya."

Hearing his brother say his name softened Volodya's heart. He wanted to make peace, though his brother had no idea he had even been offended.

"You're not mad at me, Misha?" he asked after a short silence.

"For what?"

"Just... because we argued a little... never mind."

"Not at all," the older brother said, turning slightly and patting him on the leg.

"Then forgive me, Misha, if I upset you," Volodya said quietly, turning away so his brother wouldn't see the tears welling up in his eyes.

VIII.

"Are we in Sevastopol already?" the younger brother asked as they climbed the hill.

Before them, the bay came into view, filled with ships and masts, while the distant enemy fleet floated on the horizon. White forts lined the shore, surrounded by barracks, docks, and wooden aqueducts. Above the town, thick white and purple smoke drifted into the sky, rising from the yellow hills in the warm glow of the setting sun. The golden light reflected off the rippling sea as it stretched toward the horizon.

Volodya didn't feel fear as he looked at the place he had thought about so much. Instead, he felt a strange excitement, even admiration. He was finally here. In just a little while, he would step into this chaotic and dangerous world. The scene before him seemed almost beautiful in its own way. He stared at it intently, taking in every detail as they made their way toward the northern fortification, where they needed to find out exactly where their regiment and artillery battery were stationed.

The officer in charge of supplies lived near what people called the "new town," a small settlement of wooden huts built by the families of sailors. His quarters were a tent attached to a large shelter made of freshly cut oak branches, their green leaves not yet dried out.

When the brothers arrived, they found the officer sitting at a worn-out table covered in crumbs of dried fish and bread. A glass of cold tea sat next to a tray holding a bottle of vodka. He wore only a yellowed shirt, and he was busy counting a large pile of paper money using an abacus.

But before describing the officer himself, it's important to take a look at his living space and lifestyle. His shelter, built like the ones used by generals and senior officers, was large and well-made, with sturdy walls woven tightly together. Inside, it was somewhat cozy, with benches and tables made of packed earth. The walls and ceiling were covered with thick rugs to keep the leaves from falling, and though the rugs were worn and ugly, they were clearly expensive.

Against the far wall stood an iron-framed bed, covered with a bright red velvet blanket, a torn and dirty pillow, and a raccoon fur coat. A silver-framed mirror, a dirty silver brush, and a broken comb full of greasy hair sat on the table. There was also a silver candlestick, a fancy bottle of liqueur with a gold label, a gold watch with a portrait of Peter the Great, two gold pens, a small box of pills, a crust of bread, and some worn-out playing cards. Empty and half-full bottles were scattered underneath the bed.

This officer was responsible for managing supplies for the regiment and feeding the horses. His close friend, another officer who handled administrative tasks, lived with him.

At the moment the brothers entered, the second officer was fast asleep in the shelter, while the supply officer was busy balancing the government accounts before the end of the month. He had a strong and commanding appearance, with a tall frame, a thick mustache, and a well-fed look. However, his puffy, sweaty face nearly swallowed up his small gray eyes, giving him a bloated, sluggish appearance—almost as if he had too much to drink. From his unwashed, oily hair to his bare feet resting in worn-out slippers, he gave off an air of laziness and carelessness.

"Money, money!" Kozeltzoff, the older brother, said as he stepped inside, his eyes immediately drawn to the pile of cash. "Vasily Mikhailitch, you should lend me some of that!"

The supply officer flinched when he saw them. He quickly gathered up the banknotes and gave them a polite nod without standing up.

"Oh, if only it were mine! This is government money," he replied, stuffing the bills into a chest beside him. His eyes then turned to Volodya. "And who is this you've brought with you?"

"This is my brother, fresh from the military academy. We've come to find out where our regiment is stationed."

"Sit down, gentlemen," the officer said as he got up and walked into the shelter, not paying much attention to his guests. "Would you like something to drink? Some porter, perhaps?"

"Don't trouble yourself, Vasily Mikhailitch."

Volodya was impressed by the commissary officer's large build, his relaxed attitude, and the way his older brother spoke to him with respect.

"This must be an important officer that everyone looks up to. He seems simple but welcoming and brave," Volodya thought as he sat down carefully on the sofa, trying to stay quiet.

"Where is our regiment now?" his older brother called into the wooden hut.

"What?" came the reply.

He repeated the question.

"Zeifer was here today. He said they moved to the Fifth Bastion."

"Are you sure?"

"If I said it, then it must be true! But honestly, who knows? He wouldn't hesitate to lie." Then, without much concern, the commissary officer added, "Want some porter?"

"I'll take some if you have it," Kozeltzoff replied.

"Osip Ignatievitch, will you have a drink?" the commissary officer called out, this time addressing someone inside the tent. "You've slept long enough—it's already five o'clock!"

"Why are you bothering me? I'm not even asleep," a tired, high-pitched voice replied.

"Come on, get up! We're bored without you."

The commissary officer finally stepped out to join them.

"Bring some Simferopol porter!" he shouted.

A servant entered the booth, looking proud of himself—at least in Volodya's opinion. He bumped into Volodya as he reached under a bench to grab the bottle.

They soon finished the porter and kept chatting when suddenly, the flap of the tent swung open. A short man with rosy cheeks stepped out, wearing a blue robe with tassels, a cap with a red band, and a shiny cockade. As he appeared, he smoothed his small black mustache and stared at the rug beneath him while barely nodding in greeting.

"I'll have a small glass too!" he said, sitting at the table. Then, turning politely to Volodya, he asked, "Did you just come from Petersburg, young man?"

"Yes, sir. I'm on my way to Sevastopol."

"You signed up yourself?"

"Yes, sir."

"What a strange choice!" the commissioner said, shaking his head. "If I had the chance, I'd walk all the way to Petersburg just to get out of here. I am so sick of this miserable life!"

"What's so bad about it?" the older Kozeltzoff asked. "You, of all people, shouldn't be complaining."

The commissioner glanced at him but then looked away.

"The danger, the discomforts—you can't get anything decent here," he continued, now speaking to Volodya. "I don't understand why you young men choose this. If at least there were some benefits—but there's nothing! Imagine losing a leg or an arm at your age. What kind of life would that be?"

"Some do it for the money, and some serve for honor," Kozeltzoff said sharply, clearly annoyed.

"What good is honor when there's no food?" the commissioner scoffed, turning to the commissary officer, who chuckled in agreement. "Put on something from 'Lucia.' Let's listen," he added, pointing at the music box. "I love it."

As Volodya and his brother left the shelter at dusk, heading toward Sevastopol, he asked, "Is Vasily Mikhailitch really such a great officer?"

"Not at all," his brother answered. "In fact, he's the stingiest man I've ever met! And that commissioner? I can't stand him. One of these days, I'm going to knock him flat."

IX.

Volodya wasn't really sad when they finally arrived at the big bridge over the bay in the evening, but he felt uneasy. Everything he had seen and heard was so different from what he had imagined. He remembered the bright exam hall with its shiny floors, the cheerful voices and laughter of his classmates, his crisp new uniform, and the tsar, who had tearfully called them his children as he said goodbye. None of it felt like the heroic and exciting future he had dreamed of.

"Well, here we are at last!" said his older brother as they arrived at the Mikhailovsky battery and climbed down from the cart. "If they let us cross the bridge, we'll head straight to the Nikolaevsky barracks. You can stay there for the night, and I'll go find out where your battery is stationed. Tomorrow, I'll come back for you."

"Why should we split up? Let's go together," Volodya said. "I'll come with you to the bastion. I have to get used to it sooner or later, so I might as well start now."

"It's better if you don't go."

"No, really, I want to—"

"My advice is to stay back, but if you insist…"

The night sky was deep and dark, filled with bright stars and the flickering bursts of artillery fire. The big white battery building and the start of the bridge stood out in the shadows. Every few seconds, cannon blasts and explosions shook the air, each one louder and closer. Through the constant rumbling, the sound of waves crashing could be heard, steady and rhythmic. A light breeze carried the damp, salty air in from the sea.

As the brothers stepped onto the bridge, a soldier snapped to attention, accidentally knocking his rifle against his arm, and shouted, "Who goes there?"

"Soldier," the older brother replied.

"No one's allowed to pass!" the guard warned.

"We have important business! We need to cross!" he insisted.

"Ask the officer."

The officer, half-asleep while sitting on an anchor, stood up and gave them permission to go through.

"You can go that way, but not back this way. And you wagons, where do you think you're all rushing to?" he yelled at the transport carts piled high with supplies, waiting to cross.

As they reached the first pontoon, a group of soldiers heading in the opposite direction passed by, talking loudly.

"If he already got his pay, then he's got nothing left to worry about," one of them said.

"Once you make it to the Severnaya side, you'll see a different world, brothers! The air itself feels different," another one added.

"You're right about that!" the first soldier replied. "A shell landed there the other day and tore off two sailors' legs, just like that…"

The brothers crossed the first section of the floating bridge while waiting for their wagon, then stopped on the second, where some parts were already soaked with water. The gentle breeze from earlier had turned into strong gusts, pushing against them. The bridge rocked under their feet, creaking as the waves crashed against the beams and pulled at the thick ropes and anchors.

To their right, the vast, dark sea stretched endlessly, a thin black line separating it from the starlit sky. In the distance, tiny lights flickered from enemy ships. To their left, the towering masts of one of their own warships rose above the water, the sound of waves slapping against its side. A steamer rumbled past, moving quickly as it made its way from Severnaya.

A bomb exploded nearby, lighting up the piles of gabions stacked on the deck, the foamy waves churning against the steamer, and two men standing on board. On the edge of the bridge, a man in his shirt sleeves sat with his legs dangling over the water, working on repairs. Ahead, the same flashes lit up the sky over Sevastopol, and the loud, frightening sounds of battle grew even stronger. A wave rolled in from the sea, crashing over the bridge and soaking Volodya's feet. Two soldiers trudged past, dragging their boots through the water.

Suddenly, a deafening explosion sent bright flashes across the bridge, lighting up a passing wagon and a man on horseback. Splinters from the blast rained down into the water, sending up a spray.

"Ah, Mikhaïlo Semyónitch!" called the rider, pulling his horse to a stop in front of the older Kozeltzoff. "You've recovered already?"

"As you can see. Where are you headed?"

"To the Severnaya, for cartridges. I have to report to the regiment's adjutant. We're expecting an attack at any moment."

"Where is Martzoff?"

"He lost a leg yesterday. He was sleeping in his room when it happened... Maybe you've heard?"

"The regiment is at the fifth bastion, right?"

"Yes, they replaced the M—— regiment. Go to the field hospital; some of our men are there, and they'll show you the way."

"What about my quarters on Morskaya? Are they still standing?"

"My friend, they've been completely destroyed by bombs. You wouldn't even recognize Sevastopol now. No women, no taverns, no music—the last of them left yesterday. It's miserable there now... Farewell!"

The officer rode off, leaving Volodya frozen in place. Fear suddenly gripped him. He felt certain that at any moment, a cannonball or a bomb fragment would come straight for his head. The dark, damp night, the roaring of the sea, the blasts in the distance—it all seemed to be telling him that he shouldn't go any further, that something terrible was waiting for him ahead. Maybe he would never return from the other side of the bay. Maybe it was too late to turn back. His whole body tensed, both from fear and from the cold water soaking his boots.

Volodya let out a deep breath and stepped away from his brother.

"Lord, will I be the one to die? Lord, have mercy on me," he whispered, crossing himself.

"Come on, Volodya, let's go," his brother said as their cart rolled onto the bridge. "Did you see that bomb?"

On the bridge, they passed wagons carrying the wounded, supplies, and even one piled with furniture, driven by a woman. Once they reached the other side, no one stopped them.

Sticking close to the walls of the Nikolaevsky battery, they listened in silence to the terrifying sound of bombs exploding overhead, followed by the sharp whistling of shrapnel raining down. They made their way toward a small shrine, where they learned that Volodya's assigned battery was stationed on the Korabelnaya. Despite the risk, they decided he would spend the night with his brother in the fifth bastion and head to his unit the next day.

They entered a narrow passageway, stepping carefully over the legs of sleeping soldiers stretched out along the walls, until they finally reached the place where the wounded were being treated.

X.

As they stepped into the first room, lined with cots filled with wounded men and filled with the awful smell of a hospital, two nurses walked toward them.

One was an older woman, around fifty, with dark eyes and a serious expression. She carried bandages and lint, giving firm instructions to a young assistant doctor trailing behind her. The other was a young woman, about twenty, with delicate features and pale skin. She looked nervous under her white cap, keeping her hands tucked into her apron pockets as she walked close to the older nurse, as if afraid to move away from her side.

Kozeltzoff asked them if they knew where Martzoff was—the man who had lost his leg the day before.

"He was in the P—— regiment, wasn't he?" the older nurse asked. "Are you a relative?"

"No, just a comrade."

She turned to the younger nurse and, speaking in French, told her to lead them. "Come this way," she said before moving toward a wounded soldier with the assistant.

"Come on, why are you just standing there?" Kozeltzoff said to Volodya, who had stopped to stare at the wounded men with wide eyes and a troubled look on his face.

"Ah, my God… my God…" Volodya whispered, unable to look away.

"He's new here, isn't he?" the young nurse asked Kozeltzoff, glancing at Volodya as he followed them down the hallway, still groaning softly under his breath.

"He just arrived today."

At that, the young nurse suddenly burst into tears. "My God, when will this end?" she said with despair in her voice.

Inside the officer's hut, Martzoff lay on his back. His muscular arms, bare to the elbows, were thrown over his head, and his yellowish face was twisted in pain. His leg, still in its stocking, stuck out from under the blanket, his toes twitching restlessly.

"How are you feeling?" the nurse asked gently. She lifted his bald head with her delicate hands—Volodya noticed a gold ring on one of her fingers—and adjusted his pillow. "Your comrades have come to check on you."

"Terrible, of course," he snapped. "Just leave me alone! I'll be fine." His toes wiggled even faster inside the stocking. He turned toward Kozeltzoff. "And you are…?"

Kozeltzoff said his name, but Martzoff only frowned. "Ah, yes, I remember now. Everything blurs together here," he muttered. "We lived together before, didn't we?" He barely seemed to care as he glanced at Volodya.

"This is my brother. He just arrived from Petersburg today."

"Hm. Well, I guess I'm done with my service now," Martzoff grumbled. "Ah, this pain… I just wish it would end already."

He pulled his leg back under the blanket and covered his face with his hands, his toes still twitching faster than before.

"You should leave him," the young nurse whispered, her eyes filled with tears. "He's in very bad shape."

Earlier, the brothers had agreed to go to the fifth bastion together. But as they left the Nikolaevsky battery, they seemed to silently understand that there was no need to take any extra risks. Without saying much, they decided to split up.

"How will you find your way, Volodya?" the older brother asked. "Never mind—Nikolaeff will take you to the Korabelnaya, and I'll go on my own. I'll see you tomorrow."

That was all they said before parting ways.

XI.

The cannon fire continued to roar just as loudly as before, but the street Volodya walked down, with Nikolaeff silently following behind him, was quiet and empty. In the thick darkness, all he could make out was the wide road, the white walls of large buildings—some damaged from explosions—and the stone sidewalk beneath his feet. Occasionally, a soldier or an officer passed by. As he moved along the left side of the street near the Admiralty, he noticed the acacia trees lining the sidewalk, their dusty leaves glowing in the flickering light of a fire burning behind a wall.

He could hear his own footsteps clearly, along with Nikolaeff's heavy breathing behind him. His thoughts wandered, flashing between images—the kind young nurse, Martzoff's injured leg twitching under the blanket, the bombs, the darkness, and the countless scenes of death he had imagined. His heart tightened with fear and loneliness, overwhelmed by the feeling that no one cared what happened to him, even though he was surrounded by people.

"They could kill me, I could suffer horribly, and no one would even grieve for me," he thought. It was nothing like the heroic life he had imagined, where he would fight bravely, surrounded by admiration and respect. The explosions grew louder and closer, and Nikolaeff sighed more often but still said nothing.

As they crossed the bridge to Korabelnaya, Volodya saw something fly through the sky with a high-pitched whistle before landing in the bay. For a moment, the lilac-colored waves lit up with a red glow before the water crashed upward in a foamy splash.

"It didn't go out," Nikolaeff muttered hoarsely.

"Yes," Volodya replied, his voice suddenly high-pitched and weak, surprising even himself.

They passed groups of wounded men on stretchers, wagons carrying supplies, and a regiment marching down the street. A few riders on horseback trotted past. One officer, accompanied by his Cossack, slowed his horse as he approached Volodya. He looked at him closely for a moment, then turned away and whipped his horse to keep going.

"Nobody cares if I exist or not," Volodya thought, his chest tightening as he fought the urge to cry.

As they climbed the hill past a tall white wall, they reached a street of crumbling houses, constantly lit up by the flashing bombs. A drunken woman, disheveled and stumbling, stepped out of a doorway with a sailor and bumped into Volodya.

"If only he were a proper gentleman," she grumbled, then suddenly changed her tone, "Oh, pardon me, sir!"

His heart sank even lower, and the bombs around him seemed to be whistling through the air and exploding more often. Nikolaeff, who had been silent all this time, suddenly spoke in a strange, tense voice, making Volodya feel even more uneasy.

"We rushed all the way here like it was some great thing," Nikolaeff muttered. "Now that we're here, look at this place. What was the hurry?"

Volodya, desperate to shake off his fear, answered quickly. "Well, my brother got better, so I had to come."

"Better? You call that better?" Nikolaeff scoffed. "If he was truly well, he'd still be in the hospital. What's the point of coming here? You either lose an arm or a leg, and that's all you get for it. It's almost a sin. The bastion is worse than this—it's terrifying. You walk up to it saying your prayers the whole way. Ah, you beast!" he shouted suddenly at a loud screeching noise as a shell fragment whizzed past them. "Hear that? This is what we rushed here for!"

He sighed and kept mumbling. "They told me to show you the way, so that's what I'm doing. But I had to leave our cart with some random soldier, and now all my stuff might be stolen. If anything goes missing, guess who gets blamed? Nikolaeff!"

They walked a few more steps before reaching a large open square. Nikolaeff suddenly fell silent.

"There's your artillery, sir," he finally said. "Ask the guard, he'll point you in the right direction."

A few steps later, Volodya no longer heard Nikolaeff's sighs behind him. He was alone.

The realization hit him like a crushing weight. He felt small, cold, and helpless. This was real danger. This could be death. It felt like a giant stone pressing down on his chest.

He stopped in the middle of the square, looking around for someone, anyone. Panic set in. He grabbed his head and whispered, as if speaking his fears out loud would make them go away.

"God... am I a coward? A worthless, miserable coward? How could I have dreamed of dying for my country and my tsar, and now feel like this? No, I'm just pathetic... just pathetic!"

Overwhelmed by shame, disappointment, and fear, he forced himself to ask the guard for directions to the battery commander's house and walked forward, feeling more lost than ever.

XII.

The commander's house, which the guard had pointed out, was a small two-story building with an entrance facing the courtyard. A dim candle flickered in one of the windows, its glass covered with paper. A servant sat on the porch, smoking a pipe. When Volodya arrived, the servant went inside to announce him, then led him into the house.

Inside, the room was plain and simple. Between two windows, beneath a cracked mirror, stood a table piled with paperwork. A few chairs were scattered around, and an iron bed with a clean mattress and a small rug beside it was pushed against the wall. Near the door stood a tall, serious-looking sergeant with a large mustache, wearing a saber and a cloak decorated with a cross and a Hungarian medal. In the middle of the room, a short, middle-aged officer with puffed-up cheeks, wrapped in a thin, worn-out coat, paced back and forth.

Volodya took a deep breath and recited the introduction he had memorized. "Cornet Kozeltzoff, reporting for duty to the Fifth Light Battery."

The battery commander responded with a brief nod, not shaking his hand, and motioned for him to sit down.

Volodya hesitated, then nervously dropped into a chair near the desk. His hands found a pair of scissors lying there, and he began twisting them absentmindedly. The commander continued pacing, his hands behind his back, occasionally glancing at Volodya's fidgeting fingers, as if trying to recall something.

The commander was a stout man with a bald spot on top of his head, thick mustache drooping over his mouth, and kind brown eyes. His hands were clean and well-kept, his small feet stepping confidently as he walked. Everything about him showed that he was not a man who frightened easily.

"Yes," he suddenly said, stopping in front of the sergeant. "We need to add more grain to the rations tomorrow, or the horses will start losing weight. What do you think?"

"It can be done, sir. Oats are cheap right now," the sergeant replied quickly. Though his hands rested stiffly at his sides, they twitched as if he wanted to gesture while talking. "Franchuk, the forage-master, sent word from the supply wagons saying we should buy oats now while the price is low. What are your orders?"

"Buy them, of course. He has the money for it, doesn't he?" The commander resumed his pacing. Then, stopping in front of Volodya, he suddenly asked, "Where's your gear?"

Poor Volodya was already struggling with the feeling that he was a coward. Now, he imagined that every word, every glance, carried hidden judgment. It felt like the commander had already seen through him, mocking him without saying it outright. He stammered that his belongings were still at the dock, but his brother would send them tomorrow.

The commander barely listened and turned to the sergeant. "Where should we put the ensign?"

Volodya cringed as the sergeant hesitated for a moment before replying. He gave Volodya a quick glance—one that seemed to say, This kid? An ensign?—before thinking it over.

"He can stay downstairs with the staff-captain, sir. The captain is at the bastion now, so his cot is empty."

"Will that be fine for now?" the commander asked Volodya. "You must be tired. We'll find you a better place tomorrow."

Volodya quickly stood and bowed.

"Would you like some tea?" the commander added. "I can have the samovar brought in."

But Volodya simply saluted and left.

The commander's servant led him downstairs into a small, messy room cluttered with random belongings. In the corner was an iron bed frame with no sheets or blanket. A man in a red shirt lay fast asleep on it, wrapped in a thick cloak.

Volodya assumed he was a soldier.

"Piotr Nikolaïtch," the servant said, shaking the man's shoulder. "The ensign is staying here tonight."

"This is our yunker," he added, turning to Volodya.

"Oh, please don't wake him," Volodya said quickly.

But the young man, tall and broad-shouldered, with a handsome yet somewhat dull expression, groggily sat up. He threw his cloak around himself, stretched, and without a word, left the room.

"No big deal, I'll sleep outside," he mumbled before disappearing.

XIII.

Alone with his thoughts, Volodya felt lost and uneasy. He wanted to sleep and forget everything—especially his own fears. He blew out the candle, lay down, and pulled his coat over his head, trying to block out the darkness that had scared him since he was a child. But then a terrible thought hit him—what if a bomb struck the roof and crushed him? He held his breath and listened carefully. Above him, he could hear footsteps—most likely the battery commander.

"If a bomb does fall," he reassured himself, "it will hit him first, then me. At least I won't be the only one."

That thought brought him a little relief.

But another worry quickly replaced it—what if the enemy suddenly attacked at night? What if the French broke in? How would he defend himself?

He sat up and paced around the room. His fear of real danger now felt stronger than his childhood fear of the dark. He looked around for something heavy to use as a weapon, but the only things in the room were a saddle and a samovar. A wave of disgust hit him.

"I'm a coward—a miserable coward!"

That terrible thought made his chest tighten with shame. He threw himself back onto the bed and tried not to think.

But he couldn't stop. Images from the day flooded his mind—the wounded soldiers, the blood, the sound of bombs crashing down, splinters flying through the air. He imagined a nurse, the young Sister of Mercy, gently bandaging him as he lay dying. He pictured his mother, back home, kneeling in front of an icon, tears streaming down her face as she prayed for him. His heart ached, and sleep seemed impossible.

Then, a new thought came to him—God.

He knelt beside the bed, crossed himself, and folded his hands like he had as a child. The moment he did, a wave of comfort washed over him—something he hadn't felt in a long time.

"If I have to die, then let it be your will, Lord," he thought. "Let it happen quickly. But if I need to be brave, if I must stay strong, please give me the courage. Don't let me be a coward. Show me the right path."

For the first time, he felt a little calmer. His mind was clearer, and the world seemed different. As this feeling took hold, he slowly drifted into a deep sleep, even as the distant sounds of explosions rattled the window.

Only God knew how many desperate prayers rose from the battlefield that night—from the officer who had spent the day thinking about his medals but now shook with fear, to the wounded soldier lying on the cold ground, begging for an end to his pain.

XIV.

The older Kozeltzoff, walking down the street, spotted a soldier from his regiment and headed straight for the fifth bastion with him.

"Stay close to the wall, sir," the soldier advised.

"Why?"

"It's dangerous, sir. There's one flying overhead," the soldier replied, listening to the sharp whistling of a cannonball as it crashed into the ground on the other side of the street.

Kozeltzoff ignored the warning and confidently walked down the middle of the street.

The city looked the same as when he had last been here in the spring—the same streets, the same gunfire, even more frequent now, the same wounded men, the same trenches and barricades. But something was different. Everything felt heavier, more urgent. The buildings had bigger holes in them, the windows were dark except for the Kushtchin house, which had been turned into a hospital. The usual feeling of routine, even recklessness, was gone. Now, there was only exhaustion, tension, and an unspoken anticipation of something worse to come.

They finally reached the last trench. In the dim light, a soldier from the P—— regiment recognized Kozeltzoff and called out to him. Nearby, the third battalion stood close to the wall, their shapes briefly visible when the sky lit up from cannon fire. Quiet voices murmured, and rifles clattered as soldiers shifted their grips.

"Where's the regiment commander?" Kozeltzoff asked.

"He's in the bomb shelter with the sailors, sir," a soldier quickly replied. "I can take you there if you'd like."

The soldier led Kozeltzoff through the maze of trenches until they reached a small dugout. A sailor sat outside, calmly smoking his pipe. Behind him was a wooden door, faint light escaping through the cracks.

"Can I go in?" Kozeltzoff asked.

"I'll let them know you're here," the sailor replied and disappeared inside.

Muffled voices came from the other side of the door.

"If Prussia stays neutral," one man was saying, "then Austria will have no choice but to follow…"

"Austria won't change anything," another voice responded. "As long as the Slavic lands— Well, let him in."

Kozeltzoff had never been inside this shelter before. He was surprised by how well-kept it was. The wooden floor was polished, and screens covered the doorway. Two beds stood against the wall, and in one corner, a large religious icon of the Virgin Mary hung in a golden frame, with a red lamp flickering before it.

On one bed, a naval officer lay fully dressed, fast asleep. At a small table nearby, two men sat talking—the regiment's new commander and his adjutant.

Although Kozeltzoff was never one to be intimidated, he couldn't help but feel uneasy. Just a few weeks ago, this man had been his fellow officer, but now, as regiment commander, he carried himself with an air of authority that was hard to ignore.

"It's strange," Kozeltzoff thought, studying him. "Just seven weeks ago, he was one of us. He ate alone, never invited anyone over, lived simply. And now look at him—so confident, so proud, like he knows every man here would give anything to be in his place."

"You took a long time to recover," the colonel said coldly, barely looking at him.

"I was badly wounded, sir. It hasn't fully healed yet."

"Then maybe you shouldn't have come back," the colonel replied, giving him a skeptical glance. "Are you sure you're fit for duty?"

"Yes, sir," Kozeltzoff answered firmly.

"Good," the colonel said. "You'll take command of the ninth company from Ensign Zaitzoff. That was your old unit. You'll receive your orders shortly."

"Yes, sir."

"Send the regimental adjutant to me once you get there," the commander added, giving a brief nod that signaled the conversation was over.

As Kozeltzoff left the shelter, he muttered to himself and shrugged his shoulders, looking troubled. He wasn't angry at the colonel—there was no reason to be—but something about the whole exchange unsettled him. He felt annoyed, maybe even disappointed, but he couldn't quite tell if it was with his commander, the situation, or himself.

XV.

Before joining the other officers, Kozeltzoff went to visit his company and find out where they were positioned.

The barricades, trenches, cannons, and even the broken pieces of bombs—everything lit up by flashes of gunfire—looked familiar. Three months ago, he had spent two weeks in this same spot without leaving. Even though it had been dangerous, the memories weren't all bad. In a strange way, he even felt happy to see this place again. His company was positioned near the defensive wall, facing the sixth bastion.

Kozeltzoff stepped into a long shelter where the ninth company was gathered. The entrance was wide open, and inside, the room was packed with soldiers, leaving barely any space to move. In one corner, a soldier held a bent candle, its weak flame lighting up a book another soldier was reading out loud, slowly sounding out the words. The men around him listened carefully. It was a simple book for learning how to read. As Kozeltzoff entered, he caught part of the reading:

"Pray-er af-ter lear-ning. I thank Thee, Crea-tor..."

"Blow that candle out," someone whispered. "That's a good book."

"My ... God ..." the reader continued.

When Kozeltzoff asked for the sergeant, the reading stopped. The soldiers shuffled around, clearing their throats and stretching after sitting still for so long. The sergeant, who had been standing near the reader, quickly buttoned up his coat and stepped forward, carefully avoiding the feet of the men who had no room to move.

"How are you, brother? Are all these men from our company?"

"Good to have you back, sir! Welcome!" the sergeant said with a big smile. "Are you feeling better? Thank God! It's been boring around here without you."

It was clear the soldiers respected Kozeltzoff. Quiet voices murmured in the back of the shelter—"Our old commander, Mikhaïl Semyónitch Kozeltzoff, has returned!" A few men stepped forward to greet him, and even the company drummer offered his congratulations.

"How are you, Obantchuk?" Kozeltzoff asked. "Everything alright? It's good to see you all."

A chorus of voices answered, "Good health to you, sir!"

"How's everyone holding up?"

"Not so well, sir. The French have the advantage," one soldier admitted. "Fighting from behind these barricades isn't the same as being out in the open."

"Well, maybe we'll get lucky, and God will let us fight them in the open," Kozeltzoff said. "We've done it before—we can do it again!"

"We'd love the chance, sir!" several soldiers called out.

"And what about the enemy? Are they really that brave?"

"Fearless," the drummer muttered, glancing at another soldier, as if to make sure Kozeltzoff wasn't exaggerating.

After talking with his men, Kozeltzoff left to find the other officers in the defensive barracks.

XVI.

The barracks were crowded with men—navy officers, artillery officers, and infantry officers. Some were sleeping, while others sat on wooden crates and cannon carriages, talking. A large and noisy group gathered behind an arch, sitting on two rugs spread out on the floor, drinking beer, and playing cards.

"Ah! Kozeltzoff, you're here! Great! It's good to see you! He's a brave one... How's your wound?" Voices called out from all around the room. It was clear that the men respected him and were happy he had come.

After greeting his friends, Kozeltzoff joined the group of officers playing cards. Some were familiar faces. One man, lean and good-looking, had dark skin, a long, sharp nose, and a thick mustache stretching from his cheeks. He shuffled the cards with long, pale fingers, one of which wore a heavy gold ring. His movements were quick and careless, as if he wanted to seem relaxed, but there was something else beneath the surface—nervous energy. To his right, a gray-haired major lay propped up on his elbow, playing small bets with an air of indifference, always settling up immediately. On his left, a red-faced officer, sweating slightly, laughed and joked, but it seemed forced. Whenever he won a round, his hand kept fidgeting in his empty pocket. He was betting high, though it was clear he had no cash left, which irritated the dark-haired man. A pale, thin officer with a bald head and large features paced the room, gripping a thick stack of banknotes, placing bets with real money—and winning.

Kozeltzoff took a shot of vodka and sat down with the players.

"Join us, Mikhaïl Semyónitch!" said the dealer. "You must have plenty of money with you."

"Where would I get money? I spent the last of it in town."

"Come on! Someone must have tricked you out of it in Simferopol."

"I really don't have much," Kozeltzoff insisted, though he seemed to enjoy making them doubt him. Then, he unbuttoned his coat, picked up the worn deck, and joined in.

"Alright, let's see what happens! Who knows? Luck might be on my side. But first, another drink to give me some courage."

Not long after, he had downed another glass of vodka, several of beer, and lost his last three rubles.

The red-faced officer now owed 150 rubles.

"No way he's going to pay that," he said with a shrug, flipping another card.

"Try to send it," the dealer muttered, pausing as he set down the cards, glancing at him.

"I'll pay tomorrow," the sweating officer said, rising to his feet, digging through his empty pockets as if hoping to find something.

"Hm!" The dealer grumbled, tossing the cards to the side. He finished dealing but shook his head. "This won't work. I'm done playing. We agreed—cash only."

"What, you don't trust me? That's ridiculous!"

"How can I pay out if there's no money on the table?" the dealer said.

"I won't stand for this!" the major snapped, jumping to his feet. "I'm playing against you, not him."

The red-faced officer lost his temper.

"I said I'll pay tomorrow! How dare you question me?"

"I'll say whatever I want! This is nonsense!" the major shouted back.

"Enough, Feódor Feodoritch!" the others said, trying to calm him down.

There was no point dragging out the scene. By tomorrow—or maybe even today—each of these men would walk toward battle, ready to face death without hesitation. In these grim conditions, where there was no escape and little left of normal life, their only comfort was distraction—anything to numb their thoughts. Deep down, each carried a spark of courage, waiting for the right moment to burn brightly. When the time came, that spark would ignite, pushing them forward to acts of true bravery.

XVII.

The bombardment continued just as intensely the next day. Around eleven in the morning, Volodya Kozeltzoff sat in a circle with the battery officers. He was starting to feel more comfortable around them—observing new faces, asking questions, and sharing stories.

He liked how the artillery officers spoke—calmly and with a bit of knowledge in their discussions. It made him respect them. His shy, youthful look, along with his friendly nature, made the officers take a liking to him.

The captain, the most senior officer in the battery, was a short man with light-colored hair styled in a small topknot and smoothed down at the temples. He was trained in the old artillery traditions, carried himself with charm, and liked to appear well-educated. He asked Volodya about his knowledge of artillery and recent inventions, joking about his youth and good looks. He treated Volodya almost like a father would treat a son, which Volodya found very comforting.

Sub-Lieutenant Dyadenko, a young officer with an energetic personality, spoke with a slight accent. His coat was worn out, and his hair was messy. He talked loudly, argued at every opportunity, and made quick, sharp movements. But despite his rough attitude, Volodya could sense he was a good-hearted man. Dyadenko was always offering to help him and constantly pointed out how none of the guns in Sevastopol were placed correctly.

Then there was Lieutenant Tchernovitzky. He had raised eyebrows, dressed neatly in a patched but well-maintained coat, and wore a gold watch chain over a silk vest. He was polite and spoke more formally than the others, but Volodya didn't like him. He kept asking about what the Emperor and the Minister of War were doing and told exaggerated stories about the bravery shown in Sevastopol. He also complained about the lack of true patriots. While he sounded smart and patriotic, something about him felt fake to Volodya. He also noticed that the other officers didn't really engage with him.

Among the group was Yunker Vlang, the young officer Volodya had woken up the night before. He didn't say much, just sat in the corner, laughed at jokes, reminded people of details when they forgot, passed around vodka, and rolled cigarettes for the others. Maybe it was Volodya's respectful and friendly attitude—treating him the same as the other officers, rather than looking down on him—or maybe it was Volodya's appearance. Whatever the reason, Vlang seemed completely fascinated by him. He quietly observed his every move, eager to help, almost like someone in admiration. The other officers noticed and teased him for it.

Before dinner, the staff-captain who had been on duty at the battery returned to join the group. Staff-Captain Kraut was a confident, good-looking officer with fair hair, a large reddish mustache, and thick sideburns. His Russian was excellent—too proper, almost, for a native speaker. He had a reputation for being a skilled officer, a loyal friend, and completely trustworthy with money. Yet, despite all these great qualities, something about him felt a little off—maybe because he seemed too perfect. Like many Russian-Germans, he was extremely practical, in contrast to the traditional image of a deep-thinking German.

"Ah, here he is—our hero arrives!" the captain said as Kraut entered, his spurs jingling, swinging his arms with confidence. "Friedrich Krestyanitch, what will it be—tea or vodka?"

"I already ordered tea," Kraut replied, "but a little vodka wouldn't hurt—for the soul." Then, turning to Volodya, he added, "Pleased to meet you. I hope we'll get along well."

Volodya stood and bowed politely. "Staff-Captain Kraut... The gun sergeant at the bastion told me you arrived last night."

"Thanks for the bed," Volodya said. "I slept in it."

"Hope it was comfortable? One of the legs is broken, but during a siege, we can't afford to be picky—just prop it up."

"So, how was your watch?" Dyadenko asked.

"Fine," Kraut answered. "Except Skvortzoff got hit, and we had to fix a gun carriage last night. The whole side of it was smashed."

As he spoke, he stood up and started pacing, clearly still feeling the rush that comes after surviving danger.

He patted the captain's knee. "So, Dmitri Gavrilitch, how's everything? Any updates on your promotion?"

"Nothing yet."

"There won't be," Dyadenko interrupted. "I already told you why."

"Why not?"

"The report wasn't written the right way."

Kraut grinned. "You always have to argue, don't you? Such a stubborn Little Russian! Just watch—he'll probably get promoted just to prove you wrong."

"No, he won't," Dyadenko replied firmly.

Kraut chuckled and turned to Vlang. "Bring me my pipe and fill it."

Vlang immediately jumped up to do it.

Kraut's presence livened up the group. He talked about the bombardment, asked about what had happened while he was away, and joined in on every conversation.

XVIII.

"How are things going? Have you settled in yet?" Kraut asked Volodya. "By the way, what's your full name? In the artillery, we always address each other properly. Do you have a horse yet?"

"No," Volodya replied. "I don't know what to do. I told the captain that I don't have a horse, and I won't have money for one until I get my allowance for travel and supplies. I was thinking of asking the battery commander for a horse in the meantime, but I'm afraid he'll say no."

"You mean Apollon Sergiéitch?" Kraut said, making a doubtful noise and glancing at the captain. "Not likely."

"Well, if he refuses, there's no harm in asking," the captain said. "There are extra horses that aren't being used, so it might be possible. I'll ask about it today."

"You don't know him well," Dyadenko chimed in. "He might be stingy about some things, but I doubt he'll refuse this. Want to bet on it?"

"You always have to argue," Kraut said with a grin.

"I argue because I know," Dyadenko replied. "He has no reason to say no—he doesn't lose anything by lending the horse."

"No reason? When he's paying eight rubles just for oats?" Kraut countered. "Of course, it matters whether he keeps an extra horse or not."

"Ask Skvoretz yourself, Vladimir Semyónitch!" Vlang said as he returned with Kraut's pipe. "It's a great horse."

"You mean the one you fell into a ditch with during the festival back in March?" Kraut teased.

"That's not the point," Dyadenko continued. "And why do you say oats cost eight rubles? He checked himself—it's actually ten and a half."

"You talk like he'll go broke over it. So, when you become a battery commander, you won't let any horses be taken into town?"

"When I'm in charge," Dyadenko said, "my horses will get the proper amount of feed, and I won't be hoarding money, don't worry."

"We'll see," Kraut said. "You'll do the same thing, just like everyone else—including him," he added, nodding at Volodya.

"Why do you assume he'll try to profit from it?" Tchernovitzky interrupted. "Maybe he has his own money. Not everyone has to take advantage of the system."

Volodya's face turned red. "That sounds like an insult," he said.

"Oh, come on! You're too quick to get offended," Kraut chuckled.

"It's not about that," Volodya said. "I just think that if the money wasn't mine, I wouldn't take it."

"Listen," the staff-captain said more seriously. "When you're in charge of a battery, your job is to manage things properly. That's all. The commander doesn't handle the soldiers' supplies—that's how it's always been in the artillery. If you don't manage things well, you'll end up with nothing.

"Now, let me break it down for you. First, there's the cost of shoeing your horse." He held up a finger. "Then medicine." Another finger. "Office supplies." A third. "Extra horses—those cost five hundred rubles." He kept counting. "You also have to replace the soldiers' collars, buy coal, and make sure your officers have meals. If you're a battery commander, you need to live decently. You'll need a carriage, a fur coat, and plenty of other things. But why list them all?"

The captain, who had been silent until now, finally spoke up. "The main thing, Vladimir Semyónitch, is this—imagine a man like me, who has served for twenty years. First earning two hundred rubles, then three hundred. Don't you think he deserves at least a little security in his old age?"

"There it is!" the staff-captain added. "Don't rush to judge—just keep serving and you'll understand."

Volodya felt embarrassed. He regretted speaking without thinking and muttered something under his breath, deciding to stay quiet. Dyadenko, on the other hand, jumped in, eager to argue his point.

Their discussion was interrupted when the colonel's servant arrived to call them to dinner.

"Tell Apollon Sergiéitch to give us some wine tonight," Tchernovitzky said to the captain as he buttoned his uniform. "Why is he so stingy with it? He'll die one day, and no one will get to enjoy it."

"Tell him yourself."

"No way. You outrank me—that's your job."

XIX.

The dining table had been pulled away from the wall and covered with a stained tablecloth in the same room where Volodya had met the colonel the night before. The battery commander greeted him with a handshake and asked about his trip and life in Petersburg.

"Well, gentlemen, let's have a drink. Anyone for vodka?" he said. Then, with a smile, he added, "Our ensigns don't drink."

The battery commander didn't seem as strict as he had the night before. Today, he came across as warm and welcoming—more like an experienced comrade than a superior. Still, every officer, from the senior captain to Ensign Dyadenko, showed him deep respect in the way they spoke and made eye contact when stepping forward for a drink.

Dinner consisted of a large wooden bowl of cabbage soup with chunks of beef, heavy seasoning, and bay leaves. There were mustard-covered meatballs wrapped in cabbage, meat-filled pastries, and butter that wasn't exactly fresh. There were no napkins, only pewter and wooden spoons, and just two drinking glasses. A broken-necked water decanter sat on the table. Yet, the meal was far from dull—conversation flowed nonstop.

At first, they talked about the battle of Inkerman, where the battery had fought. Everyone had their own opinions on why they hadn't succeeded, but the moment the battery commander spoke, the others fell silent, listening intently. The discussion then shifted to the weaknesses of their light cannons and new artillery models. Volodya took the opportunity to share what he knew about modern cannons.

Surprisingly, no one mentioned Sevastopol's dire situation. It was as if they had all already thought about it too much to bring it up again. To Volodya's surprise, they also said nothing about his duties or what was expected of him, as if he had come to Sevastopol just to talk about cannons and have dinner with the officers.

During the meal, a bomb exploded nearby. The walls and floor shook as if from an earthquake, and smoke from the blast darkened the window.

"I bet you don't see things like that in Petersburg," the battery commander said. "But here, it happens all the time. Vlang, check where it hit."

Vlang peeked outside and reported that the bomb had landed in the square. After that, no one mentioned it again.

Toward the end of dinner, an old clerk from the battery entered with three sealed envelopes and handed them to the commander.

"These just arrived from the artillery chief—urgent."

The officers watched closely as the commander opened one of the letters, all wondering the same thing: What could it be?

Maybe they were finally being sent away from Sevastopol for rest. Or maybe they were about to be ordered to the front lines.

"Again?" the commander muttered, tossing the letter onto the table in frustration.

"What's it about, Apollon Sergiéitch?" asked the senior officer.

"They need an officer and a crew for the mortar battery over there," the commander grumbled. "I only have four officers, and we're already short on men. And now they're asking for more. But orders are orders. Someone has to go." He paused. "The officer must be at the barrier by seven. Call the sergeant! Who's going?"

"Well, here's someone who hasn't been yet," Tchernovitzky said, nodding toward Volodya.

The commander said nothing.

"I'd like to go," Volodya said quickly. As soon as the words left his mouth, a cold sweat formed on his back and neck.

"No, you don't need to," the captain cut in. "No one here will refuse, but we shouldn't force anyone either. If Apollon Sergiéitch allows it, let's draw lots, like we did last time."

Everyone agreed. Kraut tore up pieces of paper, folded them, and placed them into a cap. The captain, trying to lighten the mood, even joked about asking the colonel for wine "to keep their courage up." Dyadenko sat in silence, looking serious. Volodya smiled nervously at something. Tchernovitzky joked that it would definitely land on him. Kraut remained calm and unreadable.

Volodya was given the first draw. He picked one slip of paper, then immediately changed his mind and chose another—smaller and thinner. He unfolded it.

"I go," it read.

"It's me," Volodya said with a sigh.

"Well, God be with you," the battery commander said, watching the unease on Volodya's face with a kind smile. "You'll be getting your first real battle experience right away. And to make things a little easier, Vlang will go with you as your gun-sergeant."

XX.

Vlang was thrilled about his new assignment. He rushed off to get ready and, once dressed, hurried to help Volodya. He tried to convince him to bring along his cot, fur coat, an old history book, a small coffee pot, and other unnecessary things. Meanwhile, the captain suggested that Volodya study his artillery manual first and copy down the firing tables for the mortars.

Volodya got to work right away. To his surprise and relief, he realized that although he still felt a bit nervous—mainly about whether he would act bravely—his fear was nowhere near as strong as the night before. The daylight, staying busy, and, most importantly, the fact that intense emotions don't last forever, all helped him regain his composure. He was starting to adjust.

At seven o'clock, just as the sun dipped behind the Nikolaevsky barracks, the sergeant arrived and told Volodya that the men were ready.

"I gave the list to Vlanga, sir. You'll need to ask him for it," he added.

Twenty artillerymen stood at the corner of the house, armed but without their loading tools. Volodya and Vlang walked over to them.

Should I say something? Volodya wondered. Maybe a little speech? Or just a simple 'Good day, men'? He decided the latter was the right thing to do.

"Good day, men!" he called out, his young voice ringing with confidence.

The soldiers responded cheerfully. The fresh, commanding tone of their new officer made a good impression. Volodya marched ahead of them, his steps firm. His heart pounded as if he had sprinted for miles, but he held himself upright, his expression steady and confident.

As they reached the Malakoff mound and climbed the slope, Volodya noticed something odd. Vlang, who had been so eager back at camp, was now shifting from side to side and lowering his head, as if every whizzing cannonball was coming straight for him. Some of the soldiers did the same, their faces showing either fear or, at the very least, nervousness. Seeing this actually made Volodya feel calmer.

So, this is the Malakoff mound—the place I imagined to be so terrifying? And here I am, walking through it without flinching! I'm not as scared as the others! Maybe I'm not a coward after all! He felt a surge of pride and confidence.

But this feeling didn't last long.

In the dimming light, he came across a grim sight near the Kornilovsky battery while searching for the bastion commander. A group of four sailors stood near the barricade, lifting the lifeless body of a man—barefoot, without a coat—by the arms and legs. Struggling under its weight, they tried to toss it over the rampart.

During the second day of the bombardment, they had run out of time to remove the dead from the battlefield, so bodies were being thrown into the trenches to keep them from getting in the way.

Volodya froze as he watched the corpse teeter at the top of the barrier before rolling into the ditch.

Thankfully, before he could dwell on it, the bastion commander appeared. He quickly gave Volodya his orders and assigned him a guide to take him to the mortar battery and the underground shelter he would be using.

That night, Volodya encountered many more harsh realities. The firing he had once imagined—precise, disciplined, like in training— was nothing like what he found here. Instead, he was given two broken mortars: one destroyed at the muzzle by a cannonball and the other sitting on a shattered platform. There were no workers available to make repairs until morning, none of the ammunition matched the weights listed in his manual, and two of his soldiers were wounded before the night was over. He came close to death at least twenty times.

Luckily, an experienced sailor was assigned to help him. This massive gunner had been manning mortars since the siege began. He assured Volodya that the weapons could still be used, showed him around the bastion with a lantern as if it were his own backyard, and promised to have everything in working order by the next day.

The bomb shelter they were taken to was carved out of solid rock, a deep underground chamber covered with thick oak planks. Volodya and his soldiers made their way inside.

As soon as Vlang saw the tiny entrance, barely big enough to crawl through, he rushed ahead, throwing himself inside first. He smacked his head hard on the stone floor but didn't even complain—he just curled up in a corner and refused to move.

Inside, the soldiers settled in along the walls. Some lit their pipes, speaking in hushed tones. Volodya set up his cot in one corner, lit a candle, and lay down, smoking a cigarette.

Outside, the bombardment continued. The muffled sound of distant artillery rumbled above them, but only one cannon—positioned right outside—was loud enough to shake the entire shelter when it fired.

Other than that, everything was quiet. The soldiers, still unsure about their new officer, spoke only when necessary—asking for a light or shifting to make space. Somewhere in the darkness, a rat scratched against the stones. Across the room, Vlang, still shaken, let out a deep sigh.

As Volodya lay in his quiet corner, surrounded by his men, illuminated only by a flickering candle, he felt something unexpected. It reminded him of playing hide-and-seek as a child—crawling under a cupboard or hiding beneath his mother's dress, holding his breath in the dark. There was a strange comfort in it. The space felt cramped, the air heavy, but deep down, he felt oddly safe.

XXI.

After about ten minutes, the soldiers started shifting around and chatting among themselves. The two most experienced men—the gun-sergeants—sat closest to Volodya's bed and the candlelight. One was an older, gray-haired man covered in medals, except for the Cross of St. George. The other was younger, a militia soldier, rolling cigarettes as he listened. The drummer, as usual, took it upon himself to serve the officer. The bombardiers and cavalrymen sat nearby, while the lower-ranking soldiers gathered in the shadows near the entrance, speaking quietly.

Their conversation was interrupted when someone rushed into the shelter.

"What's wrong, brother? Couldn't handle being outside? Weren't the songs good enough for you?" someone teased.

"They're singing songs out there like nothing I've ever heard before!" the man replied with a laugh.

"But Vasin doesn't like bombs—oh no, he does not like them," a soldier from the main group joked.

"That's ridiculous! It's different when you have to be out there," Vasin shot back. His voice carried authority, making the others go silent. "They've been firing like crazy since the 24th. And for what? You get killed for nothing, and no one even bothers to say 'thank you.'"

The soldiers laughed at his bluntness.

"There's Melnikoff—he's still standing outside the door," someone pointed out.

"Call him in," the older gunner said. "They'll kill him if he stays out there for no reason."

"Who's Melnikoff?" Volodya asked.

"A soldier from our unit, sir. He doesn't seem to be afraid of anything, and now he's just walking around outside. You should see him—he looks like a bear."

"He must know some kind of magic," Vasin said in his slow, steady voice.

Melnikoff stepped into the shelter. He was rare among soldiers— broad-shouldered and slightly overweight. He had sandy-colored hair, a large forehead, and light blue eyes that stood out on his strong face.

"Are you afraid of the bombs?" Volodya asked him.

Melnikoff shrugged. "What's there to be afraid of?" He scratched his head. "I know a bomb won't kill me."

"So, you actually want to stay here?"

"Of course! It's fun here!" He suddenly burst into laughter.

"Well then, I should sign you up for a special mission. I'll let the general know," Volodya teased, though he didn't actually know any generals.

"Why not? I'd be up for it."

Melnikoff disappeared into the group. A moment later, his voice rang out:

"Who's got a deck of cards? Let's play noski!"

Soon, a game started in the corner, followed by laughter and playful arguments.

Volodya drank tea from the samovar, which the drummer had prepared for him. He passed some to the gunners, joked with them, and chatted, wanting to earn their respect. He was pleased by how they treated him. The soldiers, noticing that their young officer didn't act superior, started speaking more openly.

One soldier insisted the siege of Sevastopol would end soon. He claimed that a sailor had told him the emperor's brother, Constantine, was coming with an American fleet to help. Supposedly, there would be an agreement to stop all firing for two weeks, and after that, if anyone shot a cannon, they'd have to pay 75 kopeks per round.

Vasin, whom Volodya had already noticed was small but had warm eyes and thick sideburns, shared a story about his last trip home. At first, his family had been happy to see him, but before long, his father started sending him off to do chores. And to top it off, the local forest officer sent a carriage to pick up Vasin's wife. The soldiers listened in silence at first, then burst out laughing.

The easy conversation and friendly atmosphere put Volodya in high spirits. He felt perfectly at ease. The cramped, stuffy air of the bomb shelter didn't bother him at all.

Many of the soldiers had already fallen asleep. Vlang was stretched out on the floor, while the old gun-sergeant laid out his coat, crossed himself, and began muttering prayers before bed.

Then Volodya suddenly had the urge to step outside and see what was happening.

"Move your legs," one soldier grumbled to another as Volodya stood up. The men shifted aside to make way for him.

Vlang, who had seemed fast asleep, suddenly lifted his head and grabbed Volodya's coat.

"Don't go!" he pleaded, his voice trembling. "You don't understand yet—they're shooting at us out there all the time! It's safer here."

But Volodya ignored him and climbed out of the shelter.

Melnikoff was already sitting at the entrance. Volodya joined him.

The fresh air felt crisp and cool after the stuffy bomb shelter. The night sky was clear, filled with stars. In the distance, cannon fire rumbled. Cart wheels creaked as supplies were hauled to the fortifications, and the voices of soldiers working on the ammunition storage echoed through the night.

Above them, streaks of fire shot across the sky—trails left by flying bombs. Just a few steps to the left, another bomb shelter entrance stood open. Through the doorway, Volodya could see the backs of soldiers inside, hear their quiet conversations.

In front of him, the raised mound of a powder magazine came into view. Bent figures hurried across it, carrying sacks of dirt. But at the very top, where bullets and bombs constantly flew past, one figure stood completely still. He was tall, wearing a black coat, hands stuffed into his pockets, calmly pressing down the dirt the others had just dumped.

Bombs exploded close by. Each time, the workers ducked and ran for cover. But the man in black never moved. He kept packing the dirt with his boots as if nothing was happening.

"Who's that?" Volodya asked Melnikoff.

"I don't know. I'll go check."

"Don't—it's not necessary."

But Melnikoff didn't listen. He walked up to the tall figure and stood beside him for a long time, just as calm and motionless. When he returned, he said, "That's the magazine officer, sir. A bomb hit the storage area, so the infantry is adding more dirt to protect it."

Sometimes, a bomb flew straight toward the shelter entrance, and Volodya instinctively shrank back into the doorway. But then he would force himself to look out again, tracking the path of the next one.

From inside the shelter, Vlang kept calling out, begging him to come back.

But Volodya sat there for hours, watching the bombs streak through the sky. There was something strangely thrilling about it— challenging fate, observing the patterns of fire. By the end of the night, he had even started to figure out where most of the shots were coming from and where they were likely to land.

XXII.

The next morning, on the 27th, after sleeping for ten hours, Volodya stepped out of the bomb shelter feeling refreshed and full of energy. Vlang tried to follow him, but the moment he heard a bullet whiz by, he panicked, flung himself backward through the entrance, and hit his head. The soldiers watching burst into laughter. Most of them had also come outside, eager to escape the stale air of the shelter and breathe in the cool morning breeze.

Only a few, including Vlang and the old gun-sergeant, preferred to stay inside. The rest scattered around the entrance, and some even climbed onto the fortifications, despite the fact that the bombardment was just as intense as the night before. Melnikoff had been out walking among the batteries since sunrise, looking up at the sky as if the bullets and cannonballs didn't bother him at all.

Near the entrance, two older soldiers sat with a young infantryman who had curly hair and was Jewish. The young soldier picked up a stray bullet from the ground, rubbed it smooth against a rock, and carefully carved a cross into it using a knife, making it look like the St. George medal. The others watched his work as they chatted. The cross turned out to be quite impressive.

"If we stay here much longer," one soldier said, "our service time will be over by the time peace comes."

"That's not true," another replied. "I still have at least four years left, and I've already been in Sevastopol for five months."

"They don't count this time toward our discharge, you know," a third soldier added.

Just then, a cannonball whistled overhead and slammed into the ground barely a few feet from Melnikoff as he walked toward them.

"That was close," one of the men said.

"I won't be killed," Melnikoff replied calmly.

"Here, take this," the young soldier said, handing him the carved cross. "For your bravery."

The conversation continued as if nothing had happened.

"No, I'm telling you, a month here counts as a whole year—that was the order," one soldier insisted.

"Believe what you want, but once peace is declared, they'll hold an imperial review at Orshava. If we don't get discharged, at least they'll let us go on indefinite leave."

Just then, a bullet zipped past them and struck a rock.

"You might get your full discharge before evening," one soldier joked.

The men laughed.

But before two hours had even passed, two of them did get their final discharge—killed by enemy fire—while five others were wounded. Yet those who remained continued joking as before.

By morning, the two broken mortars had been repaired enough to be fired again. At ten o'clock, following his orders from the bastion commander, Volodya called his unit together and led them to the battery.

Unlike the night before, when there had been some nervousness, now the men showed no signs of fear. Only Vlang still couldn't control himself, flinching and ducking at every sound. Even Vasin, usually calm, seemed uneasy—he kept shifting his position and fidgeting.

But Volodya felt something completely different. He was caught up in the excitement of the moment. He didn't even think about danger. He felt proud—proud that he was doing his duty, proud that he was not a coward, and proud that he was in charge. He knew that the twenty men under his command were watching him closely, and that thought made him even more confident. He wanted to prove himself. He even started showing off—climbing onto the fortifications, unbuttoning his coat so that his red undershirt was clearly visible, making sure everyone could see him.

The commander of the bastion, who was making his rounds, had seen many acts of bravery during his eight months of service, but even he couldn't help admiring this young officer. Volodya, with his coat open, his red shirt showing against his pale neck, his face lit up with excitement, was shouting orders—"First! Second!"—as he clapped his hands and ran along the ramparts, eager to see where the bombs landed.

By 11:30, the firing on both sides stopped. Then, at exactly noon, the enemy launched their assault on the Malakoff mound and the second, third, and fifth bastions.

XXIII.

Around midday, two naval officers stood on a hill near the telegraph station, between Inkerman and the northern fortifications. One of them was looking through a telescope at Sevastopol, while the other had just arrived with his assistant.

The sun shined high above the bay, making the water sparkle and casting a golden light over the ships, their sails, and the small boats moving smoothly across the surface. A gentle breeze barely moved the dry oak leaves near the signal pole, but it filled the sails and sent small ripples across the waves.

Across the bay, Sevastopol looked as beautiful and grand as ever. The unfinished church, the towering columns, the waterfront, the green boulevard stretching up the hill, and the elegant library building were all visible. The small blue inlets were crowded with ships, their masts forming a dense forest. Picturesque aqueducts arched over the landscape, and plumes of blue smoke rose from the city, occasionally lit by flashes of red from gunfire. The proud, majestic Sevastopol stood between the golden, smoke-covered hills on one side and the shimmering blue sea on the other.

In the distance, a long trail of black smoke stretched across the horizon from a passing steamship. White clouds gathered beyond it, hinting at an approaching storm. Along the enemy's fortifications, especially on the hills to the left, thick white smoke billowed upward, interrupted by sudden flashes of gunfire. Even in the bright midday sun, these explosions were vivid. The rising smoke shifted into different shapes as it drifted, spreading across the sky. The booming sounds of cannons and gunfire never stopped, shaking the air with their constant thunder.

By noon, the explosions became less frequent, and the air seemed to settle.

"The second bastion isn't firing back anymore," said a hussar officer on horseback. "It's completely destroyed. Terrible."

"Yes, and the Malakoff only fires once for every three shots from the enemy," replied the officer with the telescope. "It frustrates me that they're staying silent. The enemy is aiming directly at the Kornilovsky battery, and it's not responding at all."

"They always stop the bombardment at noon," the hussar officer pointed out. "It's happening again today. Let's go get breakfast—they're already waiting for us. There's nothing more to see."

"Wait, don't rush," the officer with the telescope said, suddenly more focused. "Something's happening in the trenches. There's movement—large columns of men marching."

"Yes, I see it now," the other officer said. "They're advancing. We need to send a signal."

"Look, they're coming out of the trenches."

Even without the telescope, it was clear. Dark masses of soldiers were moving down the hillside, crossing the narrow valley from the French batteries toward the Russian bastions. In front of them, thinner dark lines could be seen—these troops were already close to the Russian defenses.

Suddenly, white bursts of smoke erupted from the bastions as the Russian defenders opened fire. It looked as if gunfire was spreading in waves along the defensive line.

The wind carried the sharp crackling of musket shots—fast and steady, like raindrops hitting a window. The advancing black lines of enemy soldiers pushed forward, disappearing into the thickening smoke. The gunfire grew louder, the separate shots blending into a single, rolling roar.

The battlefield was soon covered in a dense lilac-colored haze. The smoke expanded, broke apart, then merged again. Bright flashes flickered within it, and dark figures darted through the haze. The sounds of battle became one overwhelming crash.

"It's an assault," the officer said, his face pale as he handed the telescope to the naval officer.

Along the road, messengers rode swiftly, officers on horseback rushed by, and the commander-in-chief passed in a carriage with his staff. Everyone's faces were filled with tension and anticipation.

"They couldn't have taken it," said the mounted officer.

"By God, look!" the other officer suddenly exclaimed, letting out a deep sigh as he lowered the telescope. "The French flag… on the Malakoff!"

"That's impossible!"

XXIV.

Kozeltzoff had spent the night gambling, managing to win back his money only to lose it all again—including the gold coins sewn into his cuffs. Just before sunrise, he finally collapsed into a restless sleep in the fortified barracks of the fifth battalion.

Suddenly, loud voices echoed through the room:

"Alarm!"

"Why are you sleeping, Mikhail Semyonitch? We're under attack!" someone shouted.

At first, he didn't believe it. Half-asleep, he thought it was just a young officer panicking. But then he spotted another officer running back and forth, his face pale with fear. In that instant, Kozeltzoff understood—this was real. A terrifying thought struck him: What if people think I'm afraid and hiding instead of going to my unit? That fear was worse than anything else. Without hesitation, he sprinted toward his company.

The cannon fire had stopped, but the sound of musket shots filled the air. The bullets weren't just flying one by one—they came in waves, whistling overhead like flocks of birds in autumn. Thick smoke covered the ground where his battalion had stood the night before, and in the distance, the enemy's shouting could be heard. Soldiers—both wounded and unharmed—rushed past him in every direction.

After running a little farther, he finally saw his company huddled against a wall.

"They've taken Schwartz," a young officer said in a panic. "It's over!"

"That's nonsense!" Kozeltzoff snapped, gripping his dull little sword. He took a deep breath and shouted, "Forward, men! Hurrah!"

His voice rang out with such strength that it even startled him. He charged ahead, running along the barrier, and about fifty soldiers followed, shouting as they went.

As soon as he stepped into the open, bullets rained down like hail. Two hit him—but he had no time to figure out where or how badly he was hurt.

Ahead, he could see the enemy—blue uniforms, red trousers, and foreign voices shouting. A French soldier stood on the barricade, waving his cap and yelling something.

Kozeltzoff was certain he was about to die. The thought didn't scare him. Instead, it gave him courage.

He kept running. Some soldiers overtook him, others ran alongside. The French, who had seemed so close, were now retreating toward their trenches. But all around him, the ground was littered with the dead and wounded.

When Kozeltzoff reached the last trench, everything blurred. A sharp pain shot through his chest, and everything went dark.

Half an hour later, he was lying on a stretcher near the Nikolaevsky barracks. He knew he was wounded but felt little pain. All he wanted was a cold drink and to be left alone to rest.

A short, round doctor with black sideburns came over and unbuttoned Kozeltzoff's coat. The wounded officer looked down at his own chest, watching the doctor's hands work, but he barely felt anything. The doctor pressed his shirt against the wound, wiped his hands on his coat, and walked away without saying a word.

Kozeltzoff's eyes wandered over the scene before him. He remembered fighting at the fifth bastion and felt a deep sense of pride. I did my duty. I fought bravely. I have nothing to regret. For the first time in his military career, he was completely satisfied with himself.

The doctor finished bandaging another officer and then nodded toward Kozeltzoff while speaking to a nearby priest. The priest had a thick red beard and wore a large cross around his neck.

Kozeltzoff's heart pounded. "Am I dying?" he asked.

The priest didn't answer. Instead, he began a quiet prayer and handed Kozeltzoff the cross.

He wasn't afraid. He grasped the cross with trembling hands, kissed it, and tears streamed down his face.

"Did we push them back?" he asked, his voice calm.

The priest hesitated. He knew the truth—the French flag was already raised over the Malakoff mound. But instead of telling him, he softly replied, "We held our ground everywhere."

"Thank God," Kozeltzoff murmured, not even noticing the tears streaming down his face.

For a moment, he thought of his younger brother. May God give him the same luck, he whispered to himself.

XXV.

But Volodya was not as lucky. He was listening to Vasin tell a story when suddenly, someone shouted, "The French are coming!"

His heart pounded, and for a moment, he felt all the blood drain from his face. He stood frozen, unsure what to do. Then, glancing around, he noticed that the soldiers were calmly buttoning up their coats and crawling out one by one. Someone—probably Melnikoff—even joked, "Go on, boys, offer them some bread and salt!"

Volodya, with Vlang sticking close beside him as always, crawled out of the bomb shelter and ran toward the battery.

There was no artillery fire from either side. What gave Volodya courage wasn't just the calmness of the soldiers but also the sheer panic on Vlang's face. Am I anything like him? he thought. The idea made him push forward, almost excited, as he ran up to the breastworks where his mortars stood.

He could clearly see the French troops advancing across an open area, their bayonets glinting in the sunlight. They were moving fast through the nearest trenches. One soldier, a short, broad-shouldered man in a red Zouave uniform, was leading the charge, waving a sword as he leaped over a ditch.

"Fire the grape-shot!" Volodya shouted. But before he could finish giving the order, the soldiers had already acted. The sharp, metallic hiss of the grape-shot rang out as they fired—first from one mortar, then the other.

"First! Second!" Volodya called out, running between the mortars, completely forgetting to be afraid.

Nearby, the sound of musket fire and frantic shouting filled the air.

Then, a terrified scream erupted from the left: "They're surrounding us! They're behind us!"

Volodya spun around. Twenty French soldiers had appeared in the rear. Leading them was a man with a thick black beard. He sprinted forward, stopped about ten paces away, raised his rifle, and fired straight at Volodya before charging again.

For a split second, Volodya was too stunned to move. He couldn't believe what he was seeing.

When he snapped back to reality, everything had changed. French soldiers had climbed onto the ramparts. Just ten steps away, two of them were already jamming spikes into a cannon to disable it.

The battlefield around him was empty. Melnikoff lay dead at his feet, shot down in the fight. The only person left was Vlang.

Vlang, gripping a heavy handspike, suddenly lunged forward, his face twisted in anger, his eyes fixed downward.

"Follow me, Vladimir Semyonitch! Come on!" he yelled, his voice filled with desperation.

Vlang swung the handspike hard, smashing it down on the head of the nearest French soldier. The others hesitated, startled by his sudden attack. But Vlang didn't stop—he kept looking around wildly, his voice breaking as he shouted again, "Come on, Vladimir Semyonitch! Why are you just standing there? Run!"

Without waiting, he took off toward the trenches where Russian infantry were still firing at the enemy. He jumped in, then turned back to see what had happened to Volodya.

But Volodya was no longer standing.

Something—someone—lay crumpled on the ground where he had just been.

The area was swarming with French soldiers. Gunfire filled the air. Vlang stood frozen for a moment, staring. Then he turned and ran.

XXVI.

Vlang found what was left of his battery on the second line of defense. Out of the twenty soldiers who had been with him at the mortar battery, only eight were still alive.

At nine o'clock that night, he boarded a steamer with his unit, along with wounded soldiers, cannons, and horses, all heading toward Severnaya.

The gunfire had stopped. The stars sparkled as brightly as the night before, but strong winds made the sea rough. In the distance, explosions lit up the first and second bastions, casting brief flashes of light on the wreckage and sending debris flying through the air.

Near the docks, a fire burned, its red glow reflecting off the water. The bridge, packed with people, was lit by the flames from the Nikolaevsky battery. Further away, from the Alexandrovsky battery, an enormous fire blazed, sending thick clouds of smoke into the sky. Beyond that, across the sea, the enemy fleet's lights flickered steadily, as if nothing had changed.

The wind sent waves crashing into the steamer. By the glow of the fires, the masts of sunken Russian ships could be seen sinking deeper into the bay.

No one spoke on the deck. Only the steady splash of waves, the hissing steam, the restless stomping of horses, the captain's orders, and the groans of the wounded could be heard.

Vlang, who hadn't eaten all day, pulled a piece of bread from his pocket and started chewing. But as soon as he thought of Volodya, he suddenly broke into loud sobs. The nearby soldiers heard him.

"Look at our Vlanga," Vasin said. "Eating his bread and crying at the same time."

"Unbelievable," another soldier muttered.

"See there? They've set fire to our barracks," Vasin continued with a sigh. "And how many of our brothers died there? And for what? The French just took it from us like that."

"At least we made it out alive," another soldier said. "Thank God for that."

"But it's still painful to leave it behind!"

"Why? Do you think they're happy over there? No chance! Just wait, our men will take it back. No matter how many of us fall, if the emperor gives the order, Sevastopol will be ours again. Do you really think we'll let them keep it? Never! They took nothing but bare walls. We destroyed the defenses before leaving. Even if they raised their flag over the hill, they won't get into the city."

"Just wait," another soldier added firmly. "We'll settle this later."

For months, the bastions of Sevastopol had been filled with life— waves of soldiers fighting, dying, and being replaced by others. For months, they had struck fear, hatred, and even admiration into the hearts of their enemies.

But now, not a single Russian soldier remained. The bastions were empty—deserted, eerie, ruined—but not silent.

Destruction still echoed through the air. The ground was torn apart by explosions. Shattered cannons, broken gun carriages, and the bodies of Russian and French soldiers lay everywhere. Some were crushed beneath heavy artillery. Others were half-buried in the dirt. Scattered across the ruins were shattered beams, abandoned bomb shelters, and lifeless figures in gray and blue uniforms. Every so often, the darkness was lit up by another explosion, briefly revealing the devastation before fading again.

The French sensed that something strange was happening in Sevastopol. The sudden explosions and the eerie silence on the bastions sent a chill through them. But after facing such fierce resistance all day, they hesitated to believe that their seemingly unstoppable enemy had simply disappeared. So, they stood still, watching, waiting for the night to reveal the truth.

The army of Sevastopol moved like a restless sea, flowing across the bay, over the bridge, and into the northern fortifications. Slowly, in the cover of darkness, they retreated from the place where so many of their comrades had fallen, where the earth was soaked in their blood, where they had held their ground for eleven long months against an enemy twice their size—only to be ordered to leave without a final battle.

For every soldier, this command brought overwhelming sadness.

Then came a second feeling—fear of being chased. As soon as they left the familiar trenches where they had fought for so long, they felt exposed. They huddled together at the entrance to the bridge, which swayed under the force of the wind.

The infantry pushed forward, bayonets clashing as regiments, wagons, and weapons crowded the crossing. Officers shouted orders, civilians wept and begged to be allowed through, and artillery units struggled to force their way to the bay.

Yet, beneath all the shouting and movement, one instinct united them all—the need to get away from that place of death. It was in the mortally wounded soldier lying on the cold stone pavement of the Pavlovsky quay, whispering prayers for his suffering to end. It was in the exhausted militia member pushing through the packed crowd to make way for a passing general. It was in the same general, trying to keep order among the chaos. It was in the sailor caught in the crushing crowd, gasping for breath. It was in the wounded officer, carried on a stretcher by four soldiers, who had to set him down near the Nikolaevsky battery because they couldn't move forward. It was in the artilleryman, who had served his cannon for sixteen years, now following orders he didn't understand—orders to throw their own guns into the bay. And it was in the sailors who had just sealed the portholes of the abandoned ships before rowing away.

As they stepped onto the far side of the bridge, nearly every soldier removed his cap and made the sign of the cross.

But beneath their instinct to escape was something even heavier— a feeling of shame, anger, and regret.

Standing on the northern shore, looking back at the abandoned city, many Russian soldiers sighed deeply, fists clenched, as they glared toward the enemy.

Hadji Murat

Leo Tolstoy

I

I was walking home through the fields on a warm midsummer day. The hay had already been gathered, and the rye was just starting to be harvested. The fields were bursting with colorful flowers—red, white, and pink clover with a sweet fragrance; bright white daisies with yellow centers and a spicy scent; golden rape blossoms that smelled like honey; tall bellflowers in shades of white and purple; delicate vines creeping along the ground; scabious flowers in shades of yellow, red, and pink; soft purple plantains with a hint of pink in their blossoms; deep blue cornflowers that gradually turned reddish as they aged; and tiny dodder flowers that smelled like almonds but faded quickly.

I gathered a large bouquet and was on my way home when I noticed a striking thistle growing in a ditch. It was a deep crimson color, the kind of plant people in our area called a "Tartar." No one liked to cut them because they were so prickly, and if they did, they would throw them aside to avoid getting scratched. Wanting to add it to my bouquet, I climbed down to pick it. A fuzzy bumblebee was nestled deep inside one of the flowers, fast asleep. I gently shooed it away and reached for the plant.

But plucking the thistle was harder than I expected. Its sharp spines poked through even the handkerchief I wrapped around my fingers. The stem was so tough that I had to struggle with it for several minutes, breaking the fibers one by one. When I finally tore it free, the stem was frayed, and the flower didn't look as fresh or beautiful anymore. It was stiff and rough, not fitting in with the delicate blossoms in my bouquet. Regretfully, I tossed it aside, feeling bad that I had ruined something that had looked perfect in its natural place.

"What strength and determination!" I thought. "It fought so hard to stay where it was and made me work for every inch before I could take it."

The road home led me across a vast field of freshly plowed black soil. It belonged to a wealthy landowner, and as far as I could see— on both sides and up the hill—there was nothing but rows of moist, turned earth. The field was so well tilled that not a single blade of grass or wildflower remained.

"How destructive humans are," I thought. "We wipe out countless plants just to make room for ourselves."

I glanced around, searching for any sign of life in the empty field. To my right, near the road, I saw a small cluster of plants. As I got closer, I realized it was the same type of thistle I had struggled to pick earlier.

This thistle had three branches. One was broken, sticking out like an injured arm. The other two held flowers that had once been bright red but were now blackened. One stem was bent, its flower hanging lifelessly. The other, despite being covered in dirt, still stood tall. A cart had clearly rolled over the plant, but somehow, it had managed to push itself back up. That's why it stood at an awkward angle, as if it had been torn apart but refused to fall completely.

"What incredible resilience," I thought. "Humans have crushed everything else in this field, but this one plant refuses to give in."

As I stood there, staring at the stubborn thistle, a memory from years ago came back to me. It was a story I had partly witnessed, partly heard from others, and partly imagined.

It took place in late 1851.

On a chilly November evening, Hadji Murad rode into Makhmet, a Chechen village that opposed the Russians. The air was filled with the smoky scent of burning fuel, and the call to prayer had just faded. Amid the sounds of cattle and sheep moving through the narrow, crowded streets, men's voices rose in heated arguments, while women and children talked near the village fountain.

Hadji Murad was once a powerful military leader under Shamil, known for his fearless battles. He never rode out without his banner and a group of devoted warriors who proudly displayed their skills before him. But now, things were different. Wrapped in a heavy cloak with his rifle barely visible beneath it, he rode quietly, trying not to attract attention. He was no longer a celebrated commander—he was a fugitive, traveling with just one companion, scanning the faces around him with sharp black eyes, wary of every person he passed.

As Hadji Murad entered the village, he avoided the main road leading to the open square. Instead, he turned left into a narrow side street. When he reached the second house, which was built into the hillside, he stopped and looked around. The space under the porch was empty, but on the roof, behind a freshly plastered chimney, an old man lay under a sheepskin coat.

Hadji Murad tapped him with the handle of his braided leather whip and clicked his tongue. The old man stirred, revealing a wrinkled face with red, swollen eyelids and no eyelashes. He blinked several times as if trying to unstick his eyes.

"Salaam alaikum," Hadji Murad greeted, uncovering his face.

"Alaikum salaam," the old man replied, recognizing him. He smiled, showing his toothless mouth. Slowly, he got up, sliding his feet into the wooden-heeled slippers by the chimney. Then he pulled on the sleeves of his wrinkled sheepskin coat. As he climbed down a ladder leaning against the roof, he mumbled to himself, his thin, sunburned neck shaking slightly.

When he reached the ground, he quickly grabbed Hadji Murad's horse by the bridle and reached for his stirrup as a welcoming gesture. But Hadji Murad's strong, quick-footed companion had already jumped down and stepped aside. Hadji Murad dismounted as well, walking with a slight limp as he stepped under the porch.

Just then, a boy around fifteen years old rushed out of the house. He had bright, curious eyes as dark as ripe berries and stared in wonder at the visitors.

"Run to the mosque and fetch your father," the old man instructed while hurrying to open the thin, creaky door.

As Hadji Murad entered, a slim, middle-aged woman in a yellow tunic, red jacket, and loose blue trousers walked through another doorway carrying cushions.

"May your arrival bring blessings," she said, bowing low as she placed the cushions along the front wall for him to sit on.

"May your sons live long," Hadji Murad replied, removing his heavy cloak, rifle, and sword. He handed them to the old man, who carefully hung the weapons beside those of the house's owner. The weapons were displayed between two shining basins on the clean, whitewashed clay wall.

Hadji Murad adjusted the pistol at his back and moved toward the cushions. Pulling his coat closer around him, he sat down. The old man lowered himself onto his heels beside him, closed his eyes, and lifted his hands with his palms facing upward. Hadji Murad did the same. They murmured a short prayer, then ran their hands down their faces, ending with their palms touching beneath their beards.

"Any news?" Hadji Murad asked.

"Nothing new," the old man replied, his lifeless red eyes focused not on Hadji Murad's face but on his chest. "I've been living at the apiary. I only came today to see my son… He knows."

Hadji Murad understood that the old man didn't want to discuss anything in detail. He nodded slightly and asked no further questions.

"There is no good news," the old man continued. "Only that the hares argue about how to get rid of the eagles, while the eagles keep snatching them one by one. Just the other day, the Russian dogs burned the hay in Mitchit village… May their faces be torn apart!" he added in a hoarse, angry voice.

At that moment, Hadji Murad's companion entered the room, his strong legs moving quietly over the earthen floor. Like his leader, he kept only his dagger and pistol while removing his heavy cloak, rifle, and sword. He hung them on the same nails as Hadji Murad's weapons.

"Who is he?" the old man asked, pointing at the newcomer.

"My murid. His name is Eldar," Hadji Murad replied.

"Good," the old man said, motioning for Eldar to sit on a piece of felt beside Hadji Murad. Eldar crossed his legs and sat down, his deep-set eyes locked onto the old man, who had now started speaking more freely.

The old man told them how their fighters had captured two Russian soldiers the previous week—one had been killed, while the other was sent to Shamil in Veden.

Hadji Murad listened without much attention, his focus on the door and the sounds outside. Footsteps echoed under the porch, the door creaked, and Sado, the owner of the house, walked in. He was about forty years old, with a small beard, a long nose, and deep black eyes—similar to his fifteen-year-old son, who had just returned from calling him. The boy slipped inside and sat by the door.

Sado removed his wooden slippers at the entrance, then pushed his old, worn-out cap to the back of his head. His hair had grown out, dark and unshaven. Without hesitation, he squatted in front of Hadji Murad.

Like the old man before him, he lifted his palms, recited a short prayer, and then ran his hands down his face. Only after completing this ritual did he speak.

He explained that Shamil had ordered Hadji Murad to be captured—dead or alive. Shamil's messengers had left just the day before, and the people were afraid to disobey his commands. Because of this, it was important to be careful.

"No one will harm you in my home as long as I am alive," Sado assured him. "But outside, in the open… that's another matter. We must think carefully."

Hadji Murad listened closely and nodded. When Sado finished speaking, he said, "Understood. Now we need to send someone with a message to the Russians. My murid will go, but he needs a guide."

"I'll send my brother, Bata," Sado replied, then turned to his son. "Go and get Bata."

The boy jumped to his feet as if on springs and quickly ran out of the house, his arms swinging as he hurried away. About ten minutes later, he returned with a short, muscular Chechen man, tanned dark by the sun. Bata wore a faded yellow coat with frayed sleeves and black leggings that were crumpled and worn.

Hadji Murad greeted him and got straight to the point. "Can you lead my murid to the Russians?"

"I can," Bata replied confidently. "No one else could do it as well as I can. Others might promise but never follow through. But me? I'll get it done."

"Good," Hadji Murad said. "You'll receive three for your trouble." He held up three fingers.

Bata nodded to show he understood, then added, "I'm not doing it for the money. It's an honor to help Hadji Murad. Everyone in the mountains knows how he has fought the Russian invaders."

"Enough talk," Hadji Murad replied. "A rope should be long, but words should be short."

"Then I'll say no more," Bata said with a grin.

"By the bend of the Argun River, near the cliffs, there are two haystacks in a clearing. Do you know the place?"

"I do."

"My four horsemen are waiting for me there," Hadji Murad explained.

Bata nodded.

"Find Khan Mahoma. He knows what to do. Can you take my murid to the Russian commander, Prince Vorontsov?"

"Yes, I can."

"And bring him back safely?"

"I can do that too."

"Then take him there and return to the forest. I'll be waiting."

"I will do it," Bata said. He placed a hand over his heart as a sign of respect, then left.

Hadji Murad turned back to Sado. "We also need to send someone to Chekhi," he started, reaching into one of the cartridge pouches on his coat. But before he could continue, he stopped. His eyes shifted as two women entered the room.

One was Sado's wife—the slim, middle-aged woman who had set out the cushions earlier. The other was a young girl dressed in bright red trousers and a green jacket. A necklace made of silver coins covered the front of her outfit, and a silver ruble hung at the end of her thick black braid, which rested between her shoulder blades. She had the same deep black eyes as her father and brother. Her face, though serious, sparkled with youth. She didn't look directly at the visitors, but it was clear she was aware of them.

Sado's wife carried a low, round table with tea, buttered pancakes, cheese, thin flatbread, and honey. The girl followed with a basin, a ewer, and a towel.

As they moved about, their silver jewelry jingled softly. Sado and Hadji Murad stayed silent while the women set the table. Eldar, Hadji Murad's murid, sat completely still, staring at his crossed legs. Only when the women finished their work and left, their soft footsteps fading behind the door, did he exhale in relief.

Hadji Murad pulled a bullet from one of his cartridge pouches and unrolled a small note hidden beneath it. He handed it to Sado. "This must be delivered to my son."

"Where should the reply be sent?"

"To you. Then you must forward it to me."

"It will be done," Sado promised. He tucked the note into his own cartridge pouch, then picked up the metal ewer and moved the basin toward Hadji Murad.

Hadji Murad rolled up the sleeves of his coat, revealing his strong, pale arms. He let the cold, clear water run over his hands, then dried them with a clean towel before sitting at the table. Eldar followed his example.

As they ate, Sado sat across from them, thanking them several times for their visit. His son, sitting by the door, stared at Hadji Murad in admiration, his bright eyes filled with excitement.

Even though he hadn't eaten in over a day, Hadji Murad only had a little bread and cheese. Then, pulling a small knife from his belt, he spread honey on another piece of bread.

"Our honey is good this year," the old man said proudly. "Better than ever before."

"Thank you," Hadji Murad replied, turning away from the table. Eldar wanted to keep eating, but seeing his leader step away, he did the same. He picked up the basin and ewer, offering them to Hadji Murad.

Sado knew that harboring Hadji Murad was dangerous. Shamil had issued strict orders forbidding anyone from sheltering him. The penalty for disobedience was death. The villagers could find out at any moment and demand that Sado hand him over.

But instead of fear, Sado felt a sense of pride. He believed he was doing the right thing.

"As long as you are under my roof and my head is on my shoulders, no one will harm you," he assured Hadji Murad.

Hadji Murad met his gaze, seeing the sincerity in his eyes. With quiet gratitude, he said, "May you be blessed with joy and a long life."

Sado placed a hand over his heart in silent thanks.

Before leaving the room, Sado shut the wooden shutters and placed some sticks in the fireplace. He was in a bright, almost cheerful mood as he went to the part of the house where his family stayed.

The women were still awake, whispering about the dangerous guests who had come to spend the night.

II

At Vozvizhensk, a forward military post about ten miles from the village where Hadji Murad was spending the night, three soldiers and a non-commissioned officer left the fort and stepped outside the Shahgirinsk Gate. They were dressed in the typical uniform of Caucasian soldiers at that time—sheepskin coats, fur caps, and tall boots that reached above their knees. Their heavy cloaks were rolled up and strapped across their shoulders, and they carried their rifles on their backs.

Marching in formation, they walked about five hundred paces along the road before turning twenty steps to the right, their boots crunching the dry leaves beneath them. They stopped near the charred remains of a broken plane tree, barely visible in the dim light. This tree was the usual spot where ambush parties were stationed.

The night sky was clear, filled with bright stars that had seemed to move along the treetops as the soldiers walked through the forest. Now, as they stood still, the stars shone between the bare branches.

"At least the ground is dry," said Panov, the non-commissioned officer, as he lowered his rifle and bayonet with a metallic clang and leaned it against the tree. The other soldiers did the same.

"Damn it, I've lost it," Panov muttered, annoyed. "Must have left it behind or dropped it along the way."

"What are you looking for?" asked one of the soldiers in a cheerful voice.

"The bowl of my pipe. I don't know where the hell it went."

"You still have the stem?"

"Yeah, here it is."

"Then just stick it straight into the ground," the soldier joked.

"Not worth the trouble."

"Come on, it'll be quick."

Smoking while on ambush duty was technically forbidden, but this post wasn't a real ambush—it was more of a lookout to make sure the mountain rebels didn't sneak up and fire a cannon at the fort, as they had done before. Panov didn't see any harm in having a smoke, so he agreed to the soldier's idea.

The cheerful soldier, Avdeev, pulled out a knife and carved a small hole in the dirt. He smoothed the edges, inserted the pipe stem, packed tobacco into the hole, and pressed it down. A match flared, briefly lighting up Avdeev's broad-cheeked face as he lay on his stomach. The air whistled through the pipe stem as he took the first puff, and soon, the warm, familiar smell of burning tobacco drifted up.

"Got it working?" Panov asked as he crouched down.

"Of course," Avdeev replied with a grin.

"You're a clever one, Avdeev! Smart as a judge. Alright, hand it over."

Avdeev rolled onto his side, exhaling smoke, and made room for Panov. Panov lay flat on his stomach, wiped the mouthpiece with his sleeve, and took a long inhale.

After finishing their smoke, the soldiers started talking.

"They say the commander has been dipping into the company funds again," one of them remarked lazily. "Lost it all at cards, they say."

"He'll pay it back," Panov said confidently.

"Of course he will! He's a good officer," Avdeev agreed.

"Good, huh?" the first soldier repeated with a hint of doubt. "If you ask me, the company should confront him. 'Tell us how much you took and when you'll return it.'"

"That's up to the company to decide," Panov said, handing the pipe back and settling into a comfortable position.

"Of course. 'The community is like a strong man,'" Avdeev agreed, quoting a proverb.

"But what about when we need money for oats and boots in the spring? If he's already spent it, what are we supposed to do then?" the dissatisfied soldier continued.

"I'm telling you, the company will handle it," Panov repeated. "It's not the first time. He borrows it and always pays it back."

Back then, each company managed its own supplies. The treasury gave them 6 rubles and 50 kopeks per soldier each month, and a group of chosen men handled the funds. They planted cabbages, made hay, and owned carts, taking pride in their well-fed horses. The money was stored in a chest, and only the commander had the key. Sometimes, he borrowed from it, as had happened again recently. This was what the soldiers were talking about. Nikitin, the grumpy soldier, wanted to confront the commander, but Panov and Avdeev didn't think that was necessary.

After Panov had his turn, Nikitin smoked, then spread his cloak on the ground and sat against the plane tree. The group fell silent. High above them, the wind rustled the treetops. Then, cutting through the steady whisper of the branches, came the eerie howls, whimpers, and chuckles of jackals.

"Listen to those cursed animals—how they scream!"

"They're laughing at you because your mouth is lopsided," teased the Ukrainian soldier.

The group went quiet again. Only the wind moved through the trees, making the stars appear and disappear between the shifting branches.

"Hey, Panov," Avdeev suddenly asked, "do you ever feel lonely?"

"Lonely? What for?" Panov answered reluctantly.

"I don't know... Sometimes, I feel so empty inside I don't know what I might do to myself."

"Come on now," Panov muttered.

"That time I drank all my money—it was because of that. I couldn't shake the feeling... it wouldn't leave me. So I thought, 'Might as well drink until I can't think anymore.'"

"But drinking sometimes makes it worse."

"Yeah, I know. That's happened to me too. But what else is there to do?"

"What makes you feel this way?"

"What do you think? I miss home."

"Was your family rich?"

"No, we weren't rich, but we lived well enough." Avdeev started telling his story—one Panov had already heard many times.

"You see, I joined the army willingly, in place of my brother," he explained. "He had kids. There were five of them in his family, and I had just gotten married. My mother begged me to go instead. So I thought, 'Well, maybe they'll remember this sacrifice.' I went to our landlord—he was a decent man—and he said, 'You're a good man. Go.' So I took my brother's place."

"That was the right thing to do," Panov said.

"And yet," Avdeev sighed, "that's the main reason I feel so down. I keep thinking, 'Why did I do it? He's back home, living comfortably, while I'm out here suffering.' The more I dwell on it, the worse I feel. It's just bad luck, I guess."

He fell silent for a moment.

"Maybe we should have another smoke," he suggested.

"Go ahead, set it up," Panov replied.

But they never got the chance. Just as Avdeev got up to fix the pipe, they heard footsteps on the road.

Panov grabbed his rifle and nudged Nikitin with his boot. Nikitin got up, shaking out his cloak. Bondarenko, the Ukrainian soldier, stood too.

"And I had such a strange dream, mates..." he started.

"Shh!" Avdeev hissed. The soldiers held their breath, listening.

The sound of soft boots stepping on fallen leaves and dry twigs became clearer. Then, low voices speaking in the guttural tones of Chechen dialects reached them. In the dim moonlight, two shadowy figures appeared between the trees—one taller than the other.

When they reached the soldiers' position, Panov stepped onto the road with his rifle raised. The others followed.

"Who goes there?" Panov demanded.

"Me, friendly Chechen," answered the shorter man—Bata. "Gun, no... Sword, no..." He pointed at himself to show he was unarmed. "Prince, want!"

The taller man stood beside him in silence. He, too, carried no weapons.

"He says he's a scout and wants to see the Colonel," Panov explained to the others.

"Prince Vorontsov... important talk!" Bata said in broken Russian.

"Alright, alright. We'll take you," Panov said, then turned to Avdeev. "You and Bondarenko, take them. Hand them over to the officer on duty, then come right back."

"Make sure they walk in front of you," he added in a serious tone.

Avdeev shifted his rifle, moving the bayonet as if testing its sharpness. "If they try anything, I'll just give 'em a quick stab and let the air out of them!"

"And what good would they be after that?" Bondarenko joked.

"Alright, move out!"

As soon as the sound of their footsteps faded, Panov and Nikitin returned to their post.

"What the hell brings them here at night?" Nikitin muttered.

"Must be important," Panov replied. "But it's getting cold." He unrolled his cloak, wrapped it around himself, and leaned against the tree.

Two hours later, Avdeev and Bondarenko returned.

"Did you hand them over?"

"Yep. The Colonel was still awake—they were taken straight to him. And you know what? Those bald-headed guys are alright," Avdeev said. "Really! We had such a chat."

"Of course you did," Nikitin scoffed disapprovingly.

"I'm telling you, they're just like us. One of them is married. I asked him, 'Do you have a wife?' He said, 'Yes.' 'Kids?' I asked. 'Two,' he said. We had a great conversation! Such nice guys!"

"Nice guys?" Nikitin snorted. "If you met him alone in the forest, he'd gut you in a second."

"The night's almost over," Panov said, stretching.

"Yeah, the stars are starting to fade," Avdeev murmured, settling into a comfortable position.

The soldiers fell silent once again.

III

The barracks and soldiers' houses in the fort had been dark for a while, but lights still glowed in the grandest house.

This house belonged to Prince Simon Mikhailovich Vorontsov, the commander of the Kurin Regiment, an Imperial Aide-de-Camp, and the son of the Commander-in-Chief. His wife, Marya Vasilevna, a famous beauty from St. Petersburg, was staying with him. They lived in this small Caucasian fort with a level of luxury no one there had ever seen before. However, to Vorontsov—and even more so to his wife—their life felt simple, even difficult at times. But to the local people, their way of living seemed incredibly extravagant.

It was midnight, and the prince and princess were playing cards with their guests in a large, well-furnished drawing room. The carpeted floor and heavy curtains made the space feel elegant, while the card table was lit by four candles. Vorontsov, a tall man with a long face, wore the gold cords and insignia of an aide-de-camp. His playing partner was a serious-looking young man with messy hair—a university graduate from St. Petersburg whom the princess had recently hired as a tutor for her son from a previous marriage.

Across from them sat two officers: one was a broad, red-faced man named Poltoratsky, a company commander who had transferred from the Guards; the other was the regiment's adjutant, a stiff, well-groomed officer with a cold expression on his handsome face.

Princess Marya Vasilevna, a striking woman with dark eyebrows and large, expressive eyes, sat beside Poltoratsky. Her crinoline brushed against his legs as she leaned over to look at his cards. Everything about her—her voice, her perfume, her smiles, and even the way she moved—made Poltoratsky completely forget everything except how close she was. Distracted, he kept making mistakes, frustrating his partner more and more.

"No, that's terrible! You wasted an ace again," the adjutant snapped as Poltoratsky played the wrong card.

Poltoratsky, dazed as if waking from a dream, turned his kind, dark eyes toward him, not fully understanding.

"Forgive him!" Marya Vasilevna said with a smile. "See? Didn't I tell you so?" she added, turning to Poltoratsky.

"But that's not what you said," he replied, grinning.

"Wasn't it?" she teased, giving him a playful smile that made his heart race. His face flushed red, and in his nervous excitement, he picked up the deck and started shuffling the cards.

"It's not your turn to deal," the adjutant said sharply. Without waiting, he took the cards himself and quickly began to deal, as if eager to finish the game.

Just then, the prince's valet entered the room and announced that the officer on duty needed to speak with him.

"Excuse me, gentlemen," Vorontsov said in Russian with a slight English accent. "Marya, will you take my place?"

"Is that alright with everyone?" she asked, rising gracefully to her full height. The silk of her dress rustled as she smiled brightly.

"I always agree to everything," the adjutant replied, pleased that she—who was known to be a terrible player—would now be playing against him.

Poltoratsky just spread his hands and smiled.

The game was nearly finished when Vorontsov returned. He looked cheerful and slightly excited.

"Do you know what I suggest?" he said.

"What?"

"That we open some champagne."

"I'm always up for that," Poltoratsky said eagerly.

"Why not? That sounds great!" the adjutant agreed.

"Bring some, Vasili!" the prince ordered.

"What was that all about?" Marya Vasilevna asked, curious.

"The officer on duty and someone else needed to see me," Vorontsov said, shrugging.

"Who? What did they want?" she pressed.

"I can't say," he replied with a sly smile.

"You can't say?" she repeated. "We'll see about that."

When the champagne arrived, everyone drank a glass. They finished their game, settled their scores, and the guests began to leave.

"Is your company the one going to the forest tomorrow?" Vorontsov asked Poltoratsky as they said goodbye.

"Yes, minc... why?"

"Then we'll see each other tomorrow," the prince said with a small smile.

"Glad to hear it," Poltoratsky replied, not entirely sure what Vorontsov meant. But his mind was elsewhere—he was focused on the moment when he would get to shake Marya Vasilevna's hand.

As was her custom, she not only shook his hand firmly but also gave it an extra squeeze. Then, as she reminded him of his mistake in playing diamonds, she flashed a smile that he took as affectionate and meaningful.

Poltoratsky left in a state of pure bliss, the kind only understood by men like him—men who had spent months in military life, cut off from high society, and then suddenly found themselves in the company of a woman from their own world. And not just any woman—someone as dazzling as Princess Vorontsov.

When he reached the small house he shared with his comrade, he pushed on the door, but it was locked. Annoyed, he knocked. No response. Frustrated, he kicked it and banged on it with his sword.

Finally, he heard footsteps. His servant, Vovilo, a domestic serf, unlatched the door and let him in.

"What do you mean by locking yourself in, you fool?"

"But how can that be, sir...?"

"You're drunk again! I'll show you how it can be!" Poltoratsky raised his hand to hit Vovilo but then changed his mind. "Oh, get lost! Just light a candle."

"Right away."

Vovilo was really drunk. He had been drinking at a party for the ordnance sergeant, Ivan Petrovich, whose name day they were celebrating. On his way home, he started thinking about how different his life was from Ivan Petrovich's. Ivan had a steady job, a wife, and in a year, he would be discharged from service.

Vovilo, on the other hand, had been taken in as a servant when he was just a boy. Now, even though he was over forty, he was still unmarried and spent his life traveling around with his reckless young master. Poltoratsky was not a bad man—he rarely hit him—but what kind of life was this? "He promised to free me when we get back from the Caucasus, but what will I do with my freedom? Where would I even go? This life is like a dog's!" Vovilo thought. He felt so tired that, worried someone might sneak in and steal something, he locked the door and fell asleep.

Poltoratsky entered the bedroom he shared with his friend, Tikhonov.

"Did you lose?" Tikhonov asked, waking up.

"No, actually, I didn't. I won seventeen rubles, and we drank a bottle of Cliquot!"

"And did you see Marya Vasilevna?"

"Yes, I saw Marya Vasilevna," Poltoratsky repeated.

"It'll be time to get up soon," Tikhonov said. "We leave at six."

"Vovilo!" Poltoratsky called out. "Make sure you wake me up at five!"

"How can I wake you when you start throwing punches?"

"I said wake me up! Do you hear me?"

"All right." Vovilo left, taking Poltoratsky's boots and clothes with him.

Poltoratsky got into bed, lit a cigarette, and then blew out the candle, smiling to himself. In the darkness, he pictured Marya Vasilevna's smiling face.

The Vorontsovs didn't go to bed right away. After the guests had left, Marya Vasilevna walked up to her husband and looked at him sternly.

"Well? You're going to tell me what this is about."

"But, my dear..."

"Don't call me 'my dear'! That was an emissary, wasn't it?"

"Even if it was, I can't tell you."

"You can't? Then I'll tell you!"

"You?"

"It was Hadji Murad, wasn't it?" Marya Vasilevna said. She had been hearing rumors about secret negotiations and was convinced that Hadji Murad himself had come to see her husband.

Vorontsov couldn't completely deny it, but he disappointed her by saying it wasn't Hadji Murad in person—just a messenger coming to arrange a meeting for the next day at the site where a logging crew would be working.

Life at the fortress was dull, so both of the young Vorontsovs—husband and wife—were excited by the news. They stayed up talking about how pleased his father would be to hear it. By the time they finally went to bed, it was already past two in the morning.

IV

After three nights without sleep while escaping from the warriors Shamil had sent to capture him, Hadji Murad finally dozed off as soon as Sado said goodnight and stepped out of the house.

Still dressed, he slept with his head resting on his hand, his elbow sinking into the soft red cushions his host had arranged for him. Nearby, Eldar was also asleep, lying on his back with his strong limbs stretched out. His broad chest, covered by the white Circassian coat with black cartridge pouches, rose higher than his freshly shaven head, which had slipped off the pillow and tilted backward. A faint mustache was just beginning to show on his upper lip, which moved slightly as if he were drinking something in his sleep. Like Hadji Murad, he slept with a pistol and dagger in his belt. The fire in the grate was burning low, and a small light flickered from a niche in the wall.

In the middle of the night, the wooden floor creaked, and Hadji Murad immediately sat up, his hand going straight to his pistol. Sado entered, stepping carefully on the packed earth floor.

"What is it?" Hadji Murad asked, as though he had never been asleep.

"We have a problem," Sado replied, squatting in front of him. "A woman saw you arrive from her rooftop and told her husband. Now, the whole village knows. My wife just heard that the Elders are gathered at the mosque, and they plan to stop you from leaving."

"I have to go now," Hadji Murad said firmly.

"The horses are ready," Sado answered before hurrying out of the house.

"Eldar!" Hadji Murad whispered. At the sound of his name—and more importantly, his master's voice—Eldar jumped to his feet, quickly adjusting his cap.

Hadji Murad strapped on his weapons, then threw on his burka. Eldar did the same. Without a word, they stepped out of the house into the covered entryway, where a dark-eyed boy was holding their horses. As soon as their hooves clattered against the hard dirt road, someone peeked out from a nearby house, and a man ran up the hill toward the mosque, his wooden shoes clacking against the ground.

There was no moon, but the stars were bright in the night sky, making the rooftops visible. The mosque, with its minarets, stood above the rest of the village. A low murmur of voices came from inside.

Hadji Murad grabbed his rifle, placed his foot in the stirrup, and in one smooth motion swung himself onto the saddle.

"May God bless you," he told his host while feeling for the other stirrup with his foot. He gently tapped the boy holding his horse, signaling him to let go. The boy stepped back, and the horse, as if it knew exactly what to do, started moving briskly down the narrow lane toward the main road. Eldar followed close behind. Sado, wrapped in his sheepskin coat, rushed alongside them, swinging his arms and darting from one side of the alley to the other.

As they reached the place where the roads met, dark figures appeared in their path.

"Stop! Who goes there? Stop!" a voice called out as several men stepped forward to block the way.

Instead of slowing down, Hadji Murad pulled his pistol from his belt and urged his horse forward, heading straight for the men in front of him. They quickly scattered, and without looking back, he galloped ahead. Eldar followed at a fast pace. Two gunshots rang out behind them, and the bullets whizzed past, missing them both.

Hadji Murad kept riding at the same speed, but after covering about three hundred yards, he slowed his horse, which was now breathing heavily, and listened.

Ahead, he could hear the sound of rushing water. Behind him, roosters crowed from different parts of the village, answering each other. Above it all, he heard the sound of galloping horses and men's voices approaching.

Without hesitation, Hadji Murad urged his horse forward again. The riders behind him sped up and soon caught up. There were about twenty of them—villagers who wanted to stop him, or at least make it look like they had tried so they could stay in Shamil's good graces.

As they got closer, Hadji Murad pulled his horse to a stop, loosened the reins, and with a swift, practiced motion, unbuttoned the cover of his rifle and pulled it out. Eldar did the same.

"What do you want?" Hadji Murad shouted. "Are you trying to capture me? Well, then, come and get me!" He raised his rifle, ready to fight. The men from the village hesitated, stopping in their tracks. Without waiting, Hadji Murad urged his horse down into the ravine. The mounted men followed but kept their distance.

When he reached the other side, they called out, asking him to listen to them. Instead of answering, he fired his rifle and spurred his horse into a gallop. After riding for some time, he slowed down. The voices of his pursuers had faded into the distance, and even the sound of roosters crowing had disappeared. Now, he could hear only the murmur of a nearby stream and, from time to time, the hoot of an owl.

Ahead, the dark outline of the forest was getting closer. That was where his men were waiting for him.

As soon as he reached the edge of the trees, Hadji Murad stopped and took a deep breath before whistling into the night. Then he waited. A moment later, a whistle came back in response. Without hesitation, he turned off the road and rode into the forest.

After about a hundred paces, he saw the glow of a small fire flickering among the trees. The firelight revealed the shadows of four men sitting around it and a saddled horse standing nearby, its legs tied to keep it from wandering.

One of the men quickly stood up and rushed to Hadji Murad, taking hold of his bridle and stirrup. This was his sworn brother, the man who managed his household affairs.

"Put out the fire," Hadji Murad said as he got off his horse.

The men quickly kicked apart the burning wood and stomped on the embers to smother the flames.

"Has Bata been here?" Hadji Murad asked while walking toward a blanket laid out on the ground.

"Yes, he left some time ago with Khan Mahoma."

"Which direction did they go?"

"That way," Khanefi replied, gesturing toward the opposite side from where Hadji Murad had arrived.

"Good," Hadji Murad replied. He unslung his rifle and began reloading it.

"We have to be careful—I was being followed," he warned one of the men putting out the fire.

This was Gamzalo, a Chechen warrior. Without a word, Gamzalo picked up a rifle wrapped in cloth, slung it over his shoulder, and moved to guard the side of the clearing where Hadji Murad had come from.

Eldar, who had just dismounted, took Hadji Murad's horse along with his own. Lifting their heads high, he tied them securely to two trees before grabbing his rifle and positioning himself on the opposite side of the clearing.

With the fire now completely out, the darkness of the forest didn't seem as thick as before, though the stars above still shone faintly.

Hadji Murad glanced up at the sky. Seeing the Pleiades already high above, he estimated that it was well past midnight—he had missed his nightly prayer. He asked Khanefi for a water jug, which they always carried in their packs, and then walked toward the stream.

He took off his shoes, performed his ablutions, and returned to the blanket. Sitting down with his legs folded beneath him, he placed his fingers in his ears, closed his eyes, and turned south to recite his prayer.

When he finished, he went back to where the saddle bags lay. Sitting on the blanket, he rested his elbows on his knees, lowered his head, and fell deep into thought.

Hadji Murad had always believed in his own luck. Whenever he made a plan, he felt sure it would work, and most of the time, things had gone his way. There had been a few setbacks, but overall, his military career had been filled with success. He expected the same now. He imagined leading the army that Vorontsov would give him, marching against Shamil, capturing him, and finally taking revenge. He pictured himself being rewarded by the Russian Tsar and ruling not only over Avaria but over all of Chechnya, with the people submitting to him.

With these thoughts in his mind, he drifted into sleep.

In his dream, he and his warriors charged at Shamil, shouting and singing battle songs. "Hadji Murad is coming!" they cried as they stormed in. He saw himself capturing Shamil and his wives, and he could hear their frightened sobs.

Suddenly, he woke up. The songs and cries from his dream had blended into the real sounds of the night—jackals howling and laughing in the distance.

Lifting his head, he looked up at the sky through the trees. The eastern horizon was beginning to lighten. He turned to a man sitting nearby and asked if Khan Mahoma had returned. When he learned that he had not, Hadji Murad lowered his head and quickly fell asleep again.

This time, he was awakened by the cheerful voice of Khan Mahoma, who had returned from his mission with Bata.

Khan Mahoma sat down beside Hadji Murad and began excitedly describing how they had been met by soldiers and taken directly to the prince. The prince had been pleased and had promised to meet them in the morning at a clearing beyond the Mitchik River, where the Russians would be cutting trees.

Bata, eager to add his own details, interrupted to share more about the meeting.

Hadji Murad listened closely, especially when they repeated the exact words the Russian commander, Vorontsov, had used to accept his offer to join them. Khan Mahoma and Bata both agreed that the prince had promised to welcome Hadji Murad as a guest and to ensure things would go well for him.

Satisfied, Hadji Murad asked about the route they would take. When Khan Mahoma assured him that he knew the way and could lead them straight there, Hadji Murad pulled out some money and handed Bata the promised three rubles.

Then, he gave the order for his men to take out his best weapons, decorated with gold, and his turban. He wanted them all to clean themselves up and look presentable when they arrived at the Russian camp.

As they polished their weapons, tightened their saddles, and brushed their horses, the stars gradually faded from the sky. The morning light spread across the horizon, and a cool breeze drifted through the trees, marking the start of a new day.

V

Before sunrise, while it was still dark, two groups of soldiers carrying axes, led by Poltoratsky, marched six miles beyond the

Shagirinsk Gate. When they reached their destination, they set up sharpshooters around the area and started cutting down trees as soon as the first light of day appeared.

By eight o'clock, the mist mixed with the thick, fragrant smoke from the damp branches burning in the fires. Until then, the soldiers could barely see a few feet ahead, relying only on each other's voices. But as the fog began to lift, they could finally make out the glowing bonfires and the road ahead, now blocked by fallen trees. The sun appeared as a pale spot through the mist, occasionally vanishing behind it.

A short distance from the road, in a small clearing, Poltoratsky sat on a drum alongside his deputy, Tikhonov, two other officers from the Third Company, and Baron Freze, a former officer of the Guards. Freze, who had studied with Poltoratsky at the Cadet College, had been demoted for fighting a duel. Around them, scraps of paper from food wrappers, cigarette stubs, and empty bottles were scattered on the ground. The officers had been drinking vodka earlier and were now eating while sharing a bottle of porter. A drummer was in the middle of opening their third bottle.

Even though Poltoratsky hadn't gotten much sleep, he was in high spirits. He always felt a certain excitement and carefree energy when he was out in the field with his men, especially when there was a hint of danger.

The officers were deep in conversation, discussing the latest news—the death of General Sleptsov. But instead of thinking about death as the end of a life, they focused only on the bravery of a fearless officer who had charged at the enemy with his sword, fighting until the end.

Even though most of them, especially those with battle experience, knew that in real combat, such dramatic sword fights almost never happened—except when chasing down enemies who were already running away—they still liked to believe in these heroic stories. This belief gave them a quiet sense of pride and confidence as they sat casually on their drums, some leaning back with ease, others sitting more reservedly. They joked, drank, and didn't worry about the fact that death could come for any of them at any moment, just as it had for Sleptsov.

As if to remind them of this, a sudden gunshot rang out from the left side of the road. A bullet whistled through the misty air and struck a tree nearby.

"Well, well!" Poltoratsky said with a grin. "That was aimed at our line… Looks like we've got some action." Then, turning to Freze, he added, "Kostya, here's your chance. Get back to your company. I'll take the rest of the men to back up the outpost, and we'll turn this into a proper little battle… then we can write up a great report."

Freze immediately stood up and headed toward the smoke-covered area where he had left his troops.

Poltoratsky's small dappled-bay horse was brought to him. He mounted, gathered his men, and led them toward the spot where the shots had come from.

The outpost was stationed at the edge of the forest, looking down over the open slope of a ravine. The wind was blowing toward the trees, clearing the air so that not only was the slope visible, but the opposite side of the ravine could also be seen clearly.

Just as Poltoratsky reached the front line, the sun broke through the mist, revealing a few horsemen gathered at the edge of the woods on the other side of the ravine, about a quarter of a mile away. These were the Chechen warriors who had chased Hadji Murad and were now watching him meet the Russians.

One of them fired a shot toward the soldiers. A few men returned fire, and the Chechens quickly pulled back. The shooting stopped.

Despite this, Poltoratsky gave the order to fire. Almost immediately, the whole line of sharpshooters erupted in a steady, energetic volley of gunfire. Puffs of smoke drifted into the air as the soldiers, eager for some action, loaded and fired as fast as they could.

The Chechens seemed to catch the excitement, darting forward one by one to fire a few shots of their own. One of these bullets found its mark, hitting a soldier.

The injured man was Avdeev, the same soldier who had been in the ambush the night before. When his comrades reached him, he was lying on the ground, clutching his stomach with both hands. He rocked slightly and let out soft moans of pain.

Since Avdeev was from Poltoratsky's company, Poltoratsky noticed the group gathering around him and rode over to see what had happened.

"What happened, soldier? Were you hit?" Poltoratsky asked. "Where?"

Avdeev didn't answer.

"I was just about to reload, sir, when I heard a click," said a soldier standing next to Avdeev. "I looked over and saw him drop his gun."

Poltoratsky clicked his tongue. "That's not good. Does it hurt a lot, Avdeev?"

"It doesn't hurt much, but I can't walk. A little vodka would help, sir," Avdeev replied.

One of the men quickly found some alcohol—the strong kind the soldiers drank in the Caucasus. Panov, frowning seriously, brought Avdeev a small lid filled with the drink. Avdeev took it but immediately handed it back.

"My stomach turns at the thought of it," he said. "You drink it."

Without hesitation, Panov downed the liquid.

Avdeev tried to sit up but collapsed again. The soldiers spread a cloak on the ground and carefully laid him on it.

"Sir, the colonel is coming," the sergeant-major informed Poltoratsky.

"All right, then take care of him," Poltoratsky said. With a flick of his whip, he trotted off to meet Vorontsov.

Vorontsov approached on his well-bred chestnut horse, accompanied by his adjutant, a Cossack, and a Chechen interpreter.

"What's happening here?" Vorontsov asked.

"A small group of enemy fighters attacked our front line," Poltoratsky replied.

"Come now, you set this up yourself!" Vorontsov said with a grin.

"Oh no, Prince, not me," Poltoratsky chuckled. "They made the first move."

"I heard a soldier was wounded?"

"Yes, sir. It's a shame—he's a good man."

"Is it serious?"

"I believe so... he was hit in the stomach."

"And do you know where I'm headed?" Vorontsov asked.

"No idea, sir."

"Take a guess."

"I couldn't say."

"Hadji Murad has surrendered. We're going to meet him now."

"You can't be serious!"

"His messenger came to me yesterday," Vorontsov said, clearly pleased. "He's waiting for us in the Shalin clearing. I'll meet him there in a few minutes. Position sharpshooters along the way, then come join me."

"Understood," Poltoratsky said, tipping his cap before riding back to his company. He led some of the sharpshooters to the right while the sergeant-major took men to the left.

Meanwhile, the wounded Avdeev was carried back to the fort by his fellow soldiers.

As Poltoratsky returned to join Vorontsov, he noticed several riders approaching from behind. Leading them was a man on a striking white-maned horse. He had an imposing presence, wearing a turban and carrying weapons decorated with gold. This was Hadji Murad.

As he drew closer, Hadji Murad spoke to Poltoratsky in Tartar. Poltoratsky raised his eyebrows and spread his hands, signaling that he didn't understand. He smiled, and Hadji Murad smiled back. There was something warm and almost childlike in his expression, which surprised Poltoratsky. He had expected a cold, grim warrior, but instead, he saw someone full of energy and charm. The only unusual thing was Hadji Murad's eyes—set wide apart, calm yet sharp, watching people closely.

Hadji Murad was accompanied by five men. Among them was Khan Mahoma, the same man who had gone to Vorontsov the night before. He had a round, rosy face, black eyes without eyelashes, and a lively, cheerful expression. Then there was Khanefi, a short, stocky Avar with thick, joined eyebrows. He was responsible for Hadji Murad's belongings and led a fine horse loaded with tightly packed saddle bags.

Two others stood out the most. One was a young, broad-shouldered Lesghian with a slim waist, deep brown eyes, and the beginnings of a beard. This was Eldar. The other, Gamzalo, was a Chechen with a short red beard, missing eyebrows and eyelashes, and a scar running across his nose. He was blind in one eye.

Poltoratsky pointed to Vorontsov, who had just appeared ahead. Hadji Murad rode forward, placed his right hand over his heart, and spoke in Tartar before stopping. The interpreter translated.

"He says, 'I surrender to the will of the Russian Tsar. I want to serve him. I have wanted to do this for a long time, but Shamil wouldn't let me.'"

Vorontsov listened, then extended his hand, still covered by a soft leather glove.

Hadji Murad hesitated for a moment before firmly shaking it. He spoke again, looking first at the interpreter, then at Vorontsov.

"He says he wanted to surrender only to you, because you are the son of the Sirdar, and he respects you greatly."

Vorontsov nodded in acknowledgment.

Hadji Murad gestured to his men and spoke once more.

"He says his followers will serve the Russians just as he will."

Vorontsov turned toward them and nodded. The cheerful, black-eyed Khan Mahoma nodded back and said something that made the serious Avar Khanefi grin, showing his white teeth. Gamzalo, however, barely glanced at Vorontsov before fixing his gaze on his horse's ears again.

As Vorontsov and Hadji Murad, along with their men, headed toward the fort, the soldiers who had been released from their posts gathered in small groups, whispering among themselves.

"That man has killed so many of ours, and now look at the way they treat him!"

"Well, he was Shamil's right hand… no wonder they're making a fuss over him."

"Still, you can't deny it—he's an impressive fighter, a real warrior."

"And that red-haired one? The way he looks at you—like a wild animal!"

"Yeah, he gives me the creeps. Must be a killer."

Most of them had noticed the red-haired man more than anyone else.

Near the tree-cutting site, some soldiers rushed forward to get a better look as the group passed. Their officer shouted at them to stay back, but Vorontsov stopped him.

"Let them see their old enemy up close."

He turned to a nearby soldier and, speaking slowly with his English accent, asked, "Do you know who that is?"

"No, sir."

"That's Hadji Murad... Ever heard of him?"

"Of course, sir! We've fought him more than once!"

"Yes, and he's given us trouble, too."

"That's true, sir," the soldier said, pleased to be speaking directly with his commander.

Hadji Murad, sensing that the men were talking about him, gave a bright, knowing smile.

Vorontsov, in a great mood, rode back to the fort, feeling pleased with how the day had unfolded.

VI

Young Vorontsov felt proud that he, and not anyone else, had been the one to bring in Hadji Murad—Russia's most dangerous enemy after Shamil. However, one thing bothered him. General Meller-Zakomelsky was the commander at Vozdvizhensk, and technically, everything should have gone through him. Since

Vorontsov had acted on his own without reporting it, there was a chance this could create trouble. This concern took away some of his excitement.

When he arrived home, he handed Hadji Murad's men over to the regimental adjutant and personally escorted Hadji Murad inside.

Princess Marya Vasilevna, dressed elegantly and smiling, greeted them in the drawing room along with her six-year-old son, a handsome boy with curly hair. Hadji Murad placed his hands over his heart and, through the interpreter who had entered with him, spoke solemnly. He said that because the prince had welcomed him into his home, he now considered himself his kunak, or honored guest. He explained that among his people, a kunak's entire family was treated with the same respect as the kunak himself.

Marya Vasilevna was charmed by Hadji Murad's presence and manners. She liked him even more when she noticed that he blushed slightly as she extended her hand to him. She invited him to sit and asked if he drank coffee. When it was served, he politely declined.

Hadji Murad understood some Russian but couldn't speak it well. When something was said that he didn't understand, he simply smiled—and this smile had the same effect on Marya Vasilevna as it had on Poltoratsky earlier. Her son, whom she affectionately called Bulka, stood close by, staring at Hadji Murad with wide eyes. The boy had heard many stories about him as a fierce warrior and was fascinated to see him in person.

Leaving Hadji Murad with his wife, Vorontsov went to his office to take care of the formalities. He wrote a report to General Kozlovsky, the commander of the left flank in Grozny, and sent a letter to his father. Then, feeling slightly anxious, he hurried back home. He worried that his wife might be upset with him for bringing such a feared man into their home. Hadji Murad had to be treated carefully—he must not feel insulted, but they also couldn't be too welcoming.

But when he arrived, he realized his concerns were unnecessary. Hadji Murad was sitting in an armchair, with little Bulka on his knee, listening closely to the interpreter while Marya Vasilevna laughed. She was playfully telling him that if he gave away his belongings every time a kunak admired them, he would soon be left with nothing but the clothes on his back.

As soon as Vorontsov entered the room, Hadji Murad quickly stood up, gently setting Bulka down. His face, which had been warm and playful, suddenly turned serious. He only sat back down after Vorontsov took a seat himself.

The conversation continued, and Hadji Murad explained that in his culture, if a kunak admired something, it was customary to give it to him as a gift.

"Your son, kunak?" he said in Russian, patting Bulka's curly head.

"He's amazing, your little warrior!" Marya Vasilevna said to her husband in French. "Bulka admired his dagger, and he gave it to him."

Bulka proudly showed his father the weapon.

"It's a valuable piece!" Marya Vasilevna added.

"We'll have to find a way to give him something in return," Vorontsov replied.

Meanwhile, Hadji Murad sat quietly, stroking Bulka's hair and repeating, "Dzhigit, dzhigit!"—a word used to praise a brave young man.

Vorontsov picked up the dagger, half pulling the sharp blade from its sheath. It had a ridge down the center and was beautifully made.

"A fine dagger," he said. "I thank you!"

Then, turning to the interpreter, he asked, "What can we do for him in return?"

The interpreter translated the question, and Hadji Murad answered immediately. He said he wanted nothing, but he did request a place where he could pray.

Vorontsov called for his valet and told him to take Hadji Murad somewhere he could pray in peace.

As soon as Hadji Murad was alone in his room, his face changed. The friendly and confident look he had before was gone, replaced by a cautious and tense expression. Vorontsov had treated him better than expected, but that only made him more suspicious. He worried that at any moment, he might be arrested, tied up, and sent far away to Siberia—or even killed. Because of this, he stayed on guard, ready for anything.

When Eldar entered the room, Hadji Murad immediately asked where his men were, if their weapons had been taken away, and where the horses had been placed. Eldar reported that the horses were in the prince's stables, the men had been put in a barn, and they still had their weapons. He added that the interpreter was giving them food and tea.

Hadji Murad shook his head doubtfully, but said nothing. After removing his outer garments, he performed his prayers. Then he asked Eldar to bring him his silver dagger. Once he was dressed again and had fastened his belt, he sat on the couch with his legs folded beneath him, waiting to see what would happen next.

At four in the afternoon, the interpreter arrived to invite him to dinner with the prince.

At the table, Hadji Murad barely ate. He took only some pilaf, and he deliberately scooped his portion from the same part of the dish that Marya Vasilevna had taken hers from.

"He's afraid we might poison him," Marya Vasilevna whispered to her husband. "He made sure to take food from the same spot I did."

Then, turning directly to Hadji Murad, she asked through the interpreter when he would pray again. Hadji Murad raised five fingers and pointed toward the sun.

"Then it will be time soon," Vorontsov said, taking out his watch and pressing a small button. The watch chimed, signaling the time—four and a quarter.

Hadji Murad looked surprised. He asked to hear it again and gestured to see the watch up close.

"This is the perfect chance! Give it to him," Marya Vasilevna whispered to her husband in French.

Without hesitation, Vorontsov handed the watch to Hadji Murad.

Hadji Murad placed his hand on his chest as a sign of thanks and took the watch carefully. He pressed the button a few times, listened to the chimes, and nodded approvingly.

After dinner, an officer arrived with a message from General Meller-Zakomelsky. The general, having heard of Hadji Murad's arrival, was furious that he had not been informed. He demanded that Hadji Murad be brought to him immediately.

Vorontsov responded that he would comply, then explained the situation to Hadji Murad through the interpreter, inviting him to come along.

Marya Vasilevna quickly understood that this could lead to trouble between her husband and the general. Ignoring Vorontsov's attempts to stop her, she insisted on going with them.

"You'd be better off staying—it's my business, not yours," Vorontsov told her.

"You can't stop me from visiting the general's wife!" she shot back.

"You could visit her another time."

"But I want to go now!"

Vorontsov had no choice but to agree, and the three of them set off together.

When they arrived, General Meller-Zakomelsky greeted Marya Vasilevna with stiff politeness and escorted her to his wife. Then, he ordered his aide to take Hadji Murad to a waiting room and not to let him out until further notice.

"Please," he said, opening the door to his office and motioning for Vorontsov to step inside.

Once inside, the general stood in front of Vorontsov, not offering him a seat.

"I am in charge here," he stated coldly. "All negotiations with the enemy must go through me! Why did you not report Hadji Murad's arrival to me?"

"His messenger came directly to me and said Hadji Murad would surrender only to me," Vorontsov replied, his face turning pale with frustration. He expected the general to lash out and felt his own temper rising.

"I asked you a question. Why wasn't I informed?"

"I planned to inform you, Baron, but—"

"You are to address me as 'Your Excellency,' not 'Baron!'" Meller-Zakomelsky's anger, which had clearly been building up for some time, finally burst out.

"I have served the Tsar for twenty-seven years! I will not allow men who only started their careers yesterday—men who rely on family connections—to take charge of matters that do not concern them!"

"Your Excellency, I ask you not to say things that are untrue!" Vorontsov interrupted, his voice firm.

"I am speaking the truth, and I will not allow—" the general began, growing even angrier.

At that moment, Marya Vasilevna entered, her dress rustling as she walked, followed by the general's perfectly composed wife.

"Come now, Baron! Simon never meant to offend you," Marya Vasilevna said with a charming smile.

"I am not speaking about that, Princess—"

"Oh, let's just forget it all!" she interrupted playfully. "You know what they say—'A bad peace is better than a good quarrel!' Oh, what am I saying?" She laughed at herself.

The furious general found himself softening under the spell of her laughter. A small smile appeared beneath his mustache.

"I admit, I may have been too harsh," Vorontsov said. "But—"

"And I might have overreacted," Meller-Zakomelsky admitted, extending his hand.

Just like that, the argument was over. They agreed that Hadji Murad would remain with the general for now before being sent to the commander of the left flank.

Meanwhile, in the next room, Hadji Murad sat waiting. He couldn't understand what was being said, but he understood what mattered—there was conflict over him, and his surrender was extremely important to the Russians. This meant they would not imprison or kill him. Instead, he would have the power to demand things in return.

He also realized something else. While Meller-Zakomelsky was technically in command, Vorontsov had more influence. Vorontsov was the one who truly mattered, while Meller-Zakomelsky was less important.

So, when Meller-Zakomelsky finally sent for him and began asking questions, Hadji Murad kept his posture proud and formal. He stated that he had come from the mountains to serve the White Tsar, but he would report only to his Sirdar—the supreme commander, Prince Vorontsov's father in Tiflis.

VII

The wounded Avdeev was taken to the hospital—a small wooden building with a plank roof near the entrance of the fort. He was placed on an empty bed in the shared ward, where four other patients were already resting.

One of them had typhus and was burning with fever. Another, pale and exhausted, had malaria and was waiting for his next attack, yawning constantly. The other two had been wounded in a raid three weeks earlier—one had an injured hand and was already moving around, while the other, shot in the shoulder, sat quietly on his bed.

All of them, except the feverish man, gathered around Avdeev and the soldiers who had carried him in, asking what had happened.

"Sometimes they fire dozens of shots at you, and nothing hits," said one of the men who had helped carry Avdeev. "But today, they only fired a few times, and he got hit."

"Everyone gets what fate gives them," another soldier muttered.

Avdeev groaned loudly as they placed him on the bed, trying to fight through the pain. Once he was settled, he stopped groaning, but his face remained tense. He kept his hands over his wound, his legs shifting restlessly as he stared ahead.

The doctor arrived and told the men to turn Avdeev over to check if the bullet had gone through. As they did, the doctor noticed a series of deep, crisscrossing white scars on Avdeev's back.

"What happened here?" he asked.

"That's from a long time ago, sir," Avdeev answered with a groan.

The scars were from a flogging he had received in the past—for spending money on alcohol.

The doctor turned him over again and carefully felt around the wound, searching for the bullet. After a long and painful attempt, he located it but was unable to remove it. Instead, he cleaned and bandaged the wound before applying a thick layer of medical plaster.

Throughout the procedure, Avdeev clenched his teeth and kept his eyes shut, enduring the pain in silence. When the doctor finally left, he slowly opened his eyes and looked around the room as if he had just woken from a dream. His gaze moved from the other patients to the orderly, though it seemed like he wasn't really seeing them, but something else entirely.

A little while later, his friends Panov and Serogin came to see him. But Avdeev remained still, staring blankly, his expression dazed. It took him a long time to recognize them, even though he was looking right at them.

"Hey, Peter," Panov said gently. "Do you have any message you want us to send home?"

Avdeev didn't react. His empty gaze stayed fixed on Panov's face.

"Do you want to send word to your family?" Panov asked again, touching Avdeev's large, cold hand.

Avdeev seemed to snap out of his trance.

"Ah... Panov," he mumbled.

"Yes, I'm here," Panov said. "Do you have anything to tell them? Serogin can write a letter for you."

Avdeev slowly turned his eyes toward Serogin. "You'll write it?" he asked weakly. "Alright then, write this... 'Your son Peter wishes you a long life. He used to envy his brother'... I told you about that earlier... 'but now he's happy. Don't scold him. Let him live his life. May God bless him. I am happy.' Write that."

He stopped speaking and kept his eyes on Panov for a long moment.

Then suddenly, as if remembering something, he asked, "Did you find your pipe?"

Panov didn't answer right away.

"Your pipe... I mean, did you find it?" Avdeev repeated.

"It was in my bag," Panov said.

"Good... good," Avdeev whispered. Then, after a short pause, he added, "Now bring me a candle... I'm going to die."

Just then, Poltoratsky entered the room to check on him.

"How are you holding up, my friend? Not too well?" he asked.

Avdeev closed his eyes and shook his head slightly. His pale face looked serious and calm. He didn't answer Poltoratsky but turned to Panov again.

"Bring me a candle... I'm going to die," he repeated.

A small wax candle was placed in his hand, but his fingers wouldn't close around it. Instead, someone carefully positioned it between his fingers and held it up for him.

Poltoratsky left the room. Five minutes later, the orderly pressed his ear to Avdeev's chest, then lifted his head and quietly said, "It's over."

Later, the official report sent to Tiflis described his death in simple, formal terms:

"November 23rd—Two companies of the Kurin regiment were sent from the fort for a wood-cutting operation. Around noon, a large group of enemy fighters suddenly attacked. The sharpshooters began retreating, but the 2nd Company launched a bayonet charge and pushed them back. During this skirmish, two soldiers were slightly wounded, and one was killed. The enemy suffered approximately one hundred casualties, including dead and wounded."

VIII

The day Peter Avdeev died in the hospital at Vozdvizhensk, his father, along with his brother's wife and their teenage daughter, was working on the farm, threshing oats on the frozen ground.

The night before, a heavy snowfall had covered everything, followed by a harsh frost in the morning. The old man woke up when the roosters crowed for the third time. Seeing the bright moonlight shining through the frosted window, he climbed down from the stove, put on his boots, sheepskin coat, and cap, and went outside to start work. He spent a couple of hours preparing the threshing floor before returning to the hut to wake up his son and the women.

By the time the women arrived at the threshing floor, everything was set. The snow had been cleared, a wooden shovel stood upright in the frost, and birch brooms were leaning nearby. The oat sheaves had been arranged neatly in long rows. They each grabbed a flail and started threshing in rhythm. The old man struck hard with his heavy flail, breaking the straw, the girl beat the heads of the oats with steady swings, and the daughter-in-law turned the grain over with her flail to loosen it.

As the moon disappeared and the sky brightened with dawn, they neared the end of their row when Akim, the eldest son, arrived in his sheepskin coat and cap.

"What took you so long?" the old man yelled, pausing to lean on his flail.

"I had to take care of the horses," Akim answered.

"The horses! That's your mother's job. Grab a flail! You're getting lazy, just drinking all the time," his father scolded.

"Have you been buying me drinks?" Akim muttered under his breath.

"What was that?" the old man snapped, missing a stroke.

Akim didn't reply. Instead, he grabbed a flail and joined the threshing, their blows landing in a steady rhythm.

"You've got a fat neck like some rich man!" the old man teased, swinging his flail in the air without striking, just to keep time. "Look at me—my pants are barely hanging on!"

When they finished the row, the women started clearing away the straw with rakes.

"Peter was a fool to go in your place," the old man muttered. "The army would have knocked some sense into you! He was worth five of you at home."

"That's enough, Father," the daughter-in-law said as she tossed aside the ties from the sheaves.

"Enough? I feed six people here, and not one of you works! Peter worked twice as hard as any of you. He wasn't like—"

Just then, the old man's wife appeared, walking along the packed snow path from the house. Her bark shoes crunched against the ice as she approached. The men were gathering the loose grain into piles while the women swept up the rest.

"The Elder came by," the old woman announced. "He says everyone has to go help cart bricks for the master. Breakfast is ready—are you coming?"

"Fine," the old man said. Then he turned to Akim. "Harness the roan and go help. And don't mess things up like you did last time! I still can't stop thinking about Peter."

"When he was home, you were always scolding him," Akim grumbled. "Now that he's gone, all you do is nag at me."

"Because you deserve it," his mother snapped. "You'll never be like Peter."

"Oh, alright," Akim muttered.

"'Alright' my foot!" his father shot back. "You wasted our flour money, and now you just say 'alright'?"

"Let it go," the daughter-in-law said, trying to calm things down.

The tension between the old man and Akim had started long ago, ever since Peter left for the army. The old man felt like he had traded an eagle for a crow.

It had been the right decision—at least by tradition. Peter had no children, while Akim had four, so Peter was the one who had to go. But Peter was hardworking like his father—strong, skilled, and always ready to lend a hand. If he walked past someone struggling with a task, he would step in, whether it was swinging a scythe, loading a cart, or chopping wood. The old man missed him but knew there was nothing he could do. In those days, being drafted was like a death sentence— once a man left for the army, he was gone.

The father rarely spoke about him, except when he wanted to push Akim to do better, like today. But Peter's mother thought about him often. For over a year, she had been begging her husband to send Peter a little money. He never responded.

Their family wasn't poor; the old man had savings hidden away. But he refused to touch them. This time, though, after hearing him mention Peter, the old woman decided to ask again. When the younger family members left for the master's work, she sat down with her husband and convinced him to send at least one ruble from the oat sale.

So, after they had packed ninety-six bushels of oats onto three sledges—carefully covering them with cloth pinned together with wooden pegs—she handed her husband a letter, written by the church clerk at her request. The old man promised that when he got to town, he would include a ruble and send it off.

Wearing a fresh sheepskin coat with a wool cloak over it, his legs wrapped in thick woolen bands, the old man tucked the letter into his pouch, said a prayer, climbed onto the front sledge, and set off for town. His grandson drove the last sledge behind him.

When he arrived, he asked the innkeeper to read the letter aloud. He listened carefully and nodded in approval.

Peter's mother had written about how she and the family sent their blessings. She shared small news, including the death of Peter's godfather. At the end, she mentioned that Peter's wife, Aksinya, had not wanted to stay with them and had gone to work as a servant, where they had heard she was doing well.

Then came the part about the ruble, followed by a final message from his mother. She had dictated it through tears, and the church clerk had written it down word for word:

"One more thing, my dearest child, my sweet boy, my beloved Peter. I have cried my eyes out missing you, my shining light. Why did you leave me?..."

At that point, she had broken down sobbing and told the clerk to stop writing.

But Peter would never read his mother's words. He would never receive the ruble, nor learn that his wife had left home. The letter was returned, unopened, with an official notice.

It stated that Peter had died in battle, "defending his Tsar, his homeland, and the Orthodox faith."

When Peter's mother received the news, she cried as much as time allowed, then got back to work. That Sunday, she went to church, paid for a requiem service, and had Peter's name added to the prayer list. She handed out pieces of holy bread in his memory.

Aksinya, Peter's widow, also wailed loudly when she heard the news. She mourned the husband she had only lived with for a year, cried about his brown hair, his kindness, and the hard life she now faced with their little son, Vanka. She bitterly blamed Peter for choosing to help his brother instead of staying with her.

But deep down, Aksinya wasn't just grieving. She was relieved. She was pregnant again—this time by the shopkeeper she had been living with. Now that Peter was gone, no one could judge her, and the shopkeeper could finally marry her, just as he had promised when convincing her to stay with him.

IX

Michael Semenovich Vorontsov, the son of a Russian ambassador, had been educated in England, which was unusual for Russian officials at the time. He was ambitious, polite to those below him, and skillful at handling those above him. He could not imagine life without power and control. Over the years, he had earned the highest ranks and honors and was seen as a talented military leader—some even credited him with defeating Napoleon at Krasnoe.

By 1852, he was over seventy but still energetic for his age. He moved quickly and, most importantly, had a sharp, charming mind that he used to maintain his influence and popularity. He was extremely wealthy, both from his own fortune and that of his wife, who had been Countess Branitski. As Viceroy, he earned an enormous salary and spent much of his wealth on building a palace and designing gardens along the southern coast of Crimea.

On the evening of December 4, 1852, a courier arrived at his palace in Tiflis. A troika—three horses harnessed together—pulled up, and an officer, exhausted and covered in dust from the journey, stepped out. He had been sent by General Kozlovsky with important news: Hadji Murad had surrendered to the Russians.

It was six o'clock, just as Vorontsov was about to sit down for dinner, when he was informed of the courier's arrival. He met with him immediately, which made him a few minutes late for the meal.

As he entered the drawing room, the thirty guests who had gathered—some seated beside Princess Elizabeth Ksaveryevna Vorontsova, others standing in small groups by the windows—turned to look at him.

Vorontsov wore his usual black military coat with shoulder straps but no epaulets. Around his neck hung the White Cross of the Order of St. George. His clean-shaven face, sharp and foxlike, carried a pleasant smile as he squinted slightly, scanning the room.

Moving quickly and gracefully, he apologized to the ladies for his delay, greeted the men, and then approached Princess Manana Orbelyani—a tall, elegant woman of about forty-five with striking Eastern features. Offering her his arm, he led her to the dining table.

His wife, Princess Elizabeth Ksaveryevna, gave her arm to a visiting red-haired general with stiff mustaches. A Georgian prince escorted Countess Choiseuil, a close friend of the princess. The other guests followed, some in pairs, some alone.

Footmen in formal uniforms pulled out chairs as the guests sat down, and the head servant carefully ladled steaming soup from a silver tureen.

Vorontsov took his seat at the center of one side of the long table, while his wife sat directly across from him, with the general seated to her right. On Vorontsov's right sat Princess Orbelyani, and to his left was a beautiful Georgian woman with dark hair, rosy cheeks, sparkling jewelry, and an endless smile.

"Wonderful news, my dear!" Vorontsov replied in French when his wife asked about the courier's message. "Simon has been lucky!"

Then, in a voice loud enough for all to hear, he shared the exciting news—though it was not entirely a surprise to him, since negotiations had been ongoing for some time. Hadji Murad, the most fearless and well-known of Shamil's commanders, had surrendered to the Russians. Within a few days, he would be brought to Tiflis.

The whole table fell silent. Even the younger aides-de-camp and officials sitting at the far ends—who had been quietly laughing at something—stopped talking and turned their attention to the prince.

"And you, General," the princess asked her dinner partner, the red-haired officer with the bristly mustache, "have you ever encountered Hadji Murad?"

"More than once, Princess," the general replied.

He then launched into a story about how, after the mountaineers captured Gergebel in 1843, Hadji Murad had attacked General Pahlen's troops and killed Colonel Zolotukhin right before their eyes.

Vorontsov listened to the general with a polite smile, happy that he had joined the conversation. But suddenly, his face changed—he looked distant and uneasy.

The general, caught up in his storytelling, continued talking about another time he had encountered Hadji Murad.

"It was him, sir, if you recall," the general said, "who set up the ambush that attacked the rescue party during the 'Biscuit' expedition."

"Where?" Vorontsov asked, narrowing his eyes.

What the general called a "rescue" referred to a disastrous event during the failed Dargo campaign. That mission, led by Vorontsov himself, had nearly ended in complete disaster, with an entire detachment—including Vorontsov—almost wiped out, if not for reinforcements arriving just in time. Everyone knew that the campaign had been a terrible failure. Many soldiers had died, cannons had been lost, and the entire operation had been an embarrassment. However, in reports to the Tsar, it was framed as a heroic victory.

Because of this, no one ever brought it up in front of Vorontsov—at least not in a way that hinted at failure.

But the general's use of the word "rescue" made it painfully clear what had really happened. Everyone at the table understood the blunder. Some pretended not to notice, while others shifted uncomfortably, waiting to see what would happen. A few exchanged quick glances and smirked.

Only the red-haired general with the bristly mustache was unaware of the mistake. Enthusiastic about his story, he casually repeated, "Yes, at the rescue, your Excellency."

Getting carried away, he described in detail how Hadji Murad had skillfully split the detachment in two. He kept repeating the word "rescue" as he explained that if reinforcements hadn't arrived in time, not a single soldier would have survived.

Before he could finish his thought, Princess Manana Orbelyani, realizing the tension in the room, quickly interrupted.

"Tell me, General, have you found your accommodations in Tiflis comfortable?" she asked.

The general, caught off guard, looked around. He suddenly noticed the serious stares of his aides at the far end of the table. In that moment, he understood his mistake. Without answering the princess, he frowned, went quiet, and began eating quickly, though he barely tasted the food on his plate.

The room felt tense, but the awkwardness was soon broken by the Georgian prince sitting next to Princess Vorontsova. Though not particularly intelligent, he was an expert flatterer and courtier. Acting as if nothing had happened, he smoothly changed the subject.

"Did you know," he said, "that Hadji Murad once kidnapped the widow of Akhmet Khan of Mekhtuli?"

"He rode into the village at night, took what he wanted, and escaped with her before anyone could stop him."

"Why did he take that particular woman?" the princess asked.

"He had been her husband's enemy for years," the prince explained. "He chased him many times but never managed to capture him before his death. So, he took his revenge on the widow instead."

The princess translated this for her friend, Countess Choiseuil, who sat beside the Georgian prince.

"What a terrible thing!" the countess said, closing her eyes and shaking her head.

"Oh no!" Vorontsov said with a smile. "I heard that he treated her with respect and later released her unharmed."

"Yes, but only after receiving a ransom," someone pointed out.

"Of course," Vorontsov replied, "but still, he acted honorably."

At those words, the mood at the table shifted. The guests understood that Vorontsov wanted Hadji Murad to be spoken of with admiration rather than criticism.

"He's incredibly bold—a remarkable man!" someone said.

"In 1849, he rode into Temir Khan Shura and looted the shops in broad daylight," another added.

An Armenian guest at the far end of the table, who had been in Temir Khan Shura at the time, eagerly shared the full details of Hadji Murad's daring raid.

The conversation continued, with everyone taking turns praising Hadji Murad's bravery, intelligence, and leadership. Someone mentioned that he had ordered twenty-six prisoners to be executed, but this was brushed aside with the usual saying, "What can you do? In war, things happen!"

"He is truly a great man."

"If he had been born in Europe, he might have become another Napoleon," the Georgian prince added, always ready to flatter.

He knew that any mention of Napoleon pleased Vorontsov, who wore the White Cross as a symbol of his role in defeating him.

"Well, not quite Napoleon," Vorontsov corrected, "but he would have made a fine cavalry general."

"If not Napoleon, then Murat," someone suggested.

"And his name is Hadji Murad!"

"Now that Hadji Murad has surrendered, Shamil won't last much longer," another guest said.

"They must realize that now," one man added, emphasizing the word "now" to imply that things had changed under Vorontsov's leadership.

"This is all thanks to you!" Manana Orbelyani said warmly.

Vorontsov, though attempting to downplay the praise, clearly enjoyed the admiration. In high spirits, he led his dinner partner back to the drawing room after the meal.

Later, as coffee was being served, he was especially friendly to everyone. He even approached the red-haired general, making an effort to show that he had ignored his earlier mistake.

After making the rounds and chatting with guests, Vorontsov sat down at the card table. He only played ombre, an old-fashioned card game. His playing partners included the Georgian prince, an Armenian general (who had learned the game from Vorontsov's valet), and Doctor Andreevsky, a man known for his strong influence.

Vorontsov placed his gold snuffbox—decorated with a portrait of Alexander I—beside him. He tore open a fresh deck of glossy cards and was about to deal when his Italian valet approached with a silver tray.

"Another message, sir," the valet announced.

Vorontsov set down the cards, excused himself, and opened the letter. It was from his son, describing Hadji Murad's surrender and his encounter with Meller-Zakomelsky.

His wife approached and asked what their son had written.

"It's all about the same situation," he replied in French. "He had some trouble with the garrison commander. Simon was in the wrong." Then, switching to English, he added with a grin, "But all's well that ends well."

He handed the letter to his wife and turned back to the card game.

"Shall we begin?" he said to his partners.

Feeling particularly cheerful, Vorontsov did something he only did when in a good mood. With his wrinkled white fingers, he took a pinch of fine French snuff, brought it to his nose, and gently released it.

X

When Hadji Murad arrived at the prince's palace the next day, the waiting room was already crowded with people hoping to see Vorontsov.

Among them was the red-haired general from the dinner, now dressed in full uniform with all his medals, there to say his farewells. A regimental commander, facing a court-martial for misusing government funds, waited anxiously for a chance to plead his case. A wealthy Armenian businessman, supported by Doctor Andreevsky, had come to ask for an extension on his exclusive vodka-selling rights. Sitting quietly in a black dress was the widow of an officer killed in battle, hoping to secure a pension or free education for her children. A ruined Georgian prince, wearing a magnificent traditional outfit, had arrived to request ownership of confiscated church land. An official carrying a large roll of paper held a new plan for controlling the Caucasus. Lastly, a Khan had come for no reason other than to be able to boast back home that he had met with the prince.

Each person waited for their turn, and one by one, the aide-de-camp—a handsome, fair-haired young officer—led them into the prince's office and back out again.

When Hadji Murad entered the room with his quick but slightly uneven steps, all eyes turned toward him, and whispers of his name spread through the crowd.

He was dressed in a long white Circassian coat over a brown beshmet, its collar lined with fine silver embroidery. He wore black leggings and soft black shoes that fit tightly over his feet, like gloves. On his head was a high cap wrapped in a turban-style cloth—the same turban that, years ago, had led to his arrest by General Klugenau after being reported by Akhmet Khan. That event had ultimately driven him to join Shamil.

Walking across the polished wooden floor, Hadji Murad moved with a slight sway due to his limp—one of his legs was shorter than the other. His sharp, widely spaced eyes stared straight ahead, as if he didn't see anyone around him.

The aide-de-camp greeted him politely and offered him a seat while he went to announce his arrival to the prince, but Hadji Murad refused to sit. Instead, he rested a hand on his dagger and stood tall, his foot slightly forward, glancing around the room with a look of quiet defiance.

Prince Tarkhanov, the court interpreter, approached him and spoke, but Hadji Murad responded briefly and without interest.

Just then, a Kumyk prince, who had come to file a complaint against a police officer, exited Vorontsov's office. A moment later, the aide-de-camp returned and signaled for Hadji Murad to follow him.

The Commander-in-Chief stood by his desk as Hadji Murad entered. Unlike the day before, his old, pale face no longer carried a friendly smile. Instead, he looked serious and reserved.

Hadji Murad stepped into the large office, taking in the enormous desk and tall windows covered with green blinds. He placed his small, sun-darkened hands over his chest, right where the folds of his white coat overlapped. Lowering his eyes, he began speaking slowly and clearly in Kumyk, a language he spoke well. His tone was respectful but firm.

"I place myself under the great Tsar's protection," he said. "I swear to serve him with complete loyalty, even if it costs me my last drop of blood. I hope to be of use to you in your war against Shamil, who is both my enemy and yours."

As the interpreter translated his words, Vorontsov studied Hadji Murad carefully, and Hadji Murad did the same to him.

For a brief moment, their eyes met, and in that silent exchange, they understood more about each other than words could ever express.

Vorontsov's gaze revealed his true thoughts—he didn't believe a single word Hadji Murad was saying. He saw him as an enemy of Russia, someone who had only surrendered because he had no other choice. He knew Hadji Murad would never truly serve the Russian Empire.

Hadji Murad, in turn, understood Vorontsov's doubt but continued speaking with unwavering confidence. His own eyes seemed to say, This old man should be thinking about retirement, not war. But he is clever, and I must be careful with him.

Vorontsov grasped this unspoken message, yet he still responded in the way that suited his goals.

"Tell him," Vorontsov instructed the interpreter, "that our Tsar is both powerful and merciful. At my request, he may pardon Hadji

Murad and allow him to serve in our ranks." Then, turning to look at Hadji Murad directly, he asked, "Has that been translated?"

Once the interpreter confirmed, Vorontsov continued, "Until I receive word from the Tsar, I will personally ensure that he is treated well during his stay with us."

Hadji Murad pressed his hands to his chest once more and began to speak again, his voice filled with determination.

The interpreter translated Hadji Murad's words:

"He says that back in 1839, when he ruled Avaria, he was loyal to the Russians and never would have turned against them if his enemy, Akhmet Khan, hadn't spread lies about him to General Klugenau."

"I know, I know," Vorontsov said, though if he had ever known, he had long since forgotten. "I know," he repeated, motioning for Hadji Murad to sit on the couch against the wall as he took a seat himself.

Hadji Murad, however, did not sit. He shrugged his broad shoulders as if to say that he could not bring himself to sit in the presence of such an important man. Instead, he continued speaking through the interpreter:

"Akhmet Khan and Shamil are both my enemies. Akhmet Khan is dead, so I can no longer take my revenge on him. But Shamil is still alive, and I will not die until I have repaid him for what he has done." Hadji Murad's face tightened, and his lips pressed into a firm line.

"Yes, yes, but how exactly does he plan to take his revenge on Shamil?" Vorontsov asked the interpreter. "And tell him he may sit down."

Hadji Murad once again refused to sit and explained that he had come to the Russians to help them defeat Shamil.

"Very well, very well," Vorontsov said. "But what, specifically, does he want to do? Sit down, sit down!"

This time, Hadji Murad took a seat. He said that if the Russians sent him to the Lesghian border with an army, he could guarantee that the entire region of Daghestan would rise against Shamil. If that happened, Shamil would have no chance of holding on to power.

"That would be excellent... I'll consider it," Vorontsov replied.

The interpreter repeated the words to Hadji Murad, who paused, thinking.

"Tell the Sirdar one more thing," Hadji Murad continued. "My family is still in the hands of my enemy. As long as they remain in the mountains, I am trapped and cannot fully serve you. If I openly go against Shamil, he will have my wife, my mother, and my children killed. Let the prince arrange an exchange—my family in return for the Russian prisoners he holds. Then, I will destroy Shamil or die trying!"

"Alright, alright," Vorontsov said. "I will think about it. For now, let him go to the chief of staff and explain his position, his plans, and his requests in detail."

With that, the first meeting between Hadji Murad and Vorontsov came to an end.

That evening, an Italian opera was performed at the new theater, which had been decorated in an Eastern style. Vorontsov sat in his private box when, suddenly, the striking figure of Hadji Murad appeared in the audience. He walked in with Loris-Melikov, the aide assigned to watch over him, and took a seat in the front row.

Hadji Murad sat through the first act with complete composure, his face showing neither enjoyment nor boredom. He appeared indifferent to the performance, sitting with the dignified stillness of an Eastern nobleman. Then, without any sign of emotion, he stood up, calmly looked around the theater, and left, drawing curious glances from all around him.

The next evening, the usual gathering was held at the Vorontsovs' mansion. The brightly lit ballroom was alive with music, played by a band hidden among the indoor trees. Women, both young and older, danced in elegant dresses that revealed their shoulders, arms, and chests, spinning in the arms of men dressed in glittering military uniforms.

At the refreshment table, footmen in red coats and white stockings poured champagne and served sweets to the guests. Even the prince's wife, despite her age, moved about the room in a low-cut gown, greeting visitors with a friendly smile.

When Hadji Murad arrived, she welcomed him politely through the interpreter. He looked at the gathering with the same expressionless face he had worn at the theater the night before. After the hostess spoke to him, other women—also dressed in revealing gowns—approached him, smiling boldly and asking the same question:

"How do you like what you see?"

They seemed certain that he would be amazed by the grand European ball.

Then Vorontsov himself walked up, wearing his gold epaulets and military decorations, his white cross and ribbon hanging at his chest. He, too, asked Hadji Murad what he thought of the celebration, clearly expecting him to be impressed.

Hadji Murad gave the same answer to Vorontsov that he had given the women:

"Among my people, we do not have such things."

He made no comment on whether he thought that was good or bad.

During the ball, Hadji Murad attempted to bring up the matter of securing his family's release, but Vorontsov pretended not to hear and walked away. Later, Loris-Melikov told Hadji Murad that this was not the place to discuss business.

At eleven o'clock, Hadji Murad checked the time on the watch the Vorontsovs had given him and asked Loris-Melikov if he could leave.

"You may, but it would be better if you stayed," Loris-Melikov replied.

Ignoring the suggestion, Hadji Murad left anyway. A carriage had been provided for him, and he rode back to the quarters assigned to him without looking back at the lavish event he had left behind.

XI

On the fifth day that Hadji Murad stayed in Tiflis, Loris-Melikov, the assistant to the Viceroy, came to see him on the prince's orders.

"My mind and hands are ready to serve the Sirdar," Hadji Murad said politely. He bowed his head and placed his hands over his chest. "Tell me what you need," he added, looking at Loris-Melikov with a friendly expression.

Loris-Melikov sat in a chair by the table, while Hadji Murad sat on a small couch across from him. He rested his hands on his knees, lowered his head slightly, and listened closely.

Speaking in Tartar, Loris-Melikov explained that while the prince already knew some of Hadji Murad's past, he wanted to hear the full story directly from him.

"Tell me everything, and I will write it down, translate it into Russian, and the prince will send it to the Emperor."

Hadji Murad stayed quiet for a moment. He never interrupted people and always made sure they were finished before speaking. Then, he lifted his head, adjusted his turban, and smiled. It was a warm, almost childlike smile—the same one that had charmed Marya Vasilevna.

"I can do that," he said, happy that his story would reach the Emperor.

"You must tell me everything, from the very beginning," Loris-Melikov said, taking out a notebook.

"I can, but there's a lot to tell—so much has happened!" Hadji Murad replied.

"If we don't finish today, we'll continue another time," Loris-Melikov assured him.

"Shall I start at the very beginning?"

"Yes, from the start. Where you were born and how you grew up."

Hadji Murad lowered his head, lost in thought. He stayed still for a long time. Then, he picked up a stick beside the couch, pulled out a small, sharp knife with an ivory handle decorated with gold from beneath his dagger, and began carving the wood as he spoke.

"Write this down: I was born in Tselmess, a tiny village—so small we say it's 'the size of a donkey's head' in the mountains," he began. "Not far from there, about the distance of two cannon shots, is Khunzakh, where the Khans lived. My family was close to them.

"When my oldest brother, Osman, was born, my mother became the nurse for the eldest Khan, Abu Nutsal Khan. Later, she also nursed his second son, Umma Khan, and raised him. But my second brother, Akhmet, passed away. When I was born, the Khansha had a son, Bulach Khan, and she wanted my mother to nurse him too.

"My father told her to go, but she refused. She said, 'I lost one son while nursing another, and I won't risk another child.' My father, who had a terrible temper, became furious and struck her with a dagger. He would have killed her if others hadn't stopped him.

"So she kept me with her and later wrote a song about it... but that doesn't really matter."

"It does matter," Loris-Melikov said. "Tell me everything."

Hadji Murad thought for a moment. He remembered how his mother used to put him to sleep beside her on the roof of their house, covering them both with a fur coat. He once asked her to show him where his father had cut her, and she let him see the scar on her side.

Then, he repeated the song his mother had written:

"A bright steel blade cut deep through my chest,

But I held my dear child so close to me

That his small body was covered in my blood.

And though no herbs or roots could heal my wound,

My courage kept my soul from breaking."

"My mother is now in Shamil's hands," he added. "She must be saved."

As he spoke, more childhood memories came back. He remembered the fountain at the bottom of the hill, where he would hold onto his mother's trousers while they got water. He thought about the first time she shaved his head, how he had looked in the brass water basin on the wall and found his round, smooth, bluish reflection strange. He remembered a scruffy little dog that once licked his face.

He could still smell the warm, smoky scent of the flatbread his mother used to give him—a mix of firewood and sour milk. He remembered how she carried him in a basket on her back when they visited his grandfather's farm. He could still picture his grandfather—old and wrinkled, with gray hair—and how his strong hands shaped silver with a hammer.

"My mother didn't go to be a nurse," Hadji Murad said, giving a quick nod. "The Khansha found another woman to take care of her child, but she still liked my mother a lot. She would invite us to her palace, and we played with her children.

"There were three young Khans: Abu Nutsal Khan, who was my brother Osman's foster-brother; Umma Khan, who was like a brother to me; and Bulach Khan, the youngest—the one Shamil later threw off a cliff. But that happened much later.

"I was about sixteen when the murids started coming to our villages. They would hit stones with wooden swords and shout, 'Muslims, Holy War!' The Chechens all joined them, and the Avars began to as well. At the time, I was living in the palace like a brother to the Khans. I had everything I wanted—horses, weapons, money. I enjoyed life without worries, and things went on like that until Kazi-Mulla, the Imam, was killed, and Hamzad took his place.

"Hamzad sent messengers to the Khans, warning that if they didn't join the Holy War, he would destroy Khunzakh. The Khans were unsure what to do. They feared the Russians but were also afraid of Hamzad. The old Khansha decided to send me and her second son, Umma Khan, to Tiflis to ask the Russian Commander-in-Chief for help. At that time, Baron Rosen was in charge. But when we arrived, he refused to see us. He only sent a message saying he would help but never actually did anything.

"Instead, his officers came to visit us. They played cards with Umma Khan, gave him wine, and took him to bad places. He lost all his money gambling with them. He was as strong as a bull and as brave as a lion, but he had no self-control. If I hadn't stopped him, he would have lost everything, even his last horse and weapons.

"After our trip to Tiflis, my view of the Russians changed. I went back and told the Khansha and the Khans that they should join the Holy War."

Loris-Melikov looked at him curiously. "What made you change your mind? Did you not like the Russians?"

Hadji Murad paused.

"No, I didn't like them," he said firmly, closing his eyes. "But there was another reason I decided to join the Holy War."

"What was it?"

"Near Tselmess, the Khan and I came across three murids. Two of them got away, but I shot the third one. He was still alive when I reached him to take his weapons. He looked up at me and said, 'You have killed me… I am happy. But you are a Muslim, young and strong. Join the Holy War! It is God's will!'"

"And did you?"

"I didn't at first. But his words made me think," Hadji Murad said, then continued his story.

"When Hamzad got closer to Khunzakh, we sent our village Elders to him, saying we would consider joining if he sent a wise man to explain the Holy War to us. Instead of answering properly, Hamzad humiliated them—he shaved off their mustaches, pierced their nostrils, and hung cakes from their noses before sending them back.

"They told us that Hamzad would send a teacher, but only if the Khansha gave up her youngest son as a hostage. She agreed and sent Bulach Khan. Hamzad treated him well and then sent a message, inviting the two older brothers too. He promised he would serve them, just as his father had served their father.

"The Khansha was not a smart woman—most women are foolish when they aren't guided by a man. She was scared to send both sons, so she only sent Umma Khan. I went with him. About a mile before we arrived, Hamzad's men met us. They sang, fired their guns, and performed riding tricks around us. When we got closer, Hamzad came out of his tent and walked up to Umma Khan's stirrup, greeting him with respect.

"Hamzad said, 'I have done no harm to your family and do not wish to. All I ask is that you don't try to stop me from leading people into the Holy War. If you let me live in your house, I will help you with advice, and you can do as you like.'

"Umma Khan wasn't good with words. He didn't know what to say, so he stayed silent. I stepped in and said that if Hamzad was sincere, he should come to Khunzakh, where the Khansha and the Khans would welcome him.

"But before I could finish, I was interrupted—and that was the first time I met Shamil. He was standing beside Hamzad and turned to me, saying, 'You were not asked to speak. The Khan was!'

"I said nothing after that. Hamzad took Umma Khan into his tent and later called for me. He ordered me to return to Khunzakh with his messengers. When we arrived, they began pressuring the Khansha to send her eldest son as well.

"I saw through their tricks and warned her not to send him. But women have no more sense than an egg has hair. She insisted that he go. Abu Nutsal Khan refused at first, but then she said, 'I see you are afraid!' She knew exactly how to hurt his pride.

"He turned red, stopped talking to her, and ordered his horse to be saddled. I went with him."

Hamzad welcomed us with even more respect than he had shown Umma Khan. He rode out far down the hill to meet us, about the distance of two rifle shots. A large group of horsemen followed him, carrying banners. They sang, fired their guns into the air, and showed off their riding skills.

When we reached the camp, Hamzad took the Khan into his tent while I stayed behind with the horses.

I was standing lower on the hillside when I suddenly heard gunshots from inside Hamzad's tent. I rushed there and saw Umma Khan lying face down in a pool of blood. Abu Nutsal was still fighting the murids. One of his cheeks had been slashed so badly that it was hanging down, and he was holding it in place with one hand while using his other to stab at anyone who came near. I watched as he struck down Hamzad's brother and then swung at another attacker, but the murids fired their guns at him, and he collapsed.

Hadji Murad paused. His sunburned face turned a deep red, and his eyes filled with rage.

"I was so afraid that I ran away," he admitted.

"Really? I thought you were never afraid," Loris-Melikov said.

"Never again after that," Hadji Murad replied. "From that moment on, I carried that shame with me. And whenever I remembered it, I was never afraid of anything again."

XII

"That's enough! It's time for me to pray," Hadji Murad said as he pulled a watch from the inside pocket of his coat. It was a repeater watch that Vorontsov had given him. He carefully pressed the button, and the watch chimed twelve fifteen. Tilting his head slightly, he listened to the sound, holding back a childlike smile.

"A gift from my friend Vorontsov," he said, smiling.

"It's a fine watch," Loris-Melikov replied. "Go ahead and pray, I'll wait for you."

"Good. Very well," Hadji Murad said, then left for his bedroom.

Alone in the room, Loris-Melikov took out his notebook and wrote down the key points of Hadji Murad's story. Then he lit a cigarette and started pacing back and forth. As he walked past the door to the bedroom, he heard loud voices speaking quickly in Tartar. He guessed it was Hadji Murad's murids and decided to step inside.

The room had a strong, leathery smell, the kind common among mountain people. Sitting on a felt rug on the floor was Gamzalo, a one-eyed, red-haired man wearing a greasy, worn-out coat. He was weaving a bridle and talking excitedly in his rough voice. But the moment Loris-Melikov entered, he went silent and kept working, ignoring him completely.

Standing in front of Gamzalo was Khan Mahoma, smiling wide and flashing his white teeth. His black eyes, which had no eyelashes, sparkled as he repeated something over and over. Meanwhile, Eldar, a tall, strong man, had his sleeves rolled up as he polished the leather straps of a saddle hanging from a nail. Khanefi, the one who managed their household, wasn't there—he was in the kitchen cooking their meal.

"What were you arguing about?" Loris-Melikov asked after greeting them.

"He keeps going on about how great Shamil is," Khan Mahoma said, shaking Loris-Melikov's hand. "He says Shamil is wise, holy, and a great warrior."

"If he thinks that, why did he leave him?"

Khan Mahoma grinned. "That's the question—he left him but still praises him!"

"Does he really believe Shamil is a saint?" Loris-Melikov asked.

"If he weren't a saint, people wouldn't follow him," Gamzalo said quickly.

"Shamil isn't a saint, but Mansur was!" Khan Mahoma argued. "He was the real deal. When he was Imam, people lived differently. He would ride through villages, and everyone would rush to him, kissing the hem of his coat, confessing their sins, and vowing to be better. The elders say that back then, people lived like saints. No drinking, no smoking, no skipping prayers. Even when there were feuds, they forgave each other, even if blood had been spilled. If someone found money or lost belongings, they would tie them to a stake on the roadside for the owner to find. In those days, God blessed the people—unlike now."

"They don't drink or smoke in the mountains even now," Gamzalo muttered.

"Your Shamil is just another mountaineer," Khan Mahoma said, winking at Loris-Melikov.

"Yes, and in the mountains, that's where the eagles live," Gamzalo shot back.

Khan Mahoma grinned. "Nice one! You got me there!"

Noticing the silver cigarette case in Loris-Melikov's hand, Khan Mahoma asked for a cigarette. When Loris-Melikov reminded him that smoking was forbidden, he smirked and nodded toward Hadji Murad's bedroom. "As long as he doesn't see, it's fine."

He lit a cigarette and started puffing awkwardly, blowing the smoke out with pursed lips.

"That's not right," Gamzalo said sternly and walked out of the room.

Khan Mahoma smirked after him and then turned to Loris-Melikov. "Where's the best place to buy a silk coat and a white cap?"

"Why? You suddenly have money?"

"I have enough," Khan Mahoma said with a sly wink.

Eldar looked over at him with a grin. "Ask him where he got it."

"Oh, I won it!" Khan Mahoma said quickly and launched into his story.

He explained that the day before, while walking through Tiflis, he saw a group of Russians and Armenians gambling, playing a coin-tossing game called orlyanka. The bet was big—three gold pieces and a pile of silver. He figured out how the game worked right away, jingled the few coins in his pocket, and stepped up to the group, boldly saying he would bet the whole amount.

"How could you do that? Did you have that much money?" Loris-Melikov asked.

"I only had twelve kopecks," Khan Mahoma admitted, grinning.

"And what if you had lost?"

He shrugged and pointed at his pistol. "Then this!"

"You mean you would have handed over your gun?"

"Hand it over? No! I would have run. And if anyone tried to stop me, I'd have shot them. Simple as that!"

"So, did you win?"

"Aye, I won every coin and walked away with all of it!"

Loris-Melikov had no trouble understanding what kind of men Khan Mahoma and Eldar were. Khan Mahoma was cheerful, carefree, and always looking for excitement. He had so much energy that he didn't know what to do with it. He loved taking risks, whether it was his own life or someone else's. Right now, he was on the Russians' side, but just as easily, he might switch back to Shamil if it suited him.

Eldar, on the other hand, was different. He was completely loyal to his leader. He was calm, strong, and steady.

The one person Loris-Melikov didn't understand was Gamzalo, the red-haired man. He could tell that Gamzalo wasn't just loyal to Shamil—he despised the Russians with a deep hatred. His every move showed disgust and resentment toward them. This made Loris-Melikov wonder why he had even come over to their side.

A thought crossed his mind—what if the rumors were true? Some high-ranking officials suspected that Hadji Murad's surrender wasn't real. Maybe he wasn't truly against Shamil. What if he was only pretending to be on their side so he could gather information on the Russians' weaknesses and later use it against them? If that was the case, Gamzalo's attitude only made the suspicion stronger.

"The others, even Hadji Murad, know how to hide their true intentions," Loris-Melikov thought. "But this one—his hatred is too obvious."

Loris-Melikov decided to speak to him.

"Are you bored here?" he asked.

Gamzalo didn't stop working and barely looked up. "No, I'm not," he grumbled in his rough voice, glancing sideways at Loris-Melikov with his one good eye.

Every time Loris-Melikov tried to ask him something else, Gamzalo answered in the same short, unfriendly way.

While they were talking, Hadji Murad's fourth murid, Khanefi, walked in. He was an Avar, with a thick, hairy face and a broad chest that looked almost like it was covered in moss. Strong and hardworking, he focused only on his tasks and, like Eldar, followed Hadji Murad's orders without question.

He had come to grab some rice when Loris-Melikov stopped him.

"Where are you from? How long have you been with Hadji Murad?"

"Five years," Khanefi replied. "I come from the same village as him. My father killed his uncle, and they wanted to kill me."

He said it so calmly, staring at Loris-Melikov from under his thick eyebrows, that it was clear he didn't see anything unusual about it.

"So what did you do?" Loris-Melikov asked.

"I asked them to accept me as a brother."

"What do you mean by that?"

"I didn't shave my head or cut my nails for two months. Then I went to them. They let me see Patimat, his mother. She nursed me, and from then on, I became his brother."

Just then, Hadji Murad's voice called out from the next room.

Eldar immediately wiped his hands, stood up, and walked quickly toward the sound. A moment later, he came back.

"He's asking for you," Eldar said.

Loris-Melikov handed another cigarette to the always-smiling Khan Mahoma and then headed toward the drawing room.

XIII

When Loris-Melikov stepped into the drawing room, Hadji Murad greeted him with a bright expression.

"Shall I continue?" he asked, settling comfortably on the couch.

"Yes, of course," Loris-Melikov replied. "I just had a conversation with your men... One of them is quite the lively one!"

"Ah, Khan Mahoma—he's a carefree sort," Hadji Murad said with a small smile.

"I liked the young, good-looking one," Loris-Melikov added.

"That's Eldar," Hadji Murad nodded. "He may be young, but he's strong—like iron."

For a moment, neither of them spoke.

"So, shall I go on?" Hadji Murad asked.

"Yes, yes, please!"

"I told you how the Khans were killed... After that, Hamzad took control of Khunzakh and moved into their palace. The only survivor from their family was the Khansha. He ordered her to come to him. She stood up to him, but Hamzad gave a quick signal to one of his men, Aseldar, who attacked her from behind and killed her."

"Why did he kill her?" Loris-Melikov asked.

"What choice did he have?" Hadji Murad shrugged. "When the front legs go, the back legs must follow. He wiped out the whole family. Shamil finished the job—he threw the youngest son off a cliff."

"After that, all of Avaria surrendered to Hamzad. But my brother and I refused. We wanted revenge for the Khans' blood. We pretended to submit, but we were only thinking of how to kill him. We spoke with our grandfather and decided to wait for a chance to attack him when he left his palace.

"But someone overheard us and told Hamzad. He summoned our grandfather and warned him, 'If it's true that your grandsons are plotting against me, all three of you will hang from the same beam. I serve God, and no one will stand in my way. Remember that!'

"Our grandfather came home and told us what Hamzad had said. That's when we realized we couldn't wait any longer. We had to act. So we decided to do it on the first day of the feast, in the mosque.

"Our friends didn't want to be part of it, but my brother and I were determined.

"We each took two pistols, put on our cloaks, and went to the mosque. Hamzad arrived with thirty murids, all holding drawn swords. Aseldar—the same murid who had killed the Khansha—spotted us. He shouted at us to remove our cloaks and started walking toward me. I had my dagger ready. I struck him down with it, then ran at Hamzad. But before I could reach him, my brother Osman had already shot him.

"Even after being shot, Hamzad still tried to attack my brother with his dagger. But I landed a final blow to his head.

"There were thirty of them, and only two of us. They killed my brother Osman, but I fought them off, jumped through a window, and escaped.

"When word spread that Hamzad was dead, the people rose up. The murids ran for their lives. Those who didn't escape were killed."

Hadji Murad stopped and took a deep breath.

"That was a great victory," he continued, "but everything fell apart after that.

"Shamil took Hamzad's place. He sent messengers to tell me I should join him in fighting the Russians. He warned that if I refused, he would destroy Khunzakh and kill me.

"I told him I wouldn't join him—and I wouldn't let him come near me either..."

"Why didn't you go with him?" Loris-Melikov asked.

Hadji Murad frowned and stayed silent for a moment.

"I couldn't," he finally said. "He had the blood of my brother Osman and Abu Nutsal Khan on his hands. I refused to join him. Instead, General Rosen sent me an officer's commission and put me in charge of Avaria. That would have been fine, but then Rosen appointed Mahomet-Murza as Khan of Kazi-Kumukh, and later replaced him with Akhmet Khan—both of whom hated me.

"Akhmet Khan had been trying to arrange a marriage between his son and the Khansha's daughter, Sultanetta, but she refused. He blamed me for this. He despised me so much that he sent his men to kill me, but I managed to escape. Then he spread lies about me to General Klugenau, accusing me of telling the Avars not to supply wood to Russian soldiers. He even said that I had put on a turban—this one right here," Hadji Murad said, touching it, "and that it meant I had joined Shamil.

"The general didn't believe him and ordered that I be left alone. But as soon as the general left for Tiflis, Akhmet Khan did whatever he wanted. He sent a group of soldiers to capture me, put me in chains, and tied me to a cannon.

"They kept me like that for six days," Hadji Murad continued. "On the seventh day, they untied me and began taking me to Temir-Khan-Shura. There were forty soldiers, all with loaded guns, escorting me. My hands were tied, and I knew they had orders to kill me if I tried to escape.

"As we got near Mansokha, the path became narrow. On my right, there was a steep drop—about a hundred and twenty yards deep. I walked close to the edge. A soldier tried to pull me back, but I jumped, dragging him down with me. He died instantly, but I, as you can see, survived.

"My ribs, head, arms, and leg were all broken. I tried to crawl but got dizzy and passed out. When I woke up, I was covered in blood. A shepherd found me and called for help. Some villagers carried me to their aoul. My ribs and head healed, and so did my leg, though it remained shorter than before," he said, stretching out his crooked leg. "But it still works, and that's all that matters."

As word spread, people began coming to see him. "I recovered and returned to Tselmess. The Avars called on me to lead them again," he said with quiet but firm pride, "and I agreed."

He stood up quickly, pulled a portfolio from his saddlebag, and took out two old letters, handing one to Loris-Melikov. They were from General Klugenau.

Loris-Melikov read the first one:

"Lieutenant Hadji Murad, you served under me, and I was pleased with you. I believed you to be a good man.

"Akhmet Khan has informed me that you are a traitor, that you have put on a turban and are working with Shamil, and that you have encouraged the people to disobey the Russian government. Because of this, I ordered your arrest. But you escaped. I do not know if this will help or harm you, as I do not know whether you are guilty or not.

"Now listen. If your conscience is clear, if you have done nothing against the great Tsar, come to me. Do not be afraid. I will protect you. Akhmet Khan has no power over you—he is under my command. So you have nothing to fear."

The letter went on to say that Klugenau was an honest man who always kept his word, urging Hadji Murad to come to him.

When Loris-Melikov finished reading, Hadji Murad spoke before handing him the second letter.

"I wrote back explaining that I wore a turban not for Shamil but for my own faith. I told him I had no desire to join Shamil, nor could I, because Shamil was responsible for the deaths of my father, my brothers, and many of my relatives.

"But I also told him I could not serve the Russians either. I had been humiliated by them. In Khunzakh, while I was bound, a man spat on me. I could not fight alongside your people until that man was dead. But most of all, I did not trust Akhmet Khan."

Hadji Murad handed Loris-Melikov the second letter.

Loris-Melikov read:

"You have replied to my first letter, and I thank you. You say that you are not afraid to return, but you refuse because of the insult you suffered. You should know that Russian law is fair, and the man who wronged you will be punished before your very eyes. I have already given orders for an investigation.

"Listen to me, Hadji Murad. I have reason to be disappointed that you do not trust me, but I forgive you because I know how suspicious mountaineers can be. If your conscience is clear, if you wear a turban only for your faith, then you have nothing to fear. You may stand before me and the Russian government without shame. I promise you, the man who dishonored you will be punished, and your property will be returned to you. You will see that Russian law is just.

"Unlike you, we Russians see things differently. The insult you suffered does not lower your worth in our eyes.

"I have allowed the Chimrints to wear turbans, and I understand their customs. So once again, I tell you—there is no need to fear. Come to me with the man delivering this letter. He is loyal to me, not to your enemies, and is a friend of someone highly respected by the government."

The letter continued with more promises, urging Hadji Murad to surrender to the Russians.

"I didn't believe him," Hadji Murad said once Loris-Melikov had finished reading. "So I never went to Klugenau. My priority was revenge against Akhmet Khan, and I knew the Russians wouldn't help me do that.

"Then Akhmet Khan surrounded Tselmess, planning to capture or kill me. I had too few men to fight him off. Around that time, a messenger arrived from Shamil, bringing a letter. He promised to help me defeat and kill Akhmet Khan. He also offered to make me ruler over all of Avaria.

"I thought long and hard about it. In the end, I went to Shamil. From that moment on, I fought the Russians without stopping."

Hadji Murad then described his many battles, some of which Loris-Melikov had already heard about. His campaigns were known for his incredible speed, his daring attacks, and his constant victories.

"There was never any real friendship between me and Shamil," Hadji Murad said as he finished his story. "He feared me, but he also needed me.

"At one point, I was asked who should be Imam after Shamil. I answered, 'The one with the sharpest sword will be Imam.'

"Someone repeated my words to Shamil. After that, he wanted to get rid of me. He sent me to Tabasaran. I went and captured a thousand sheep and three hundred horses. But he claimed I had done the wrong thing. He removed me from my position as Naib and ordered me to hand over all the money. I sent him a thousand gold pieces. Then he sent his men, and they took everything I had left.

"Next, he demanded that I go to him. But I knew he wanted me dead, so I refused. That's when he sent his murids to capture me. I fought back and instead fled to Vorontsov.

"But I could not take my family with me. My mother, my wives, and my son are still in Shamil's hands.

"Tell the Sirdar that as long as Shamil has my family, I can do nothing."

"I will tell him," Loris-Melikov assured him.

"Do everything you can," Hadji Murad said. "What is mine is yours—just help me convince the prince. Right now, I am trapped, and Shamil is holding the other end of the rope."

XIV

On December 20th, Vorontsov wrote a letter in "I didn't write to you in my last message, dear Prince, because I wanted to make a decision about Hadji Murad first. Also, I haven't been feeling well for the past few days.

"In my last letter, I mentioned Hadji Murad's arrival. He got to Tiflis on the 8th, and I met him the next day. Over the past week, I've spoken with him several times, trying to figure out how we might use him in the future and what to do with him now.

"He is deeply worried about his family, and I believe he is being completely honest when he says that as long as they are under Shamil's control, he is helpless. He insists that he cannot serve us or truly show his gratitude for our kindness and forgiveness until he knows his family is safe."

"His concern for his family makes him restless. The people I have assigned to stay with him tell me that he hardly sleeps, barely eats, prays constantly, and only asks to be allowed to go riding—always accompanied by several Cossacks. This is the only form of activity he is used to and the only way he can get some relief. Every day, he comes to me, asking if there is any news about his family. He keeps pleading with me to gather all the prisoners we hold and offer them to Shamil in exchange for his loved ones. He would even be willing to pay a ransom, and there are people who could provide him with the money for that.

"He keeps repeating to me: 'Save my family, and then give me a chance to serve you.' He believes he would be most useful on the Leshghian border and even says, 'If within a month I do not prove my worth to you, punish me however you see fit.'

"I have told him that his request is reasonable, but at the same time, many people among us do not fully trust him while his family remains in the mountains, effectively hostages of Shamil. I assured him that I would do everything possible to gather prisoners at our frontier. However, according to our laws, I cannot provide him with money to ransom his family, beyond whatever amount he can raise himself. I did tell him that I would try to find another way to assist him.

"I was also completely honest with him—I told him that I do not believe Shamil will ever release his family. I warned him that Shamil might try to convince him to return by offering a full pardon, promising to reinstate him in his former position, or even threatening to kill his mother, wives, and six children if he does not surrender. I asked him what he would do if that happened.

"He looked up to the sky, raised his hands, and said that everything is in God's hands. However, he insisted that he would never go back to Shamil because he knows Shamil would never truly forgive him and would likely have him killed. As for his family, he doubted that Shamil would go so far as to harm them. He believed that killing them would only make him more dangerous and that even in Daghestan, there were important people who would try to prevent Shamil from doing such a thing.

"Still, he keeps saying that, for now, his only concern is getting his family back. He has begged me, in the name of God, to help him and allow him to return to an area near Chechnya. There, with the cooperation of our commanders, he believes he could find ways to communicate with his family and get updates on their condition. He also thinks he could gather intelligence on how best to secure their release. According to him, there are people in that region—including some of Shamil's Naibs—who still have ties to him. He believes that among the neutral or Russian-controlled areas, it would be easy, with our help, to establish valuable connections that could be useful to our cause. He says that once his family is safe, he will be able to serve us fully and prove his loyalty.

"He asks to be sent to Grozny, escorted by twenty or thirty specially selected Cossacks. They would protect him from his enemies while also serving as a guarantee of his loyalty to us.

"You can imagine, dear Prince, how difficult this decision is for me. No matter what I choose, the responsibility falls on me. If we trust him completely, it would be extremely risky. But if we want to make sure he has no chance to escape, we would have to imprison him, and I believe that would be both unfair and unwise.

"If we treat him like a prisoner, word will spread quickly across Daghestan, and it will damage our position. There are many people there who are already questioning Shamil's leadership, some even considering openly opposing him. They are watching carefully to see how we handle Hadji Murad, one of Shamil's most respected and fearless warriors, now that he has put himself in our hands. If we lock him up, we will lose the opportunity to turn others against Shamil.

"For that reason, I feel I have made the right choice, even though I know I may be blamed if Hadji Murad decides to escape. In military service, and especially in complicated situations like this, it is nearly impossible to follow a clear and safe path without making mistakes or taking on serious risks. But once I believe a course of action is right, I must follow it—no matter what happens."

"I ask you, dear Prince, to bring this matter to His Majesty the Emperor for his consideration. I would be honored if our most esteemed ruler approves of my decision.

"Everything I have written here, I have also shared with Generals Zavodovsky and Kozlovsky so that Kozlovsky knows how to handle direct communication with Hadji Murad. I have warned Hadji Murad not to take any actions or go anywhere without Kozlovsky's approval. I also told him that it would benefit both of us if he rode with our convoy, so that Shamil could not spread false rumors that we are holding him as a prisoner. However, I made him promise never to go to Vozdvizhensk. My son, who was the first to accept his surrender and whom he considers a close friend, is no longer in command there. If Hadji Murad were to go, it could lead to misunderstandings. Also, Vozdvizhensk is too close to a heavily populated enemy settlement. If he wants to stay in touch with his allies, Grozny is a much safer and better option.

"In addition to the twenty Cossacks he requested to stay close to him, I am also sending Captain Loris-Melikov—a capable, intelligent officer who speaks Tartar and has built a good relationship with Hadji Murad. It seems that Hadji Murad fully trusts him. During the ten days Hadji Murad has been here, he has stayed in the same house as Lieutenant-Colonel Prince Tarkhanov, who commands the Shoushin District and is currently here on official business. Tarkhanov is an excellent officer whom I trust completely. He has also earned Hadji Murad's confidence, and since he speaks Tartar fluently, he has been the main person handling sensitive and secret discussions with him.

"I have spoken with Tarkhanov about Hadji Murad, and he agrees with me that we had only three options—handle things as I have done, imprison Hadji Murad under the strictest security, or remove him from the region altogether. However, the last two choices would have caused us to lose all the advantages of Hadji Murad's conflict with Shamil. They also would have slowed down the growing resistance among the people against Shamil's rule and possibly prevented a future uprising.

"Tarkhanov has no doubts about Hadji Murad's honesty and believes that he is convinced Shamil will never forgive him and will eventually have him executed, no matter what promises of pardon he may offer. The only thing Tarkhanov has noticed that could be a concern is Hadji Murad's strong religious faith. He does not deny that Shamil could try to influence him through that. But as I have already said, Hadji Murad will never believe that Shamil would spare his life if he returned.

"This, dear Prince, is everything I can tell you about this situation."

XV

The report was sent from Tiflis on December 24, 1851. By New Year's Eve, a courier, after exhausting a dozen horses and brutally beating several drivers, delivered it to Prince Chernyshov, who was then the Minister of War. On January 1, 1852, Chernyshov brought Vorontsov's report, along with other documents, to Emperor Nicholas.

Chernyshov disliked Vorontsov. He resented the respect and admiration that Vorontsov received, as well as his vast wealth. Unlike Chernyshov, who had risen from a lower rank, Vorontsov was a true aristocrat. Most of all, Chernyshov was jealous of the Emperor's favoritism toward Vorontsov. Because of this, he always looked for ways to undermine him.

The last time he reported on Caucasian affairs, Chernyshov had managed to turn the Emperor against Vorontsov by pointing out that, due to poor leadership, almost an entire Russian detachment had been wiped out by the mountaineers. This time, he planned to make Vorontsov look bad by criticizing how he handled Hadji Murad. Chernyshov wanted to suggest that Vorontsov was too lenient with the native people, even favoring them over Russians. He planned to argue that allowing Hadji Murad to stay in the Caucasus was a mistake. After all, Hadji Murad could very well be a spy, pretending to have defected while secretly gathering intelligence on Russian defenses. Chernyshov believed the safer option would be to send him to Central Russia, where he could only be trusted after his family was rescued and his loyalty was proven.

But Chernyshov's plan failed—not because of any argument Vorontsov made, but because on that particular New Year's Day, Emperor Nicholas was in a terrible mood. He wasn't willing to listen to anyone, let alone Chernyshov, whom he only tolerated because he was useful. Nicholas actually despised him, knowing that Chernyshov had once tried to have his own relative, Zachary Chernyshov, convicted during the Decembrist trials just so he could claim his estate. Thanks to the Emperor's bad mood, Hadji Murad was allowed to stay in the Caucasus, and his situation remained unchanged. Had Chernyshov chosen a different day to make his case, things might have turned out very differently.

At 9:30 in the morning, through the freezing winter mist, Chernyshov's carriage pulled up to the entrance of the Winter Palace. The temperature was brutally cold—13 degrees below zero. His coachman, a stocky man with a thick beard, sat hunched over on the driver's seat, wearing a bright blue velvet cap with sharp edges. He gave a friendly nod to another coachman, who had been waiting outside for a long time after dropping off Prince Dolgoruky. The second coachman sat on his reins, rubbing his frozen hands together, wrapped in a thick, heavily padded coat.

Chernyshov was dressed in a long cloak with a high collar made of silver beaver fur. On his head, he wore a military hat decorated with cock feathers. He pushed back the bearskin covering his carriage and carefully freed his stiff, frozen feet. He took pride in the fact that he never wore extra shoes in the winter, believing it made him look tougher. With a loud clank of his spurs, he stepped out with a show of confidence, climbed the carpeted palace steps, and entered through the door, which a porter respectfully opened for him.

Inside, an elderly servant quickly stepped forward to take his coat. Chernyshov walked to a large mirror, took off his three-cornered hat, and adjusted his wig. With a practiced motion, he smoothed the curls at his temples and the tuft of hair above his forehead. Then he straightened his uniform, making sure his medals, shoulder knots, and large epaulets were perfectly in place.

He climbed the gently sloping stairs, though his aging legs struggled slightly with the steps. As he passed through the hallway, royal servants in their formal uniforms bowed deeply as he walked by.

When he reached the waiting room, he was greeted by a young aide-de-camp who had recently been assigned to the Emperor. The officer's uniform was spotless, his epaulets and shoulder knots shining as if they had never been worn before. His face was fresh and youthful, with a small black mustache. His sideburns were styled in a way that mimicked the Emperor's own look.

Prince Vasili Dolgoruky, the Assistant Minister of War, greeted Chernyshov with a bored expression. His dull face was framed by whiskers, mustaches, and carefully styled hair, mimicking Emperor Nicholas's look.

"The Emperor?" Chernyshov asked the aide-de-camp, glancing toward the door leading to the office.

"His Majesty has just arrived," the aide-de-camp replied, clearly enjoying the sound of his own voice. He walked toward the door with such careful precision that, had he balanced a glass of water on his head, not a drop would have spilled. With great reverence, he stepped inside and disappeared.

Meanwhile, Dolgoruky checked his portfolio to make sure all the necessary documents were inside. Chernyshov, frowning, paced the room, trying to warm his cold feet while reviewing what he planned to say to the Emperor. Just as he reached the office door, it opened again. The aide-de-camp reappeared, looking even more respectful than before, and motioned for the minister and his assistant to enter.

The Winter Palace had been rebuilt after a fire, but Nicholas still preferred to stay in the rooms on the upper floor. His office was a big room with high ceilings and four tall windows. A huge painting of Emperor Alexander I hung on the front wall. Between the windows, there were two desks, and several chairs were neatly lined up against the walls. In the middle of the room sat a large writing table with a big armchair for Nicholas and extra chairs for visitors.

Nicholas sat at his desk, wearing a black coat with shoulder straps but no decorations. His large body was squeezed into his uniform to hide his growing belly. He leaned back in his chair, watching as the men entered. His pale face, framed by carefully styled hair that blended smoothly into his wig, looked even colder and more lifeless than usual. His tired eyes seemed dull, his thin lips were pressed tightly under his curled mustache, and the stiff high collar holding up his chin only made him seem more annoyed. His freshly shaved cheeks, along with his neatly trimmed sideburns, added to the impression that he was in a bad mood.

His foul mood came from exhaustion. The night before, he had attended a masquerade ball. As always, he had walked confidently among the crowd, dressed in his Horse Guards' uniform with a decorative bird on his helmet. Wherever he passed, people stepped aside respectfully, intimidated by his towering presence.

At the previous masquerade, he had noticed a masked woman with striking beauty, pale skin, and a soft voice that had stirred his interest. She had disappeared that night but had promised to meet him again at the next ball.

When he spotted her again at the most recent masquerade, he did not let her slip away. He led her to a private box, specially reserved for moments like these, where they could be alone. When they reached the door, Nicholas glanced around for the attendant, but no one was there. Annoyed, he pushed the door open himself and let the woman step inside first.

"There's someone here!" she whispered, stopping abruptly.

Inside, a young officer from the Uhlan regiment was sitting close to a fair-haired woman who had removed her mask. They were leaning into each other on the small velvet sofa. When they saw Nicholas, the woman hurriedly pulled her mask back on. The officer, frozen in fear, simply stared at the Emperor, unable to move.

Nicholas was used to seeing people terrified of him, and he enjoyed it. At times, he liked to surprise them by acting friendly. This was one of those times.

"Well, my friend," he said to the officer, "you're younger than I am—you should give up your seat for me."

The officer jumped up instantly. His face turned pale, then bright red. Bowing deeply, he silently hurried out of the box, leading his companion away.

Now alone with the masked woman, Nicholas soon learned that she was only about twenty years old, the daughter of a Swedish governess. She confessed that she had fallen in love with him as a child, just from seeing his portraits. She adored him and had planned for years to get his attention. Now that she had succeeded, she wanted nothing more—at least, that's what she told him.

Nicholas took her to his usual private location, where he spent over an hour with her.

Later that night, when he returned to his room, he lay on his small, stiff bed, which he took pride in using. He pulled his cloak over himself—the same cloak he often compared to Napoleon's famous hat. Sleep didn't come easily. He kept thinking about the young woman's excited and nervous expression. Then, his mind drifted to his longtime mistress, Nelidova, and her fuller, stronger figure. He found himself comparing the two.

He never once thought he had done anything wrong, even though he was a married man. If anyone had pointed it out, he would have been truly shocked.

Still, even with his confidence, a feeling of unease lingered. To ignore it, he clung to the one idea that always gave him comfort—the belief in his own greatness.

Even though he had gone to bed late, he was up before eight. He followed his usual morning routine—rubbing his large, well-fed body with ice—and then said his prayers. He repeated the same ones he had learned as a child, including the prayer to the Virgin, the Apostles' Creed, and the Lord's Prayer, but the words had little meaning to him. Afterward, he left the palace through a smaller entrance, wearing his military cloak and cap, and walked toward the embankment.

There, he came across a student in the uniform of the School of Jurisprudence. The young man was just as tall as he was. Nicholas frowned when he recognized the uniform since he disliked the school for its more open-minded views. But seeing how serious the student looked as he stood tall and saluted, sticking out his elbow on purpose, softened Nicholas's irritation.

"What's your name?" he asked.

"Polosatov, Your Imperial Majesty."

"...Good man!"

The student remained still, his hand firmly raised in salute.

Nicholas paused. "Do you want to join the army?"

"Not at all, Your Imperial Majesty."

"Fool!" Nicholas muttered before turning away and continuing his walk. He began saying random words aloud, not paying attention to their meaning.

"Kopervine… Kopervine…" he repeated a few times. It was the name of a girl from the night before. "Terrible… terrible…" He wasn't really thinking about what he was saying—he was just trying to push away his feelings.

"Where would Russia be without me?" he wondered as frustration returned. "Not just Russia—what about all of Europe?" Thinking about his brother-in-law, the King of Prussia, and how weak and clueless he was, Nicholas shook his head.

As he neared the small entrance to the palace, he noticed a carriage approaching. It belonged to Helena Pavlovna, and her footman wore a bright red uniform.

To Nicholas, Helena Pavlovna represented a group of people he found annoying—those who not only talked about science and poetry but also thought they knew how to govern a country better than he did. He knew that no matter how much he tried to suppress such ideas, people like her always reappeared. His thoughts drifted to his brother, Michael Pavlovich, who had passed away recently. A mix of sadness and irritation settled over him, and once again, he started mumbling meaningless words under his breath. He only stopped when he stepped back inside the palace.

Returning to his private rooms, he adjusted his whiskers, smoothed the hair at his temples, and straightened his wig. He twisted the ends of his mustache upward in front of the mirror before heading straight to his office to receive reports.

The first person he met was Chernyshov, who immediately noticed that Nicholas was in an especially bad mood. Knowing about what had happened the night before, Chernyshov had a good idea why. Nicholas greeted him coolly, motioned for him to sit, and fixed him with a blank stare.

Chernyshov started his report. First, he talked about a recently uncovered case of government officials stealing money. Then, he gave Nicholas an update on troop movements near the Prussian border. After that, he listed people who had been mistakenly left out of the New Year's honors and needed to be included. He then shared a report from Vorontsov about Hadji Murad. Finally, he mentioned a disturbing event—a medical student had tried to harm a professor.

Nicholas listened to the report about the embezzlement without saying a word. His lips were pressed together, and his large white hand, which had a single ring on the fourth finger, absentmindedly stroked some papers. His eyes remained fixed on Chernyshov's forehead, particularly on the small tuft of hair above it.

Nicholas believed that everyone in government stole. He knew he had to punish the commissariat officials now and decided to send them to serve as regular soldiers. But he also knew that those who replaced them would likely do the same thing. Corruption was just a part of how officials behaved, and even though he was tired of dealing with it, he knew it was his duty to punish them.

"It seems there is only one honest man in Russia!" he said.

Chernyshov immediately understood that Nicholas was talking about himself and gave him an approving smile.

"It certainly looks that way, Your Imperial Majesty," he replied.

"Leave it—I will decide what to do," Nicholas said, taking the document and placing it on the left side of the table.

Chernyshov then moved on to the next topics—rewards for the New Year and troop movements near the Prussian border.

Nicholas looked at the list of names, crossed some out, and then firmly ordered two divisions to be moved closer to Prussia. He still hadn't forgiven the King of Prussia for allowing his people to have a constitution after the revolutions of 1848. While Nicholas acted friendly toward his brother-in-law in letters and conversations, he felt it was necessary to keep an army near the border just in case. He might need those troops to protect the Prussian throne if the people there decided to rebel—he always saw the potential for uprisings everywhere. A few years earlier, he had sent troops to put down the revolution in Hungary, and these soldiers could serve the same purpose. Keeping them there also made his advice to the King of Prussia carry more weight.

"Yes… what would Russia be like without me?" he thought again.

"What else is there?" he asked.

"A courier from the Caucasus," Chernyshov answered, then reported what Vorontsov had written about Hadji Murad's surrender.

"Well, well!" Nicholas said. "That's a good start!"

"It's clear that Your Majesty's strategy is working," Chernyshov added.

Nicholas was especially pleased to hear this. He liked to think of himself as a brilliant strategist, but deep down, he knew that wasn't really true. He now wanted to hear more praise.

"What do you mean?" he asked.

"I mean that if Your Majesty's approach had been followed earlier—moving forward slowly, cutting down forests, and destroying their food supplies—the Caucasus would have been conquered long ago. Hadji Murad must have realized that they can't hold out any longer."

"That's right," Nicholas agreed.

In reality, this slow approach of advancing by cutting forests and destroying supplies had been developed by Ermolov and Velyaminov, not Nicholas. His own strategy had been very different—he believed in launching direct attacks, like the 1845 campaign to take Shamil's stronghold, which had resulted in heavy losses. But now, he convinced himself that the slow and steady strategy had been his idea all along. Somehow, he managed to take pride in both plans, even though they completely contradicted each other.

Years of constant flattery from those around him had made him blind to these contradictions. He no longer questioned whether his orders made sense. To him, everything he commanded—no matter how unfair, illogical, or inconsistent—was automatically the right decision simply because he had made it.

His next decision, regarding the case of the medical student, was a perfect example of this kind of thinking.

The case was as follows: A young man had already failed his exams twice and was being tested for a third time. When he failed again, he became overwhelmed with frustration. His nerves were on edge, and he believed he was being treated unfairly. In a sudden outburst of anger, he grabbed a small penknife from the table and lunged at the professor, causing a few minor injuries.

Nicholas looked up. "What's his name?" he asked.

"Bzhezovski."

"A Pole?"

"He's of Polish descent and a Roman Catholic," Chernyshov answered.

Nicholas frowned. He had done terrible things to the Polish people. To justify it, he convinced himself that all Poles were dishonest. The more harm he caused them, the more he hated them.

"Wait a moment," he said, closing his eyes and lowering his head.

Chernyshov had seen this many times before. Whenever Nicholas had to make a decision, he would pause, as if waiting for inspiration, and then choose what he believed was the best option with absolute confidence. This time, he was thinking about how to punish the student in a way that satisfied his hatred of the Poles. The answer came to him quickly.

He grabbed the report and scribbled a note in large, clumsy handwriting, making three spelling mistakes:

"Deserves death, but thank God we have no capital punishment, and it is not for me to introduce it. Make him run the gauntlet of a thousand men twelve times. — Nicholas."

He signed it with a dramatic flourish.

Nicholas knew that this punishment—twelve thousand blows with military rods—was not just a death sentence, but a slow, painful one. He also knew that even five thousand strokes were enough to kill a strong man. But he took pleasure in being ruthless, while also telling himself that Russia had abolished the death penalty.

When he was done, he slid the paper toward Chernyshov.

"There," he said. "Read it."

Chernyshov read the order and nodded, pretending to admire Nicholas's wisdom.

"Yes, and make sure all the students watch," Nicholas added. "They need to learn a lesson! I will crush their rebellious spirit completely," he thought.

"It will be done," Chernyshov said. He smoothed his hair and moved on to the next report.

"What should I write in response to Prince Vorontsov's message?" he asked.

"Tell him to follow my orders—burn their homes, destroy their food, and keep attacking them," Nicholas replied.

"And what about Hadji Murad?" Chernyshov asked.

"Well, Vorontsov wants to use him in the Caucasus."

"Isn't that risky?" Chernyshov asked cautiously, avoiding Nicholas's eyes. "I fear Prince Vorontsov is too trusting."

"What do you think?" Nicholas asked sharply, noticing that Chernyshov was trying to make Vorontsov's decision seem foolish.

"I would have thought it was safer to send him to Central Russia," Chernyshov suggested.

"You would have thought?" Nicholas repeated mockingly. "I don't think so. I agree with Vorontsov. Write to him accordingly."

"It will be done," Chernyshov said, bowing before leaving.

Dolgoruky, who had barely spoken except to answer a question about army movements, also bowed and left.

Next, Nicholas met with Bibikov, the Governor-General of the Western Provinces. He praised him for the way he handled rebellious peasants who refused to convert to the Orthodox faith. Then, he ordered that those who continued to resist should be tried by a military court—just a formality before sentencing them to death by running the gauntlet.

He also commanded that a newspaper editor be forced to serve as a common soldier for publishing news about the transfer of thousands of state peasants to imperial land.

"I am doing this because it is necessary," Nicholas said. "And I will not allow anyone to question it."

Bibikov knew how cruel this was. He also understood that moving state peasants—who were among the only free peasants in Russia—meant turning them into royal serfs. But he also knew that if he disagreed, he would lose everything he had worked for over forty years to achieve. So, he simply bowed his head and accepted the orders without protest.

When the meeting ended, Nicholas stretched, feeling satisfied with his decisions. He glanced at the clock, then went to get dressed for the day's events.

He changed into a formal uniform decorated with medals, epaulets, and a ribbon, then stepped into the reception hall. Over a hundred people—men in military uniforms and women in elegant dresses—stood in their assigned places, waiting anxiously for his arrival.

Nicholas entered, standing stiff and upright, his chest pushed forward, his stomach pressing against his tight uniform. Feeling the weight of every eye in the room, he straightened even more, making himself seem even more powerful. As he walked, he stopped to speak with people he recognized, switching between Russian and French. He listened to them with a cold, piercing gaze.

After receiving New Year's greetings, he went to church. Just like the courtiers, the priests praised him endlessly. Even though he was tired of all the ceremonies, he accepted their admiration as something natural. He believed that the happiness and stability of the world depended on him, so even when exhausted, he would not deny people his presence.

At the end of the service, the choir sang a chant for his long life. As their deep voices filled the church, Nicholas's eyes wandered across the room. He spotted a woman, Nelidova, standing near a window. Comparing her to the girl from the night before, he decided that Nelidova was the better of the two.

After church, he spent a short time with his family, joking with his children and speaking with his wife. Then, as he passed through the Hermitage, he stopped to see Volkonski, the Minister of the Court. Among other things, he ordered that a yearly pension be given to the mother of the girl he had been with the night before, paid from a special fund.

Later, he went for his usual afternoon drive.

That evening, dinner was held in the Pompeian Hall. Along with his younger sons, the guests included Baron Lieven, Count Rzhevski, Dolgoruky, the Prussian Ambassador, and the aide-de-camp of the King of Prussia.

As they waited for the Emperor and Empress to arrive, Baron Lieven and the Prussian Ambassador talked about the latest troubling news from Poland.

"Poland and the Caucasus—those are Russia's biggest problems," Lieven said. "We need at least ten thousand troops in each region."

The Ambassador raised an eyebrow.

"You say Poland—?" he began.

"Oh yes, it was clever of Metternich to leave us to deal with that problem alone…"

At that moment, the Empress entered, smiling slightly as her head trembled. Nicholas followed her into the room.

During dinner, Nicholas spoke about Hadji Murad's surrender, saying the war in the Caucasus would soon end because of his strategy. He explained his plan: limit the movement of the mountain tribes by cutting down their forests and building small forts.

The Prussian Ambassador glanced at the aide-de-camp. That morning, they had spoken about Nicholas's tendency to see himself as a brilliant military strategist. Now, they knew they had to flatter him.

"What an excellent plan!" the Ambassador said, praising Nicholas's military genius.

After dinner, Nicholas attended the ballet, where hundreds of dancers performed in revealing costumes. One of them caught his eye, so he called for the German ballet master and ordered that she be given a diamond ring.

The next morning, Chernyshov returned with reports. Nicholas repeated his orders to Vorontsov—now that Hadji Murad had surrendered, the Chechens should be attacked even more aggressively, and the blockade around them should be tightened.

Chernyshov wrote the orders, and another courier set off at full speed toward Tiflis, pushing his horses to their limits and leaving another trail of exhausted, beaten drivers behind him.

XVI

Following Nicholas's orders, a raid was carried out in Chechnya that same month, January 1852.

The unit assigned for the mission included four infantry battalions, two companies of Cossacks, and eight cannons. As the column moved forward, soldiers in tall boots, sheepskin coats, and fur hats marched alongside it, climbing up and down the uneven terrain with rifles slung over their shoulders and ammunition strapped to their belts.

Since they were passing through enemy land, they kept as quiet as possible. The only sounds were the occasional clatter of weapons, a cannon jolting as it crossed a ditch, or a horse snorting, unaware that silence had been ordered. Sometimes, a frustrated officer would mutter sharply at his men for walking too far from the column or spreading out too much.

The silence was only broken once when a gazelle with a white chest and gray back leaped out from a patch of bushes, followed closely by another with small, curved horns. Startled, the animals bounded toward the soldiers. Some men, laughing and shouting, tried to chase them down with their bayonets, but the gazelles quickly darted through the line and disappeared toward the mountains, pursued briefly by a few horsemen and barking dogs.

Though it was still winter, the sun had risen high by midday, making the soldiers sweat. Its brightness was almost blinding, reflecting sharply off the steel bayonets and gleaming brass cannons. Behind them, they had just crossed a fast-flowing stream, while ahead lay open fields and meadows leading toward dark, forested hills. Beyond the trees, jagged rocks jutted out, and far in the distance, snow-covered peaks shimmered in the light like diamonds.

Leading the 5th Company was Butler, a tall, striking officer who had recently transferred from the Guards. He marched in a black coat and tall cap, holding his sword at his side. He felt a rush of excitement—a mix of joy, danger, and the thrill of being part of something vast, all moving under a single command. This was only his second time heading into battle, and he imagined the moment the enemy would start firing. He saw himself standing tall, refusing to duck when shells flew overhead, his expression calm and confident as he looked around at his fellow officers and soldiers, even making casual conversation as if nothing was happening.

The unit turned off the main road onto a rough, barely used path cutting through a dried-out maize field. As they neared the forest, a sudden sharp whistling sound sliced through the air. A shell landed near the baggage wagons, exploding into the dirt.

"It's starting," Butler said with a grin, glancing at the officer beside him.

And he was right. Moments later, a large group of Chechen horsemen appeared from behind the trees, waving their banners. In the center of the group, a tall green flag stood out, and an old sergeant, known for his sharp eyesight, pointed it out to Butler. "That must be Shamil himself," he said, referring to the famous leader.

The horsemen rode down the hill, aiming for the highest point in the valley nearest to the advancing soldiers. Just then, a short general in a thick black coat and fur cap trotted up on his horse and gave Butler new orders—move to the right to intercept the attackers.

Without hesitation, Butler led his men in that direction, but before they reached the valley, the thunder of cannon fire erupted behind them. Turning back, he saw thick clouds of smoke rising from two cannons. The Chechen riders, clearly not expecting artillery, immediately changed course and pulled back.

As the enemy retreated, Butler's soldiers opened fire, filling the valley with thick smoke. The mountaineers were still firing back as they scrambled up the hills, but the Cossacks chased them relentlessly. Butler's company pushed forward, and soon they spotted a village nestled in the next ravine.

Following the Cossacks, Butler and his men rushed into the village, only to find it abandoned. The soldiers were ordered to burn everything—grain, hay, and houses. Soon, thick smoke filled the air as men moved through the village, dragging out whatever they could find. Some ran after chickens left behind, laughing as they caught and shot them.

The officers sat a little way from the smoke, eating and drinking. The sergeant-major brought them honeycombs on a wooden board. There was no sign of any Chechens, and by early afternoon, the order was given to retreat. The soldiers formed into a column behind the village, with Butler's company assigned to the rear guard.

As soon as they began moving, Chechen fighters appeared, trailing behind them and firing shots. But once the soldiers reached open ground, the attacks stopped.

None of Butler's men were injured, and he returned in high spirits, feeling full of energy. When they forded the same river they had crossed that morning, the troops spread out over the maize fields and grassy meadows. Soon, each company's singers stepped forward, and their voices filled the air with marching songs.

"Very different, very different, Fagers are, Fagers are!" sang the men from Butler's unit. His horse trotted in rhythm with the tune, while the company's shaggy gray dog, Trezorka, ran ahead, its tail curled up like a commander leading the way.

Butler felt lighthearted and confident. To him, war seemed simple—it was about facing danger, risking death, and earning rewards. His comrades admired him, and he knew that his friends back in Russia would too. Strangely, he never thought about the darker side of war—the deaths and injuries of soldiers, officers, and enemy fighters. He avoided looking at the fallen, as if ignoring them would keep his idealized view of battle intact. So, when three soldiers were killed and twelve wounded that day, he barely glanced at the body of a fallen man lying on his back. He only caught a glimpse of a stiff, pale hand and a dark red stain on the man's head before walking past without stopping. To Butler, the enemy was nothing more than mounted warriors he had to fight off.

"You see, my friend," said Major Petrov, during a break between songs, "this isn't like Petersburg—'Eyes right! Eyes left!' Here, we do our job, then we go home, and Masha sets a pie and some good cabbage soup on the table. That's what life is all about, don't you think? Now, let's have 'As the Dawn Was Breaking!'" he called out, requesting his favorite song.

The air was crisp and clear, with no wind. The snowy mountains, though nearly a hundred miles away, looked so sharp and bright that they seemed much closer. Between songs, the steady rhythm of boots hitting the ground and the occasional jingle of weapons filled the silence.

The song Butler's company sang had been written by a cadet in honor of their regiment. It had a lively dance tune, with a chorus that repeated, "Very different, very different, Fagers are, Fagers are!"

Riding beside Major Petrov, Butler felt deeply grateful for his decision to leave the Guards and come to the Caucasus. The real reason he had transferred was because he had lost everything he owned gambling. He feared that if he stayed in Petersburg, he wouldn't be able to resist playing again, even though he had nothing left to lose. But here, everything was different. His old life—filled with smoky card rooms, lost bets, and the bitterness of watching others win—was gone. In its place was this thrilling, adventurous life in the Caucasus, surrounded by soldiers, officers, and battle-hardened men. The war, the camaraderie, the wild, untamed land—it all felt too good to be real.

Major Petrov lived with the daughter of a military surgeon's assistant. Her name had once been Masha, but now she was called Marya Dmitrievna, a more formal name. She was a fair-haired, heavily freckled woman in her thirties. Though she had no children, she had become a devoted companion to Petrov, taking care of him like a nurse—a necessary role, since he often drank himself into oblivion.

When they arrived at the fort, everything happened just as the major had predicted. Marya Dmitrievna welcomed them with a warm, hearty meal. Butler, the major, and two other officers from the unit sat down to eat, enjoying the rich food and plentiful drinks. The major kept drinking until he could no longer speak, then stumbled off to his room to sleep.

Butler, having had more chikhir wine than was wise, went to his own quarters, feeling tired but deeply content. He barely managed to take off his uniform before collapsing onto his bed, falling into a deep, dreamless sleep, his hand tucked under his curly head.

XVII

The home that had been destroyed was the same one where Hadji Murad had spent the night before joining the Russians. When the Russian troops approached, Sado and his family had fled the village. When they returned, they found their house in ruins—the roof had collapsed, the doorway was burned, and the inside was a mess.

Sado's son, the bright-eyed boy who had looked at Hadji Murad with such admiration, was brought back to the village, lifeless. His small body was draped over a horse covered with a rough cloak. He had been stabbed in the back with a bayonet.

The boy's mother, the same woman who had served Hadji Murad when he was in their home, now stood over her son's body in despair. Her smock was torn open, her gray hair hung loose, and her face was streaked with blood where she had clawed at it in grief. She wailed without stopping.

Meanwhile, Sado picked up a spade and a pickaxe and went with his relatives to dig his son's grave. The old grandfather sat quietly by the wrecked house, carving a stick and staring blankly ahead. He had just returned from his beekeeping area, only to find everything destroyed. The two stacks of hay had been burned, the apricot and cherry trees he had planted were broken and scorched, and worst of all, all the beehives were gone, the bees burned along with them.

All around the village, the sounds of crying filled the air. Women sobbed, and small children clung to their mothers, wailing alongside them. Even the cattle, left without food, lowed hungrily. The older children, usually busy playing, now wandered silently, their wide eyes filled with fear.

The destruction had been deliberate. The village fountain had been polluted, making the water undrinkable. The mosque had been defiled in the same way, and the mullah and his assistants were working to clean it.

No one spoke of revenge. Their feelings went beyond hatred. They did not even see the Russians as humans but as creatures—like venomous spiders, rats, or wild wolves. Their cruelty was so senseless and disgusting that wiping them out seemed as natural as defending oneself from a deadly threat.

Now, the villagers faced a terrible decision. They could stay and try to rebuild everything that had been so cruelly and needlessly destroyed, knowing that at any moment, the Russians might return and do it all over again. Or they could surrender, even though it went against their faith and filled them with disgust and shame.

The elders gathered to pray. In the end, they all agreed—they would send envoys to Shamil and ask for his help. And without wasting any time, the villagers got to work, determined to rebuild what had been lost.

XVIII

The morning after the raid, Butler stepped out onto the back porch, wanting to take a short walk and get some fresh air before breakfast, which he usually had with Petrov. The sun was already high in the sky, and the bright light reflecting off the white walls of the houses on the right side of the street made it difficult to look in that direction. Instead, he turned to the left, where the dark green hills rose and fell, leading up to the distant snow-covered peaks that always looked like they could be clouds. Breathing in deeply, he felt a rush of happiness—he was alive, in this beautiful place, and it felt good just to exist in that moment.

He was also feeling quite proud of himself. He had done well in the raid the day before, both during the attack and especially during the retreat, when things had gotten intense. He also thought back to the dinner that Marya Dmitrievna—Petrov's mistress—had prepared for them when they returned. She had been warm and welcoming to everyone, but Butler liked to think she had been especially kind to him.

Marya Dmitrievna, with her thick braid of hair, broad shoulders, and high, full chest, had a warmth and friendliness that drew him in. Her face, freckled but always smiling, made her even more appealing. As a young, healthy bachelor, Butler couldn't help but notice her, and at times, he even thought she might be interested in him too. But he respected Petrov, his good-natured and simple-hearted friend, and he felt that getting involved with her would be wrong. So he kept his distance, treating her with politeness and restraint, and felt pleased with himself for doing so.

He was lost in these thoughts when the sound of many horses approaching snapped him back to reality. Hooves clattered against the dusty road, and he looked up to see a group of horsemen coming toward him at a slow pace. Leading the group of about twenty Cossacks were two men—one in a white Circassian coat with a tall turban wrapped around his head, the other an officer in a Russian uniform, with dark features, a sharp nose, and silver decorations on his clothing and weapons.

The man in the turban rode a strong chestnut horse with a flowing mane and tail in a lighter shade. Its small head and intelligent eyes made it clear that it was a fine animal. The officer rode a large, well-built Karabakh horse. Butler, who loved horses, immediately noticed the power and quality of the first horse and stopped to get a better look at the riders.

The officer turned to him. "This the house of commanding officer?" he asked in broken Russian, his accent making it clear he was not a native speaker.

Butler nodded. "Yes, it is," he answered. Then, looking at the man in the turban, he asked, "And who is that?"

"That Hadji Murad. He come here to stay with the commander," the officer replied.

Butler had heard about Hadji Murad and knew he had recently joined the Russians, but he hadn't expected to see him here, in this small fort. Hadji Murad met his gaze with a friendly look.

"Good day, Kotkildy," Butler said, repeating a Tartar greeting he had learned.

"Saubul!" ("Be well!") Hadji Murad replied with a nod. He rode up closer and extended his hand, holding his whip between two fingers.

"You the chief?" he asked.

"No, the chief is inside. I'll go get him," Butler said, turning to the officer.

He climbed the steps to the entrance and pushed the door, but it was locked. He knocked, but no one answered. Frowning, he walked around to the back door. He called for his orderly but got no response. Neither of the two orderlies was anywhere to be seen.

Finally, he stepped into the kitchen, where Marya Dmitrievna was busy making pies. A scarf was tied around her head, and her sleeves were rolled up, revealing her plump, fair arms. She was rolling out dough, cutting it into small pieces, and shaping it into pastries, her hands covered in flour.

"Where are the orderlies?" Butler asked.

"They went off drinking," she answered without looking up. "What do you need?"

"I need the front door opened. There's a whole crowd of mountaineers outside. Hadji Murad is here!"

Marya Dmitrievna glanced up and smirked. "Come up with a better joke."

"I'm serious—he's standing by the porch!"

"Are you really telling the truth?" she asked, setting down her dough.

"Why would I lie? Go see for yourself. He's right there at the entrance!"

"Oh no, here we go!" said Marya Dmitrievna as she pulled down her sleeves and checked her thick braid to make sure her hairpins were in place. "I'll go wake up Ivan Matveich."

"No, I'll do it myself. And you, Bondarenko, go open the door," he told Petrov's assistant, who had just arrived.

"Alright, that works for me!" said Marya Dmitrievna, then went back to what she was doing.

When Ivan Matveich Petrov, the major, heard that Hadji Murad was at his house, he wasn't surprised at all. He already knew Hadji Murad had arrived in Grozny. Still in bed, he sat up, rolled a cigarette, lit it, and started getting dressed, grumbling loudly about the higher-ups who had sent "that devil" to him.

Once he was ready, he told his assistant to bring him his "medicine." The assistant knew that "medicine" really meant vodka and brought him some.

"Mixing drinks is the worst," the major muttered after taking a shot and biting into a piece of rye bread. "Had some chikhir yesterday, and now I've got a headache... Alright, I'm ready," he said and walked into the sitting room. Butler had already led Hadji Murad and the officer who came with him inside.

The officer handed the major a written order from the commander of the left flank. It said that the major should let Hadji Murad stay and allow him to communicate with the mountain people through spies—but under no circumstances should he leave the fort without a group of Cossack guards.

After reading the order, the major stared at Hadji Murad, then back at the paper. He did this several times before finally locking eyes with Hadji Murad and saying, "Alright, Bek, alright! He can stay here, but tell him I have strict orders not to let him out. Orders are orders!" Then he turned to Butler. "Where do you think we should put him? The office?"

Before Butler could respond, Marya Dmitrievna, who had just come from the kitchen, spoke up from the doorway. "Why not keep him here? He can stay in the guest room and the storeroom. That way, we can keep an eye on him," she said, glancing at Hadji Murad. But when their eyes met, she quickly looked away.

"You know, I think Marya Dmitrievna has a good point," Butler added.

"Enough, enough! This isn't women's business," the major said, frowning.

Hadji Murad sat silently through the conversation, resting his hand on his dagger and smirking slightly. He said it didn't matter to him where he stayed, as long as he was allowed to contact the mountain people, just as the Sirdar had agreed.

The major assured him that this would be arranged and asked Butler to keep their guests company while food was prepared and their rooms were set up. Meanwhile, he himself would go to the office to take care of the necessary paperwork and give some orders.

Hadji Murad's relationships with the people in the fort became clear from the start. He immediately disliked the major and treated him with arrogance. But he had a different attitude toward Marya Dmitrievna, who prepared and served his meals. He liked her kindness and, more than that, found her beauty unusual and intriguing. He could sense that she was drawn to him, which affected him in ways he didn't want to admit. He tried not to look at her or talk to her, but his eyes kept following her movements anyway.

With Butler, however, he became friendly right away. They had long conversations—Hadji Murad asked about Butler's life and shared details about his own. He even told Butler the news his spies brought about his family and asked for his advice on what to do next.

Unfortunately, the news from the spies was bad. In the first four days of his stay, they visited twice, and each time, they had nothing but bad news.

XIX

After Hadji Murad left to join the Russians, his family was taken to Vedeno and kept under guard while waiting for Shamil's decision. His elderly mother, Patimat, along with his two wives and their five young children, were locked inside the home of an officer named Ibrahim Raschid. Meanwhile, Hadji Murad's 18-year-old son, Yusuf, was thrown into a prison pit over seven feet deep, along with seven criminals who were also waiting to learn their fate.

Shamil's decision was delayed because he was away fighting the Russians.

On January 6, 1852, he returned to Vedeno after a battle. The Russians claimed he had lost and fled, but he and his warriors insisted they had won and pushed the Russians back. During the fight, he had personally fired his rifle—a rare thing for him to do—and had even drawn his sword, ready to charge. His men had to hold him back, and two of them were killed right beside him.

It was midday when Shamil, surrounded by his devoted warriors, rode into town. His men showed off, firing their rifles and pistols while singing "Lya illya il Allah!" The entire village came out to see him, standing in the streets and on rooftops. As a sign of victory, they also fired their weapons into the air.

Shamil rode a white Arabian horse that pulled against its reins as they neared his home. The horse's gear was simple—no gold or silver, just a red leather bridle with a stripe down the middle, metal stirrups, and a red saddlecloth barely visible under the saddle. Shamil himself wore a brown cloak lined with black fur, tightly fastened around his slim waist with a black belt that held a dagger. His tall cap had a black tassel, and a white turban was wrapped around it, one end hanging down his back. He wore green slippers and black leggings with simple trim.

He had no flashy decorations—no gold or silver. Dressed plainly, yet standing tall and commanding, he was surrounded by warriors whose outfits sparkled with metal and fine details. This contrast was intentional. Shamil knew exactly how to make an impression. His pale face, framed by a reddish beard, remained expressionless. His eyes were always squinting, giving him a look as if his face had been carved from stone. As he passed through the village, hundreds of eyes followed him, but he looked at no one.

Hadji Murad's wives stepped outside with the rest of the household to watch Shamil's arrival. Only his mother, Patimat, stayed inside. Sitting on the floor with her gray hair loose, she wrapped her long arms around her thin knees and stared at the dying fire. Her dark eyes burned with hatred. She had despised Shamil for years, just like her son, and now she hated him even more. She had no interest in seeing him.

Hadji Murad's son, Yusuf, also missed the event. Sitting in the dark, smelly pit of his prison, he could only hear the gunfire and chanting from above. It was a torture beyond words for someone so young and full of life to be trapped like this. Instead of fresh air and freedom, all he could see were the other prisoners—weak, bitter, and filled with resentment toward one another. He burned with envy for those outside, who got to ride their horses freely, circling around their leader, shouting and firing their weapons in celebration.

After riding through the village, Shamil entered a large courtyard that led to his private quarters. Two armed guards stood by the open gate, watching as a crowd of people filled the courtyard. Some had traveled from far away to ask for help, others had come with requests, and some were there because Shamil had summoned them for judgment.

As soon as he entered, the crowd greeted him with deep respect—some placed their hands on their chests, while others knelt and stayed on their knees as he passed. Shamil recognized many faces in the crowd, including people he disliked and those who often came to him with tedious requests. But he ignored them all, keeping the same cold, unreadable expression as he made his way through.

Once he reached his private courtyard, he dismounted at the entrance of his residence. He was exhausted—not physically, but mentally. Despite claiming victory, he knew the truth: the campaign had been a failure. Many Chechen villages had been burned and destroyed. The people, who were always quick to change sides, were beginning to doubt him. Those closest to the Russian border were even considering surrendering to the enemy.

Shamil had many things to deal with, and it weighed heavily on him. At that moment, he didn't want to think about anything. All he wanted was to rest, spend time with his family, and enjoy the company of his favorite wife, Aminal—a lively, dark-eyed eighteen-year-old. He was certain she was just on the other side of the fence that separated the men's and women's quarters, peeking through a small gap as he got off his horse. But he couldn't go to her. In fact, he couldn't even relax on his soft cushions.

First, he had to perform the midday prayers. He didn't feel like doing it, but as the religious leader of his people, he had no choice. Besides, prayer was as much a part of his life as eating. So, he performed his ritual washing, said his prayers, and then called in those who were waiting to speak with him.

The first to enter was Jemal Eddin—his father-in-law and former teacher. He was a tall, dignified old man with white hair, a snow-colored beard, and a reddish face. After saying a prayer, he started asking Shamil about the recent battle and updating him on what had happened in the mountains while he was away.

There had been many incidents—murders from ongoing blood feuds, stolen cattle, and people caught breaking religious laws by drinking wine or smoking. But one report stood out: Hadji Murad had tried to have his family smuggled over to the Russians. His men had been caught, and the family was brought back to Vedeno, where they were now under guard, waiting for Shamil's decision.

In the next room, a group of Elders had gathered to discuss these and other matters. They had already been waiting for three days, so Jemal Eddin advised Shamil to settle everything quickly and send them home.

After finishing his meal—served to him by Zeidat, his eldest wife, a sharp-nosed woman he did not love—Shamil moved into the guest chamber.

Six old men, his advisors, stood as he entered. They had different colored beards—white, gray, and red—and wore tall hats, some with turbans, others without. Each was dressed in clean beshmets and traditional coats, with their belts holding their daggers. Shamil, taller than all of them, greeted them. As he entered, they all raised their hands, palms upward, closed their eyes, recited a prayer, then ran their hands down their faces, ending at their beards. Once this was done, they sat, with Shamil taking a larger cushion than the others, and began discussing the matters at hand.

The first issue was the criminals. Punishments were decided according to religious law. Two men were sentenced to have a hand cut off for stealing. Another was ordered to be executed for murder. Three were pardoned.

Then they moved on to the most pressing issue—how to stop the Chechens from joining the Russians. To fight against this, Jemal Eddin wrote a declaration:

"I wish you peace with God Almighty!

I have heard that the Russians are trying to win you over, flattering you and urging you to surrender. Do not believe them. Do not give in. Stay strong. If you do not see your reward in this life, you will receive it in the next.

Remember what happened before when you gave up your weapons! If God had not guided you back to the right path in 1840, you would be Russian soldiers today, and your wives would be disgraced.

Learn from the past. It is better to die as an enemy of the Russians than to live among unbelievers. Hold on a little longer. I will come with the Quran and the sword and lead you into battle. Until then, I strictly forbid you not only from surrendering but from even thinking about it!"

Shamil approved the message, signed it, and had it sent out.

Finally, they discussed Hadji Murad's situation. This was a serious matter for Shamil. Though he wouldn't say it aloud, he knew that if Hadji Murad had been fighting on his side, things in Chechnya would have turned out differently. It would be best to reconcile and bring him back. But if that wasn't possible, he couldn't let him fight for the Russians either.

There were two options: either send someone to Tiflis to assassinate him, or lure him back and kill him here. The best way to get him to return was to use his family, especially his son, whom Shamil knew he loved deeply.

The council talked through these plans. Then, Shamil closed his eyes and sat in silence.

The councilors understood that Shamil was deep in thought, believing he was receiving guidance from the Prophet. They remained silent as he closed his eyes in concentration.

After five minutes of stillness, he opened his eyes, squinting more than usual, and said, "Bring me Hadji Murad's son."

"He is already here," replied Jemal Eddin. In fact, Yusuf—Hadji Murad's son—was standing at the gate of the outer courtyard, waiting to be called inside. He was thin, pale, dressed in rags, and smelled awful after days in captivity. Yet, despite his rough appearance, he still had a strong, handsome face. His dark eyes burned with the same intensity as his grandmother Patimat's.

Unlike his father, Yusuf did not hold any hatred toward Shamil. He didn't fully understand the reasons behind his father's long-standing feud with the Imam. He had grown up as the son of a respected leader, living a comfortable life in Kuhzakh, and he saw no reason to oppose Shamil. In fact, part of him admired the powerful ruler. In his eyes, Shamil was a great and almost legendary figure, someone to be respected and even worshipped.

With nervous excitement, Yusuf stepped into the guest chamber. As soon as he entered, he felt the sharp gaze of Shamil's half-closed eyes. He hesitated, then walked forward and kissed the Imam's long, slender hand.

"You are Hadji Murad's son?"

"I am, Imam."

"You know what he has done?"

"I do, Imam, and I regret it."

"Can you write?"

"I was studying to become a Mullah."

"Then write to your father. Tell him that if he returns to me before the Feast of Bairam, I will forgive him, and everything will be as it was before. But if he stays with the Russians…" Shamil's expression darkened. "I will divide your grandmother, mother, and the rest of your family among different villages, and I will behead you."

Yusuf did not flinch. His face remained calm as he bowed his head, signaling that he understood.

"Write it and give it to my messenger."

Shamil studied Yusuf in silence for a long moment before speaking again.

"Write that I have shown mercy and will not kill you—but I will blind you, as I do to all traitors… Now go."

Yusuf managed to remain composed in front of Shamil, but the moment he stepped out of the guest chamber, his emotions erupted. He lunged at his attendant, grabbed the man's dagger, and tried to stab himself. Before he could succeed, the guards seized him, tied his arms, and dragged him back to the pit.

Later that evening, after finishing his prayers, Shamil put on a white fur-lined cloak and crossed over to the women's quarters. He went straight to Aminal's room but found it empty. She was with the older wives.

Not wanting to be seen, Shamil hid behind a door and waited for her. But Aminal had no intention of going to him. She was upset because he had gifted some fine silk to Zeidat instead of her. She had noticed him sneaking into her room, searching for her, and she found it amusing. Standing near Zeidat's door, she quietly laughed at the sight of Shamil's white-cloaked figure pacing in and out of her room, looking for her.

After waiting for her in vain, Shamil finally gave up and returned to his own quarters. By then, it was already time for the midnight prayers.

XX

Hadji Murad had been staying at the major's house inside the fort for a week. Marya Dmitrievna often argued with Khanefi, the rough and wild-looking man who was one of Hadji Murad's two companions (the other was Eldar). She had even kicked him out of her kitchen once, and he had nearly attacked her in response. Despite this, she had a special respect and sympathy for Hadji Murad.

She no longer served him his meals—that task had been given to Eldar—but she still found reasons to see him and help him in any way she could. She was deeply interested in the negotiations about his family and knew exactly how many wives and children he had, along with their ages. Whenever a spy came to give him information, she tried her best to find out what was happening with his family.

During this time, Butler and Hadji Murad became quite close. Sometimes Hadji Murad would visit Butler's room, and other times Butler would go to his. They talked either through an interpreter or using gestures, expressions, and smiles when words failed them.

Hadji Murad clearly liked Butler, which was obvious from the way Eldar treated him. Whenever Butler entered Hadji Murad's room, Eldar would greet him with a big smile, showing his bright teeth. He would quickly bring a cushion for Butler to sit on and, if he was carrying a sword, take it from him.

Butler also got to know Khanefi, Hadji Murad's sworn brother, and they developed a friendly bond. Khanefi knew many traditional mountain songs and had a beautiful singing voice. To entertain Butler, Hadji Murad would often ask Khanefi to sing, carefully choosing songs he thought were the best.

Khanefi had a clear, high-pitched voice that was full of emotion. One song that Hadji Murad especially loved caught Butler's attention. It had a sad and solemn melody, and Butler was so moved that he asked the interpreter to translate the lyrics.

The song was about the blood feud between Khanefi and Hadji Murad. The words went like this:

The sun will dry the earth on my grave,

Mother, oh Mother!

And you will forget me.

Tall grass will grow over me,

Father, oh Father!

And you will not miss me.

When your dark eyes no longer weep,

Sister, dear Sister!

Your sorrow will fade away.

But you, my older brother, will never forget,

Because my revenge was never taken.

And you, my younger brother, will still grieve,

Until you rest beside me.

Death came quickly, but I did not fear it.

It served me—I did not serve it.

And you, dark earth, crushed beneath battle,

Will now hold my body forever.

Death is cold, but I was its master.

My body falls to the ground, but my soul rises faster to the sky.

Hadji Murad always listened to the song with his eyes shut. When the final note slowly faded away, he would open them and say in Russian, "A good song. A wise song."

Being around Hadji Murad and his men made Butler even more drawn to the mountain way of life. He was so fascinated by it that he bought a beshmet, a traditional Circassian coat, along with leggings. He pictured himself as a mountaineer, experiencing the same adventurous and free life they lived.

On the day Hadji Murad was leaving, the major invited several officers to say goodbye. Some sat at a table where Marya Dmitrievna was serving tea, while others stood by another table with vodka, chekhir, and light snacks.

Then Hadji Murad walked in, ready for his journey. His steps were quiet but swift, and his limp was hardly noticeable.

Everyone stood up and shook his hand. The major offered him a seat on the divan, but Hadji Murad politely declined and chose to sit on a chair by the window instead.

The room fell silent after he entered, but he didn't seem bothered. He calmly looked around at the faces in the room before resting his gaze on the tea table with the samovar and snacks.

Petrovsky, a lively officer meeting Hadji Murad for the first time, asked through the interpreter if he liked Tiflis.

"Alya!" Hadji Murad replied.

"He says 'Yes,'" the interpreter translated.

"What did he like the most?"

Hadji Murad answered, and the interpreter relayed, "He liked the theater best."

"And what about the ball at the commander-in-chief's house?"

Hadji Murad frowned. "Every nation has its own customs. Our women do not dress that way," he said, glancing at Marya Dmitrievna.

"So, he didn't enjoy it?"

Hadji Murad responded with a proverb. "The dog gave meat to the donkey, and the donkey gave hay to the dog, and both stayed hungry." He smiled. "Each nation likes its own ways."

The conversation didn't go much further. Some officers drank tea, while others enjoyed different refreshments. Hadji Murad accepted a glass of tea but simply placed it in front of him.

"Would you like some cream and a bun?" Marya Dmitrievna asked, offering them to him.

Hadji Murad gave a small bow of his head in response.

"Well, I guess this is goodbye," Butler said, touching his knee. "When will we meet again?"

"Goodbye, goodbye!" Hadji Murad said in Russian, smiling. "Kunak bulug. Strong kunak to thee! Time—ayda—go!" He nodded in the direction he was headed.

Eldar stepped into the doorway, carrying a large white item over his shoulder and holding a sword in his hand. Hadji Murad signaled for him to come over. Eldar crossed the room in long strides and handed him the white burka and the sword.

Hadji Murad stood up, took the burka, and draped it over his arm. Then he said something to the interpreter before handing it to Marya Dmitrievna.

"He says you admired the burka, so he wants you to have it," the interpreter translated.

"Oh, but why?" Marya Dmitrievna asked, blushing.

"It is necessary. Like Adam," Hadji Murad replied.

"Well, thank you," she said, accepting the burka. "May God help you rescue your son," she added. Then she turned to the interpreter and said, "Tell him I wish him success in freeing his son."

Hadji Murad looked at her and gave a small approving nod. Then he took the sword from Eldar and handed it to the major.

The major accepted the sword and said to the interpreter, "Tell him to take my chestnut gelding. I have nothing else to give in return."

Hadji Murad waved his hand in front of his face, signaling that he didn't want anything and would not accept it. Then, he pointed to the mountains, then to his heart, and walked out.

The household followed him to the door, while the officers who stayed inside drew the sword from its scabbard, examined its blade, and agreed that it was a genuine Gurda.

Butler walked with Hadji Murad to the porch, unaware that something unexpected was about to happen—something that could have cost Hadji Murad his life if not for his sharp instincts, quick thinking, and speed.

The people of Tash-Kichu, a Kumukh village that supported the Russians, had great respect for Hadji Murad. Many had come to the fort just to get a glimpse of the famous warrior. A few days earlier, they had even sent word inviting him to visit their mosque on Friday.

However, the Kumukh princes who lived in Tash-Kichu despised Hadji Murad because of an old blood feud. When they heard about the invitation, they told the people they wouldn't allow him inside the mosque. This caused an uproar, leading to a fight between the villagers and the princes' supporters. The Russian authorities stepped in to stop the conflict and warned Hadji Murad not to go.

He listened to the warning, and it seemed like the issue was over.

But just as he was about to leave, with his horses waiting outside, Arslan Khan—one of the Kumukh princes—rode up to the house. He was an acquaintance of both Butler and the major.

As soon as Arslan Khan spotted Hadji Murad, he pulled a pistol from his belt and aimed. But before he could fire, Hadji Murad— despite his limp—moved like lightning, rushing down the porch toward him. The shot missed.

In an instant, Hadji Murad grabbed the bridle of Arslan Khan's horse with one hand and pulled out his dagger with the other. He shouted something in Tartar.

Butler and Eldar quickly jumped in and grabbed both men by the arms before the fight could escalate. Hearing the commotion, the major hurried outside.

"What do you think you're doing, Arslan?" he said after learning what had happened. "Starting a fight on my doorstep? That's not right! Fight your enemy on the battlefield, not in front of my house."

Arslan Khan, a small man with a black mustache, climbed off his horse. He was pale and shaking with anger. Without a word, he shot Hadji Murad a furious look and followed the major inside.

Meanwhile, Hadji Murad, still breathing heavily but smiling, returned to his horse.

"Why did he try to kill him?" Butler asked the interpreter.

Hadji Murad's answer was simple: "It is their law," the interpreter explained. "Arslan Khan had to avenge the blood of a relative, so he tried to kill him."

"And what if he catches up to him on the road?" Butler asked.

Hadji Murad smiled. "If he kills me, then that is Allah's will," he said. Then, switching to Russian, he added, "Goodbye," as he grabbed his horse by the withers.

Looking around at everyone who had gathered to see him off, his eyes rested on Marya Dmitrievna.

"Goodbye, my lass," he said to her. "I thank you."

"May God help you," she replied. "May He help you save your family."

Hadji Murad didn't understand her words, but he could feel her kindness. He nodded in appreciation.

"Don't forget your kunak," Butler reminded him.

"Tell him I am his true friend and will always remember him," Hadji Murad said through the interpreter. Then, with unexpected ease, he lifted himself into the high saddle, barely using the stirrup. Without thinking, he adjusted his sword and made sure his dagger was in place.

Sitting tall and proud, like only a true mountain warrior could, he rode away from the major's house.

Khanefi and Eldar mounted their horses as well. After saying their goodbyes to their hosts and the officers, they followed their leader at a steady trot.

As always after a departure, those left behind began to talk about the ones who had just left.

"What a brave man! He went after Arslan Khan like a wolf! His whole face changed in that moment!"

"But he's a tricky one," Petrovsky remarked. "I wouldn't trust him. He's a dangerous rogue, if you ask me."

Marya Dmitrievna suddenly turned to him with frustration. "Too bad we don't have more Russian rogues like him!" she snapped. "He stayed with us for a week, and all we saw was good. He is polite, wise, and fair."

"And how do you know that?" someone asked.

"No matter how, I just do!" she shot back.

"She's smitten, that's for sure," the major said as he walked into the room.

"Well, so what if I am?" Marya Dmitrievna replied. "Why speak badly about him when he's a good man? He may be a Tartar, but he is still a good man!"

"You're right, Marya Dmitrievna," Butler said. "And you're right to defend him."

XXI

Life in the Russian forts along the Chechen border continued as usual. Since the last major attack, there had been two alarms where soldiers were called into action, and militiamen rode out in a hurry.

But both times, the mountain fighters escaped. In one incident at Vozdvizhensk, they killed a Cossack and managed to steal eight horses while they were being watered.

There hadn't been any more large raids since the destruction of the village, but a new campaign was expected soon. This was because a new commander, Prince Baryatinsky, had been appointed to lead the left flank. He was a close friend of the Viceroy and had previously commanded the Kabarda Regiment. As soon as he arrived in Grozny, he gathered a detachment to continue carrying out the Tsar's orders, which had been passed down through Chernyshov to Vorontsov.

The troops, stationed at Vozdvizhensk, marched toward Kurin, where they set up camp and began cutting down trees. Young Vorontsov lived in a large, elegant tent, and his wife, Marya Vasilevna, often visited the camp and even spent nights there. Everyone knew about Baryatinsky's relationship with her, and the officers who weren't part of the elite circles, as well as the soldiers, spoke about her in crude terms. They were especially annoyed because her presence meant extra duties for them.

The mountain fighters would sometimes fire long-range guns at the camp, but their shots usually missed. Normally, the Russians didn't take any special precautions against these attacks. However, now that Marya Vasilevna was there, soldiers were ordered to stand guard at night to prevent gunfire from scaring or harming her. This extra work frustrated both the soldiers and the lower-ranking officers, and they began calling her unpleasant names behind her back.

During this time, Butler got permission to leave his fort and visit the camp. He wanted to see some of his old friends from the cadet corps and fellow officers from the Kurin regiment, who now served as adjutants and orderlies.

At first, he had a great time. He stayed in Poltoratsky's tent, where he was warmly welcomed by old friends. He also visited Vorontsov, whom he knew slightly from their time serving in the same regiment.

Vorontsov greeted him kindly, introduced him to Prince Baryatinsky, and invited him to a farewell dinner for General Kozlovsky, who had been in charge of the left flank before Baryatinsky took over.

The dinner was extravagant. Several tents were set up in a row, and a long table was decorated with fine dishes and bottles of wine, making the camp feel like a grand gathering in St. Petersburg.

Lunch was served at two o'clock. Kozlovsky sat in the center on one side of the table, with Baryatinsky across from him. Vorontsov and his wife sat on either side of Kozlovsky. Officers from the Kabarda and Kurin regiments filled the seats along the table. Butler sat next to Poltoratsky, laughing and drinking with the others.

As the meal went on, the orderlies filled everyone's glasses with champagne. When the roast was served, Poltoratsky turned to Butler with real concern in his voice.

"Our Kozlovsky is going to embarrass himself," he whispered.

"Why?" Butler asked.

"He has to give a speech! And he's terrible at it," Poltoratsky said. "It's not like leading an attack under fire. And with a lady next to him and all these aristocrats watching…"

"Honestly, it's painful to watch," some officers murmured to each other.

Then, the moment everyone had been dreading arrived. Baryatinsky stood, raised his glass, and gave a short speech honoring Kozlovsky.

When he finished, Kozlovsky stood up. He had a habit of saying the word "how" too often, and it made his speech awkward. Nervously, he began:

"In obedience to the Tsar's orders, I must leave… I am saying goodbye to you, gentlemen." He paused, shifting uncomfortably. "But know that I will always be with you in spirit."

He struggled to continue. "There is a saying: 'One man alone is no warrior,' and you all understand this well, gentlemen. That is why… every honor I have received… every act of kindness from our noble Emperor… my rank… my reputation… everything I have… all of it…" His voice wavered. "I owe it all to you, my friends!"

His lined face tightened, and suddenly, his eyes filled with tears.

"From the bottom of my heart, I give you my deepest, most sincere thanks!" he said, his voice breaking.

Kozlovsky couldn't continue speaking. Overcome with emotion, he turned and hugged the officers. The princess hid her face in her handkerchief, while the prince blinked, his mouth twisting as he held back tears. Many officers' eyes grew misty, and even Butler, who barely knew Kozlovsky, couldn't stop himself from tearing up. He found the whole scene deeply moving.

More toasts followed. They raised their glasses to Baryatinsky, Vorontsov, the officers, and the soldiers. By the time the gathering ended, the guests left the table not only drunk on wine but also on the excitement of military life, something they were always eager to embrace.

The weather was perfect—sunny, calm, and fresh. The smell of bonfires filled the air, and songs echoed throughout the camp. It felt like a celebration, as if everyone were rejoicing over some great event.

Butler, feeling happy and sentimental, headed to Poltoratsky's tent, where several officers had gathered around a card game. An adjutant started the game with a hundred rubles. Butler paced in and out of the tent a few times, gripping the money in his pocket. He had promised both his brother and himself that he wouldn't gamble, but in the end, he couldn't resist. He sat down to play.

Less than an hour later, his face was flushed, his shirt damp with sweat, and his hands covered in chalk from marking the bets. Leaning on the table with both elbows, he scribbled numbers under the bent cards, keeping track of his losses. He had lost so much that he was afraid to count. But he already knew—without adding it up—that even if he borrowed money in advance and sold his horse, it wouldn't be enough to cover what he owed the adjutant, a man he barely knew.

He wanted to keep playing, hoping to win back some of his money, but the adjutant firmly set down his cards and totaled Butler's losses. Embarrassed, Butler stammered out an excuse, saying he couldn't pay everything at once but would send the money from home. As he spoke, he noticed the change in the room. The officers looked at him with pity. Even Poltoratsky avoided making eye contact.

That was the moment Butler realized how badly he had messed up. If only he had stayed away from the game. If only he had accepted the Vorontsovs' invitation instead. Everything could have been fine. But now, nothing was fine. It was a disaster.

The next morning, after saying goodbye to his fellow officers, Butler rode back to the fort. He went straight to bed and slept for 18 hours—the kind of deep sleep that comes after a crushing loss.

When he woke up the next day at noon, the weight of his debt hit him all over again. He wished he could fall back into sleep and forget, but there was no escaping it. He had to find a way to pay back the 470 rubles he owed.

His first move was to write to his brother, confessing what had happened and begging, one last time, for a loan of 500 rubles in exchange for their shared mill as security. Next, he wrote to a wealthy but stingy relative, offering to borrow 500 rubles at whatever interest she wanted.

Finally, he turned to the major. He knew that between him and Marya Dmitrievna, they had some money, so he asked for a loan.

"I'd give it to you right away," the major said, "but Masha won't allow it! Women are so tight-fisted—who can understand them? Still, you need to get out of this mess somehow. Damn it! Maybe that crook who runs the canteen has something?"

But there was no point asking the canteen-keeper for money. Butler's only hope now was that either his brother or his stingy relative would agree to help.

XXII

After failing to achieve his goal in Chechnya, Hadji Murad returned to Tiflis. Every day, he went to Vorontsov's residence, and whenever he was granted an audience, he begged the Viceroy to gather the mountain prisoners and exchange them for his family. He insisted that without his family's release, he couldn't fully commit to helping the Russians and defeating Shamil.

Vorontsov made vague promises, saying he would handle the matter once General Argutinski arrived in Tiflis so they could discuss it together.

Hadji Murad then asked for permission to stay in Nukha, a small town in Transcaucasia. He believed he could negotiate more effectively from there, as it was closer to Shamil's territory and the people loyal to him. Also, since Nukha was a Muslim town, it had a mosque where he could pray more easily. Vorontsov sent a request to St. Petersburg for approval but allowed Hadji Murad to go to Nukha in the meantime.

For Vorontsov, the Russian authorities, and most people who knew Hadji Murad's story, his defection seemed like a fortunate event in the Caucasian war—something interesting, but not personal. However, for Hadji Murad, it was a life-or-death situation.

He had escaped from the mountains partly to save himself and partly because he hated Shamil. The escape had been dangerous, but he had succeeded. At first, he was pleased and even made real plans to fight Shamil. But the one thing he had thought would be simple—rescuing his family—turned out to be the hardest part.

Shamil had taken his family hostage, threatening to give the women away to different villages and either blind or kill his son. Now, in Nukha, Hadji Murad planned to use his loyal supporters in Daghestan to free his family—either by force or by trickery.

The most recent spy who had come to see him in Nukha brought news: the Avars, who were devoted to him, were preparing to capture his family and deliver them safely to the Russians. However, there weren't enough of them to risk attacking Vedeno, where his family was being held. Their only chance would be if the family was moved to another location, in which case they could attack during the journey.

Hadji Murad sent word to his allies, offering a reward of 3,000 rubles for his family's safe rescue.

In Nukha, he was given a small five-room house near the mosque and the Khan's palace. His guards, interpreter, and personal attendants stayed with him. Most of his time was spent waiting for messengers from the mountains or riding in the surrounding areas, which he was allowed to do under supervision.

On April 24th, after returning from one of these rides, he learned that an official had arrived from Tiflis while he was out. The visitor had been sent by Vorontsov. Although Hadji Murad was eager to know the message, he went to his bedroom first to complete his noonday prayers. Only after finishing did he enter the reception room, where the officer in charge and the visitor were waiting.

The visitor was Councillor Kirillov, who informed Hadji Murad that Vorontsov wanted him to return to Tiflis by the 12th to meet with General Argutinski.

"Yakshi!" Hadji Murad responded sharply, clearly annoyed. He didn't like the official. "Did you bring money?"

"I did," Kirillov answered.

Hadji Murad raised his hands, then four fingers, to show how long he had been waiting. "For two weeks now. Give it here!"

"We'll give it to you right away," Kirillov said, reaching into his bag for his purse. Then, in Russian, he muttered, "What does he even need the money for?" assuming Hadji Murad wouldn't understand.

But Hadji Murad did understand. His expression darkened as he glared at the man.

As Kirillov counted out the money, he tried to start a conversation so he would have something to report to Prince Vorontsov. Through the interpreter, he asked if Hadji Murad found it boring living in Nukha.

Hadji Murad gave him only a brief look, his eyes showing clear disdain. To him, the official was just a powerless, overweight man in ordinary clothes—someone unworthy of his attention. He saw no need to respond.

The interpreter asked the question again.

"Tell him I don't want to talk! Just give me the money!" Hadji Murad said, then sat at the table, prepared to count it.

Hadji Murad was given five gold coins a day as an allowance. Kirillov carefully counted the money, stacking it into seven piles of ten gold coins each before pushing them toward him. Without hesitation, Hadji Murad swept the gold into the sleeve of his Circassian coat, stood up, and—without warning—slapped Councillor Kirillov on his bald head before walking away.

Kirillov jumped to his feet, furious. He ordered the interpreter to tell Hadji Murad that he had no right to treat him that way—he held a rank equal to that of a colonel! The officer in charge agreed, backing up Kirillov's demand. But Hadji Murad simply gave a slight nod to show that he had heard them, then walked out of the room.

"What can you do with a man like that?" the officer in charge muttered. "Try to reason with him, and he'll just stab you! You can't argue with these devils. He's getting more and more frustrated—I can see it."

As night fell, two spies arrived from the hills. They wore hoods that covered their faces up to their eyes. The officer in charge led them to Hadji Murad's room. One was a dark-skinned, heavyset Tavlinian; the other was a thin old man.

Their news was bad. Hadji Murad's allies, who had promised to help rescue his family, had now completely refused. They were too afraid of Shamil, who had warned that anyone who assisted Hadji Murad would face the most brutal punishments.

Hearing this, Hadji Murad sat with his elbows resting on his knees, his head bowed beneath his turban. He stayed like that for a long time, deep in thought.

His mind raced. He knew this was the final moment to decide. There was no more time to wait.

At last, he lifted his head, handed each messenger a gold coin, and said, "Go!"

"What should we tell them?" one spy asked.

"Tell them whatever God wills... Now go!"

The messengers stood and left. Hadji Murad remained sitting on the carpet, still leaning on his knees, lost in thought.

"What should I do?" he wondered. "Should I take Shamil at his word and return to him?"

No—that was impossible. Shamil was as cunning as a fox and would surely deceive him. Even if he didn't, surrendering to that "red liar" was unthinkable. Besides, after staying with the Russians, Shamil would never trust him again.

A fable came to Hadji Murad's mind. It was about a falcon that had been captured and lived among men before returning to the wild. When he came back to his fellow falcons, he still wore the silver bells that had been tied to his legs. The other falcons wouldn't accept him.

"Fly back to those who put those bells on you!" they told him. "We have no bells and no straps here."

The falcon didn't want to leave his home, so he stayed. But the other falcons refused to let him belong to their flock and pecked him to death.

"They would do the same to me," Hadji Murad thought bitterly.

"Should I stay here, fight for the Russian Tsar, and try to conquer the Caucasus? Earn wealth, power, and titles?"

It was possible. He remembered his meetings with Vorontsov and the flattering promises the prince had made.

"But I must decide now," he thought. "If I wait any longer, Shamil will destroy my family."

That night, Hadji Murad did not sleep. He stayed awake, thinking.

XXIII

By midnight, Hadji Murad had made up his mind. He decided that he had to escape to the mountains, gather the Avars who were still loyal to him, break into Vedeno, and either save his family or die trying. What he would do after rescuing them—whether to return to the Russians or go to Khunzakh to fight Shamil—he hadn't yet decided. The only thing he knew for sure was that he had to get away from the Russians and make it to the mountains. Without wasting any time, he began putting his plan into action.

He pulled his black padded beshmet from under his pillow and stepped into the hallway. His men's room was on the other side. As he moved through the open doorway, the cool night air wrapped around him. The moonlight shone brightly, and the garden was filled with the whistles and songs of nightingales.

Crossing the hall, he entered his men's room. It was dark, but the dim moonlight coming through the window faintly lit the space. A table and two chairs sat on one side, while four of his men lay sleeping on carpets or burkas spread across the floor. Khanefi was outside with the horses.

The door creaked as Hadji Murad stepped inside. Gamzalo stirred, turned to see who it was, then, realizing it was his leader, lay back down. But Eldar, who was next to him, jumped up and quickly put on his beshmet, ready to follow orders. Khan Mahoma and Bata remained asleep.

Hadji Murad placed the beshmet he was carrying on the table with a heavy thud—the sound of the gold sewn inside.

"Sew these in too," he said, handing Eldar the gold coins he had received that day. Eldar took them, stepped outside into the moonlight, and pulled a small knife from under his dagger. He immediately began unstitching the lining of the beshmet to hide the coins inside.

Hadji Murad turned to Gamzalo. "Tell the men to check their rifles and pistols. Make sure the ammunition is ready. We have a long journey tomorrow."

"We have bullets and powder. Everything will be ready," Gamzalo replied, then shouted something loud and unclear. He knew exactly why Hadji Murad wanted the weapons loaded. From the beginning, Gamzalo had only wanted one thing—to kill as many Russians as possible and escape to the mountains. That desire had grown stronger each day. Now that Hadji Murad was finally ready for action, Gamzalo was satisfied.

As soon as Hadji Murad left, Gamzalo woke the others. The four men spent the rest of the night preparing their weapons—checking rifles, cleaning pistols, sharpening their swords and daggers, and rubbing tallow on the blades to keep them from rusting. They replaced damaged parts, sprinkled fresh gunpowder into the rifle pans, and packed bullets wrapped in oiled cloth into measured powder charges.

Just before dawn, Hadji Murad stepped into the hallway again to get water for his morning prayers. The nightingales, now at their loudest, sang endlessly. From the men's room, the steady grinding sound of metal against stone echoed as daggers were sharpened.

He filled his hands with water from a tub, then turned to go back to his room. But as he reached his door, he heard Khanefi's voice rise above the scraping of blades. He had begun to sing.

The song told the story of a warrior named Hamzad, who, along with his brave men, stole a herd of white horses from the Russians. A Russian prince chased them past the Terek River, bringing an army as vast as a forest. Rather than be captured, Hamzad and his warriors killed the horses, used their bodies as a barricade, and fought fiercely until they ran out of bullets, knives, and even their own strength. Before he died, Hamzad looked up and saw birds flying in the sky. He called out to them:

Fly back home, birds, and hurry!

Tell our mothers and sisters,

Tell the young women we fell in battle

For Ghazavat! Let them know

We will never rest in a grave.

Wolves will rip us apart,

Ravens and vultures will eat our eyes.

The song came to an end, and as the final words were sung in a sorrowful tune, Bata's strong voice joined in with a loud cry of "Lya-il-lyakha-il Allakh!" followed by a high-pitched scream. Then everything fell silent again, except for the steady sounds of the nightingales chirping in the garden and the sharp, rhythmic noise of iron sliding against a whetstone behind the door.

Hadji Murad was so deep in thought that he didn't realize he had tilted his jug too far until water started spilling out. He shook his head at himself and stepped back into his room. After washing up for the morning, he checked his weapons and sat down on his bed. There was nothing else to do. If he wanted to ride out, he would need permission from the officer in charge, but the sun hadn't risen yet, and the officer was still asleep.

Khanefi's song reminded him of a tune his mother had created when he was born—a song meant for his father that he had once shared with Loris-Melikov. As the memory played in his mind, he saw his mother clearly—not as the elderly woman he had last seen, with gray hair and gaps in her teeth, but as she had been in her youth. She was strong and beautiful, carrying him on her back in a basket across the mountains when he was a chubby five-year-old boy.

Thinking of himself as a child made him remember his son, Yusuf—the boy whose hair he had shaved for the first time. Now, Yusuf had grown into a brave young man. He pictured him as he was the last time they met in Tselmess. Yusuf had brought him his horse, ready to ride alongside him. He was already dressed and armed, leading his own horse by the bridle. His bright, youthful face and tall, lean frame showed strength, courage, and excitement for life. Though he was still young, his broad shoulders, slim waist, and strong arms gave him the look of a warrior. Hadji Murad had always been proud of him.

"You should stay behind. You'll be the only man at home now. Take care of your mother and grandmother," Hadji Murad had told him. He remembered the determined and confident look on Yusuf's face when he replied that as long as he was alive, no one would dare harm them. But still, Yusuf had mounted his horse and followed his father to the stream before turning back. Since that day, Hadji Murad had not seen his wife, mother, or son. And now, Shamil was threatening to blind Yusuf! He couldn't even bear to think about what might happen to his wife.

Frustration and impatience took over, making it impossible for him to stay still. He sprang to his feet, hurried to the door despite his limp, and flung it open, calling for Eldar. Though the sun had not yet risen, the sky was already light, and the nightingales continued their song.

"Tell the officer I need permission to ride out, and get the horses ready," he said.

XXIV

The only thing that brought Butler any comfort during this time was the excitement of war, which he threw himself into both on duty and in his free time. Dressed in his Circassian outfit, he carried himself with confidence, riding around and trying to look the part of a warrior. Twice, he joined Bogdanovich on an ambush mission, but both times, they found no one and accomplished nothing. Still, Butler enjoyed being close to Bogdanovich, who was known for his bravery, and felt that their friendship made him seem more like a true soldier.

He had managed to pay off his debt, but only by borrowing money from a Jewish lender at an extremely high interest rate—pushing his problems down the road instead of actually solving them. He did his best not to think about his troubles, losing himself not just in the thrill of battle but also in alcohol. Each day, he drank more than the last, and with every drink, he felt himself growing weaker inside. He was no longer the same self-controlled man he had once been around Marya Dmitrievna. Instead, he shamelessly pursued her, only to be met with firm rejection that left him embarrassed.

At the end of April, a new detachment arrived at the fort, part of Baryatinsky's plan to push through Chechnya—an area that had always been considered impossible to cross. This group included two companies from the Kabarda regiment, and following the usual Caucasian tradition, they were treated as honored guests by the Kurin companies. The soldiers were housed in the barracks and given a meal of buckwheat porridge and beef, along with plenty of vodka. The officers, meanwhile, were welcomed into the quarters of their Kurin counterparts, where they were treated to a special dinner. The regimental singers performed, and as expected, the evening turned into a drinking party.

Major Petrov was completely drunk, and instead of his usual flushed face, he had gone pale. Sitting backward on a chair, he waved his sword around, pretending to fight invisible enemies. He kept switching between swearing and laughing—one minute, he was throwing his arms around someone in a hug, and the next, he was dancing to his favorite song.

Shamil led an uprising

In the past so long ago;

Try, ry, rataty,

Many years have come and gone!

Butler was there as well. He tried to find the thrill of war in what was happening, but deep inside, he felt bad for the major. There was no way to stop him, though. As the alcohol started to affect him too, Butler quietly left and made his way home.

The moon shined over the white houses and the rocky road. It was so bright that even tiny pebbles, bits of straw, and patches of dust could be seen clearly. As Butler got closer to his house, he noticed Marya Dmitrievna coming his way, her shawl wrapped around her head and neck. Ever since she had turned him down, he had been keeping his distance, feeling embarrassed. But now, under the soft glow of the moon and still warmed by the effects of the wine, he was happy to run into her and wanted to make amends.

"Where are you going?" he asked.

"I'm off to check on my husband," she said with a smile. Though she had been firm in turning Butler down, she didn't like how he had been avoiding her.

"Why bother? He'll be back soon."

"But what if he doesn't?"

"If he doesn't, someone will bring him home."

"That's not how it should be," she said. "But do you really think I shouldn't go?"

"I do. It's better if we just head back."

Marya Dmitrievna hesitated but then turned around and walked with him. The moon shone so brightly that their shadows cast a soft glow around them as they moved. Butler watched the shimmering outline and thought about telling her he still cared for her, but he wasn't sure how to begin. She waited for him to speak, but neither of them said anything. They were almost home when they spotted horsemen turning the corner.

"Who's coming now?" Marya Dmitrievna asked, stepping aside. The moon was behind the riders, making it hard to see their faces until they got closer. Then she recognized Peter Nikolaevich Kamenev, an officer who had once served with the major.

"Is that you, Peter Nikolaevich?" she asked.

"It's me," Kamenev said. "Ah, Butler, how are you? Still awake? Taking a walk with Marya Dmitrievna? You'd better be careful, or the major will make you pay for it. Where is he?"

"Over there," Marya Dmitrievna replied, pointing toward the sound of drums and singing. "They're celebrating."

"Why? Are your men throwing a party?"

"No, some officers from Hasav-Yurt arrived, and they're being welcomed."

"Ah, perfect! I got here just in time. I need to speak with the major."

"On official business?" Butler asked.

"Yes, just a small matter."

"Good or bad?"

"Depends," Kamenev said with a smirk. "Good for us, bad for someone else." He chuckled to himself as they reached the major's house.

"Chikhirev!" Kamenev called to one of his Cossacks. "Come here!"

A Don Cossack rode up, dressed in his usual uniform with tall boots and a cloak. A pair of saddlebags hung behind him.

"Bring it out," Kamenev ordered as he climbed down from his horse.

The Cossack got off his horse and took a sack from his saddlebag. Kamenev grabbed it and reached inside.

"Want to see something interesting? You're not scared, are you, Marya Dmitrievna?"

"Why would I be?" she asked.

"Here it is!" Kamenev said, pulling out a severed head and lifting it into the moonlight. "Do you know who this is?"

The head was shaved, with thick eyebrows, a short black beard, and mustache. One eye was open while the other was half-closed. A deep wound ran across the skull, though it didn't go all the way through, and dried blood covered the nose. A bloodstained cloth was wrapped around the neck. Despite the injuries, the blue lips still held a strange, almost childlike softness.

Marya Dmitrievna stared at it for a moment, then turned away without a word and hurried into the house.

Butler couldn't look away from the horrifying sight. It was the head of Hadji Murad—the same man he had spent so many evenings talking with not long ago.

"What does this mean? Who killed him?" he asked.

"He tried to escape but got caught," Kamenev replied, handing the head back to the Cossack before following Butler inside.

"He died like a warrior," Kamenev added.

"But how did it happen?"

"Just wait. I'll tell you everything when the major arrives. That's why I'm here. I'm taking it around to all the forts and villages to show them."

The major was sent for, and he soon arrived, accompanied by two officers who were just as drunk as he was. He greeted Kamenev with a sloppy embrace.

"And I brought you Hadji Murad's head," Kamenev announced.

"No way… He's dead?"

"Yes. He tried to run."

"I knew he'd fool them! Where is it? The head, I mean… Let me see it."

The Cossack was called in and brought the bag forward. He pulled out the head, and the major stared at it for a long time with his glazed, drunken eyes.

"He was a brave man," he muttered. "I should kiss him!"

"Yes, he fought well," one of the officers agreed.

After they had all examined it, the Cossack put the head back into the bag, making sure it didn't hit the floor too hard.

"Kamenev, what do you say when you show it to people?" one officer asked.

"No! Let me kiss him! He gave me a sword!" the major shouted.

Butler stepped outside onto the porch.

Marya Dmitrievna was sitting on the second step. When she saw Butler, she turned her face away in anger.

"What's wrong, Marya Dmitrievna?" he asked.

"You're all butchers! I hate it! Nothing but killers!" she snapped, standing up.

"It could happen to anyone," Butler said awkwardly. "That's war."

"War? You call this war? You're murderers, all of you! The dead should be buried with respect, not laughed at! Butchers, that's what you are!" she said again before storming off and disappearing into the house through the back door.

Butler went back inside and turned to Kamenev. "Tell us exactly what happened," he said.

And Kamenev began his story.

This is what had happened.

XXV

Hadji Murad was allowed to ride around the town, but he was never permitted to go without a group of Cossacks escorting him. There were only about 20 Cossacks in Nukha, and half of them were already assigned to the officers. If all 10 were sent out with Hadji Murad each time, the same men would have to go every other day. To avoid that, they decided that after the first day, only five Cossacks would accompany him, and he was asked not to take all of his men with him. However, on April 25th, he rode out with all five of his men anyway.

As he mounted his horse, the commander noticed and reminded him that he wasn't allowed to take everyone. Hadji Murad acted as if he didn't hear, nudged his horse forward, and the commander chose not to argue.

One of the Cossacks assigned to ride with him was Nazarov, a young and strong soldier who had won the Cross of St. George for bravery. He had light brown hair, a fresh, healthy face, and looked full of life. He was the eldest in a poor family of Old Believers, raised without a father, and had been supporting his mother, three sisters, and two brothers.

"Stay close to him, Nazarov!" the commander called out.

"Yes, sir!" Nazarov replied. He adjusted the rifle on his back, stood in his stirrups for a moment, and then trotted forward on his strong roan horse.

Behind him rode four more Cossacks: Ferapontov, a tall, skinny man known for stealing and smuggling (he had once sold gunpowder to Gamzalo); Ignatov, a strong-built peasant who often bragged about his strength, though he was nearing the end of his service; Mishkin, a frail young soldier who was often the target of jokes; and Petrakov, a cheerful, fair-haired man who was his mother's only son.

The morning had been foggy, but as the sun rose, the mist cleared, revealing bright green grass, fresh sprouting crops, and the fast-moving river rippling to the left of the road. The sunlight made everything shine.

Hadji Murad rode at a slow pace, with the Cossacks and his men following behind. They passed women carrying baskets on their heads, soldiers transporting supplies, and wagons creaking under the weight of goods as buffaloes pulled them along. After about a mile and a half, Hadji Murad lightly kicked his white Kabarda horse, making it pick up speed. His men and the Cossacks had to urge their horses into a quick trot to keep up.

"That's a fine horse he's riding," said Ferapontov. "If he were still our enemy, I'd take him down in no time."

"You bet. Someone in Tiflis offered 300 rubles for that horse," another Cossack added.

"But I can outrun him on mine," Nazarov said confidently.

"You think you can get ahead? Not a chance!"

Hadji Murad kept picking up speed.

"Hey, friend, slow down! You can't do that!" Nazarov shouted as he pushed his horse to catch up.

Hadji Murad glanced back but didn't say anything. He just kept riding at the same pace.

"Watch out! They're up to something, those devils!" Ignatov warned. "Look at the way they're speeding up!"

For nearly a mile, they rode toward the mountains.

"I'm telling you, this isn't allowed!" Nazarov shouted again.

Still, Hadji Murad didn't answer or even turn his head. Instead, he urged his horse into a full gallop.

"You're not getting away that easily!" Nazarov yelled, his pride stung. He lashed his roan horse with his whip and leaned forward, racing full speed after Hadji Murad.

The sky was clear, the air was crisp, and Nazarov felt alive as he and his powerful horse moved as one, chasing after Hadji Murad on the smooth road. It never crossed his mind that something terrible could happen. He was just happy, knowing that with each stride, he was gaining on his target.

Hadji Murad, hearing the sound of the horse closing in behind him, knew he was about to be caught. With his right hand, he grabbed his pistol, while with his left, he lightly pulled the reins to steady his excited horse.

"You need to stop, I'm warning you!" Nazarov shouted, now nearly side by side with Hadji Murad. He reached out to grab the reins of Hadji Murad's horse, but before he could, a gunshot rang out.

"What are you doing?!" Nazarov screamed, clutching his chest. "Attack, men!" He wobbled in the saddle and then collapsed forward onto his horse's neck.

The mountaineers were faster to react than the Cossacks. They fired their pistols and slashed at their enemies with swords.

Nazarov's lifeless body hung over his horse, which circled around the group in confusion. Ignatov's horse stumbled and fell, trapping his leg beneath it. Before he could free himself, two of Hadji Murad's men swung their swords, cutting at his arms and head.

Petrakov tried to rush in to help Ignatov, but before he could, two bullets struck him—one in the back and one in the side. He fell from his horse like a heavy sack, landing on the ground with a thud.

Mishkin panicked, turned his horse around, and galloped back toward the fortress. Khanefi and Bata chased after him but soon realized he was too far ahead. Unable to catch him, they gave up and returned to the others.

Petrakov lay on his back, his stomach torn open, his young face staring up at the sky. His chest heaved as he gasped for air, like a fish struggling out of water.

Gamzalo finished off Ignatov with his sword, then turned and struck Nazarov, knocking him off his horse. Bata quickly took the cartridge pouches from the fallen soldiers. Khanefi tried to capture Nazarov's horse, but Hadji Murad ordered him to leave it. Without wasting another moment, he charged ahead.

His men followed, driving away Nazarov's horse as it tried to run after them. They had already covered more than six miles, riding through rice fields, when a warning shot fired from a tower in Nukha signaled the alarm.

"Oh Lord! Oh God! What have they done?" the fort commander shouted, grabbing his head with both hands when he heard about Hadji Murad's escape. "They've ruined me! They let him get away, those fools!" he cried as he listened to Mishkin's report.

The alarm was sounded, and soldiers were sent out right away. The local Cossacks were ordered to chase Hadji Murad, and militia from nearby pro-Russian villages were also called to help. A reward of 1,000 rubles was offered for capturing him, whether alive or dead. Within two hours of his escape, over 200 men on horseback, led by an officer, were racing after him, determined to catch him.

After riding for miles along the main road, Hadji Murad finally slowed his horse. The animal was soaked in sweat, its white coat now looking almost gray.

To the right of the road, the houses and mosque towers of the village Benerdzhik were visible. To the left, there were fields, and beyond them, the river. Although the mountains were to the right— where his pursuers would likely expect him to go—Hadji Murad decided to turn left instead. His plan was to leave the road, cross the Alazan River, and then take the high road on the other side, where no one would think to look for him. From there, he could ride into the forest, recross the river, and finally make his way to the mountains.

Confident in his plan, he turned left, but reaching the river turned out to be impossible. The rice fields they had to cross had just been flooded for the spring season, turning them into a deep, muddy swamp. As soon as the horses stepped in, their hooves sank past their ankles.

Hadji Murad and his men tried to find drier ground, turning left and right, but the entire field was soaked. With each step, the horses struggled to pull their legs free from the thick mud, making a sucking sound like a cork being pulled from a bottle. Every few steps, they had to stop to catch their breath. They kept going like this for so long that the sun began to set, and they still hadn't reached the river.

Up ahead, they spotted a slightly higher patch of land covered in shrubs. Hadji Murad decided they should stop there until nightfall, letting the exhausted horses rest and graze. The men also took a break, eating some bread and cheese they had brought with them.

Night finally arrived, and at first, the moon cast light over the land. But soon, it disappeared behind a hill, leaving everything in darkness. The area was full of nightingales, and two of them were singing from the nearby bushes. While Hadji Murad and his men had been moving, the birds had been silent, but as soon as they settled down, the nightingales started calling to each other again.

Lying awake, Hadji Murad listened to the sounds of the night. The bird songs reminded him of the one he had heard about Hamzad the night before, when he had gone to fetch water. He knew that, at any moment, he could end up just like Hamzad. The thought weighed on him, and suddenly, he felt deeply serious.

He laid out his burka, said his evening prayers, and had just finished when he heard a noise. It was the faint sound of multiple horses splashing through the muddy field, getting closer to their hiding spot.

Bata, who had sharp eyesight, ran to the edge of the bushes and looked into the darkness. He could make out dark shapes—men on foot and horseback. On the other side, Khanefi saw the same thing. It was Karganov, the district's military commander, leading a group of soldiers.

"Then we'll fight like Hamzad," Hadji Murad thought.

When the alarm was raised, Karganov and his men, including militia and Cossacks, had rushed out to chase Hadji Murad. At first, they couldn't find any trace of him. He had almost given up and was heading back when, just before evening, he met an old man and asked if he had seen any riders. The man said he had—he had spotted six horsemen struggling through the rice fields before they disappeared into a clump of bushes, where he had been gathering wood. Karganov immediately turned back, taking the old man with him. When he arrived and saw the tied-up horses, he was sure Hadji Murad was there. That night, he surrounded the area and waited for morning to capture him, dead or alive.

Realizing they were trapped, Hadji Murad spotted an old ditch among the shrubs. He decided to make a defensive position there and fight for as long as they had strength and ammunition. He explained the plan to his men and ordered them to build a barrier in front of the ditch. Without hesitation, his men got to work—cutting branches, digging up dirt with their daggers, and stacking up a makeshift defense. Hadji Murad worked alongside them.

As dawn approached, the militia leader rode up close and shouted, "Hey, Hadji Murad! Surrender! There are many of us and only a few of you!"

A rifle shot rang out in response. A small cloud of smoke rose from the ditch, and a bullet struck the officer's horse. The animal staggered, then collapsed. Immediately, the militia opened fire, their rifles cracking one after another. Bullets whistled through the air, snapping leaves and branches and hitting the dirt barrier, but none reached Hadji Murad's men.

Only Gamzalo's horse, which had wandered from the others, was hit in the head. It didn't fall right away; instead, it broke free from its ties and ran through the bushes, bleeding as it pushed itself toward the other horses.

Hadji Murad and his men fired only when they had a clear target, and they rarely missed. Three militia fighters were wounded. Instead of attacking, the others grew more hesitant, pulling back and only shooting from a distance without aiming properly.

The standoff lasted for over an hour. The sun had risen halfway above the trees when Hadji Murad began thinking about jumping on his horse and making a run for the river. But suddenly, loud shouting filled the air—more men had arrived.

Hadji Aga of Mekhtuli had arrived with about 200 men. He had once been Hadji Murad's friend and had lived with him in the mountains, but later, he betrayed him and sided with the Russians. With him was Akhmet Khan, the son of Hadji Murad's longtime enemy.

Hadji Aga, like Karganov, ordered Hadji Murad to give up. But just as before, Hadji Murad responded with a gunshot.

"Draw your swords, men!" Hadji Aga shouted, pulling out his own. A hundred voices roared as the fighters charged into the bushes.

The militia charged forward, but gunfire erupted from behind Hadji Murad's barricade. One shot after another rang out. Three attackers fell, causing the rest to hesitate and take cover at the edge of the bushes, where they fired back. Slowly, they tried to move closer, running from one shrub to the next. Some made it through, but others were struck down by Hadji Murad and his men.

Hadji Murad's shots never missed. Gamzalo, too, rarely wasted a bullet and let out a triumphant shout whenever he hit his mark. Khan Mahoma, sitting at the edge of the ditch, sang "Il lyakha il Allakh!" while firing slowly, often missing. Eldar trembled with impatience, eager to charge at the enemy with his dagger. He fired wildly, barely aiming, constantly glancing at Hadji Murad as if waiting for permission to attack.

Khanefi, with his sleeves rolled up, focused on reloading. Even in battle, he worked like a servant, carefully stuffing bullets wrapped in greasy rags into the barrels and pouring dry powder onto the pans. Bata didn't stay in the ditch like the others. Instead, he kept running back and forth, moving the horses to a safer spot. He screamed as he fired without aiming properly. He was the first to be hit—a bullet struck his neck. He sat down, coughing up blood and cursing.

Then, Hadji Murad was shot. The bullet tore through his shoulder. Without hesitation, he ripped some cotton from the lining of his beshmet, stuffed it into the wound, and kept shooting.

"Let's charge them with our swords!" Eldar pleaded for the third time. He crouched behind the barricade, ready to attack. But just as he leaned forward, a bullet struck him. He staggered and fell back onto Hadji Murad's leg.

Hadji Murad glanced at him. Eldar's deep, animal-like eyes stared at him with a serious, almost childlike expression. His lips twitched, but he didn't speak. Hadji Murad pulled his leg from under him and continued shooting.

Khanefi bent over Eldar's body, taking the unused bullets from his coat. Meanwhile, Khan Mahoma kept singing as he reloaded and fired at a slow, steady pace.

The militia kept advancing, darting between bushes and yelling as they came closer.

Another bullet hit Hadji Murad, this time in the side. He fell back into the ditch and once again plugged the wound with cotton. But this time, he knew the injury was fatal. He felt himself slipping away.

His mind raced with images—flashes of memories from his life. He saw the strong and fearless Abu Nutsal Khan, holding his severed cheek as he rushed at his enemy. Then, he pictured Vorontsov, the frail old man with his pale, cunning face and soft voice. He saw his son Yusuf, his wife Sofiat, and finally, the cold, red-bearded face of his enemy Shamil with his half-closed eyes. These thoughts passed through his mind, but they no longer meant anything to him. There was no anger, no sadness, no longing—just a quiet understanding that everything was coming to an end.

But his body still fought. Using the last of his strength, he pushed himself up, aimed his pistol at an approaching soldier, and fired. The man dropped to the ground.

Hadji Murad then climbed out of the ditch, dragging himself forward with heavy steps. Holding his dagger, he moved straight toward the enemy.

Gunshots cracked. His body jerked, and he collapsed.

With victorious cries, several militiamen ran toward him. But just as they reached his fallen body, it moved. His bloodied, shaved head lifted off the ground. He grabbed a nearby tree trunk and pulled himself up.

The men froze in place.

For a moment, he looked terrifying, like a warrior refusing to die.

Then, his body shuddered. He lost his grip on the tree and fell forward, landing face-down. He stretched out, unmoving, like a thistle that had been cut down in a field.

He no longer moved, but he could still feel.

Hadji Aga was the first to reach him. He lifted his dagger and struck Hadji Murad's head. The blow felt like a hammer crashing down, but Hadji Murad no longer understood what was happening or why. That was the last thing he felt.

His enemies began kicking and hacking at his body, but it was no longer him—it was just a lifeless shell.

Hadji Aga stepped on Hadji Murad's back. With two swift cuts, he severed his head, then pushed it aside with his foot, careful not to get blood on his shoes. Bright red blood streamed from the neck, while thick, dark blood flowed from the head, staining the grass.

Karganov, Hadji Aga, Akhmet Khan, and the rest of the soldiers gathered around, standing over the bodies of Hadji Murad and his men. The survivors—Khanefi, Khan Mahoma, and Gamzalo—were tied up as prisoners. Smoke from the gunfire still hung in the air as the victors celebrated.

The nightingales, which had gone silent during the battle, began to sing again. First, one called out nearby, then others answered from a distance.

I thought of this death when I saw a crushed thistle in the middle of a plowed field.

Thank You for Reading

Dear Reader,

We hope this timeless classic has sparked your imagination and enriched your literary journey. Now that you've turned the final page, we want to share a vision for the future of reading—one where every classic you've ever wanted to explore is at your fingertips, in a format that best suits your life.

We'd like to invite you to gain immediate, unlimited digital & audiobook access to hundreds of the most treasured literary classics ever written—along with the option to secure deluxe paperback, hardcover & box set editions at printing cost. Together, we can spark a new global literary renaissance alongside our small, independent publishing house called "The Library of Alexandria."

Thousands of years ago, the Library of Alexandria stood as a beacon of knowledge—until it was lost to history. We aim to reignite that spirit of preservation and discovery right now, in the modern age—only this time, it's accessible to all, in every language and every format.

Picture a world where every timeless classic, novel, poem, or philosophical treatise is not only available to read but also updated for today's readers—modernized, translated into any language or dialect, and ready to enjoy in any format you choose, whether that is in an eBook, audiobook, paperback, or deluxe hardcover & box set version a printing cost.

By joining our movement to rebuild the modern Library of Alexandria, you become part of an unprecedented mission to offer:

- **Unlimited Audiobook & eBook Access** to the Greatest Classics of All Time

  Instantly explore thousands of legendary works, from Plato and Shakespeare to Jane Austen and Leo Tolstoy. All are instantly ready to read or listen to, giving you a complete literary universe at your fingertips.

- **Paperback & Deluxe Editions at Printing Costs:**

  Purchase any title in a paperback, deluxe hardbound, or deluxe boxset edition at printing costs, shipped right to your doorstep. Curate your personal library of Alexandria with editions worthy of display—crafted to last, designed to captivate, and delivered straight to your door.

- **Modern translations for Contemporary Readers** in all languages and dialects

  Discover a vast selection of classics reimagined in clear, current language—no more struggling with outdated phrases or obscure references. Next to the original versions, we aim to offer translations in as many languages and dialects as possible.

  As we continue our translation efforts and add new languages, readers everywhere can connect with these works as if they were written today. By bridging linguistic divides, you're contributing to ensuring that these timeless stories become more meaningful, accessible, and inspiring for people across the globe.

- **Your Personal Library of Alexandria:**

  Over the months and years, you'll curate a unique physical archive of classics—each volume a testament to your taste, curiosity, and love of knowledge. It's not just about owning books—it's about curating a cultural legacy you'll cherish and pass down for generations to come.

- **Join a Global Literary Renaissance:**

  Your support fuels an ongoing mission: allowing us to reinvest in offering deluxe print editions (including special boxsets) at their true cost, broaden the range of available formats and translations, and extend the reach of these works to new audiences worldwide. By joining today, you're not just preserving a legacy of masterpieces; you set in motion a powerful wave of literary accessibility.

  We are more than a publisher—we're a movement, and we can't do it alone. Your support lets us scale our mission, preserving and reimagining history's greatest works for tomorrow's readers.

Become a Torchbearer of knowledge.

Thank you for picking up this book and allowing us into your literary journey. As you turn the pages, know that you're part of something larger: a global effort to keep these stories alive, share their wisdom across borders and generations, and spark a true cultural revival for the modern era.

If this resonates with you—please consider taking the next step by visiting:

www.libraryofalexandria.com

With gratitude and a shared love of knowledge,

The Modern Library of Alexandria Team

Visit:

www.libraryofalexandria.com

Or scan the code below:

www.ingramcontent.com/pod-product-compliance
Lightning Source LLC
Chambersburg PA
CBHW011351010726
47494CB00008B/2265